I0611158

Slot Attendant

A Novel About A Novelist

"exceptionally brilliant and rewarding"

Also featuring
Engelhard's Guide to Writing
and more bonus essays

by

JACK ENGELHARD

DayRay Literary Press
British Columbia, Canada

Slot Attendant: A Novel About A Novelist

Copyright ©2009, 2013 by Jack Engelhard
ISBN-13 978-1-77143-111-8
Second Edition

Library and Archives Canada Cataloguing in Publication
Engelhard, Jack, 1940-, author
Slot attendant / by Jack Engelhard. – Second edition.
Issued in print and electronic formats.
ISBN 978-1-77143-111-8 (pbk.).--ISBN 978-1-77143-112-5 (pdf)
Additional cataloguing data available from Library and Archives Canada

Jack Engelhard may be contacted through: **www.jackengelhard.com**

Front cover artwork: Original photo used © Christopher Johnson.

Previously published in 2009 by CreateSpace.

DayRay Literary Press is a literary imprint
of CCB Publishing: www.ccbpublishing.com

DayRay Literary Press
British Columbia, Canada
www.dayraypress.com

International Bestselling Novelist Jack Engelhard
Author of _Indecent Proposal_

Translated into more than 22 languages and turned into a Paramount motion picture of the same name starring Robert Redford and Demi Moore.

Slot Attendant

A Novel About A Novelist

Exceptionally brilliant, masterful and rewarding – and here it is from the mighty pen of novelist Jack Engelhard, the highs and lows, warts and all of making it as a writer. Here the sweetness of success is given its proper place, as are the moments of failure and despair, and you will never forget the refrain, especially if you're a writer, "Nobody cares." Engelhard opens the door into the world of New York publishing with equal access into the world of gambling and casinos. A triumph, and an absolute must-read.

Also featuring

Engelhard's Guide to Writing

and more bonus essays

Praise received for *Slot Attendant*

"Jack Engelhard combines personal experience, the experience of others, and a truly vivid, thoroughly grounded imagination to paint this compelling portrait of a novelist. The dialogue is sharp and engrossing. The elements of both mystery and deeply personal conflict are introduced and compelling from the very beginning. The ending is anyone's guess, and guess you will...it's guaranteed. Yet no wisdom was ever imparted more entertainingly...not to mention at times emotionally. For a quick, brisk read brimming with pathos and dignity, humor and mystery, hope and despair, love and lust, corporate autocracy and little guys who won't knuckle under...you don't want to miss *Slot Attendant*."
- John W. Cassell, author of *Crossroads: 1969*

"Engelhard takes you on a literary cruise. Truly the author of this era."
- Len J. Jones, Amazon reviewer

"*Slot Attendant* is a page turner. You won't be able to put it down. It is such a fantastic read that I wonder, can any reviewer ever do it justice?"
- Gisela Hausmann, author and blogger

"With his usual energetic ease of edgy, efficient expression, Engelhard's *Slot Attendant* provides an electrifying, edifying, and entertaining read."
- Linda G. Shelnutt, mystery novelist

Also by Jack Engelhard

Indecent Proposal: Fiction.
Translated into more than 22 languages and turned into a Paramount motion picture of the same name starring Robert Redford and Demi Moore.

Compulsive: A Novel: Fiction.

Escape From Mount Moriah: Memoir.
Award-winner for writing and film.

The Days of the Bitter End: Fiction.

The Girls of Cincinnati: Fiction.

The Prince of Dice: Fiction.

The Bathsheba Deadline: Fiction.

The Horsemen: Non-fiction.
Excerpted in *The New York Times*

* * * * *

A new Spanish language edition of *Indecent Proposal* was released in 2013 in both print and e-book editions and made available for purchase worldwide.

"Precise, almost clinical language...Is this book fun to read? You betcha."
- *The New York Times,* for *Indecent Proposal*

"Well-wrought characters, exhilarating pace...funny and gruff...a fast and well-crafted book."
- *Philadelphia Inquirer,* for *Indecent Proposal*

"*Compulsive* is enormously enjoyable, and so easy to get into."
- Kenneth Slawenski, (Random House) bestselling author of *J.D. Salinger: A Life* - www.deadcaulfields.com

"Engelhard tells the story of *The Girls of Cincinnati* with precision through his masterful narration. Every word has a place and every page has a quote you will want to remember."
- Lois Sack, author of *Her Brightness in the Darkness*

"A towering literary achievement."
- Letha Hadady, author, for *The Bathsheba Deadline*

"Savor it...it may be the best, sharpest, most vivid portrait of life around the racetrack ever written."
- Ray Kerrison, *New York Post* columnist
writing for the *National Star,* for *The Horsemen*

"The refugee stories Engelhard preserves are boyhood memories of an almost Tom Sawyer character... adventurous, humorous, sometimes wonderfully strange."
- Chris Leppek, *Jewish News (Denver),*
for *Escape from Mount Moriah*

"What a great story. If you missed the 60s – if you missed the excitement, the passion, the radicalism, the thrills, the hopes and dreams – this book brings it all alive. I could not put it down."
- Kmgroup review, for *The Days of the Bitter End*

Dedicated to
Leslie, David, Rachel, Sarah, Toni...and Siena!

...and to the loving memory of my parents
Noah and Ida

Immeasurable gratitude to
Jeffrey Farkas, John W. Cassell, Linda Shelnutt

Engelhard's Guide to Writing
and other bonus essays featured herein
were previously published in the Communities
section of *The Washington Times*, except for
The Obit Uris Never Got.

Engelhard's Guide to Writing
(for a world gone berserk)

*"Everyone is a genius at something.
The trick is to find out what it is."*

NEW YORK, September 18, 2013 -- Tips on writing, from any writer, should be ignored. But here we go anyway because the world needs you.

1. Keep it simple.

2. Write for yourself. If you do not trust yourself, write for your best friend.

3. Do not write for the public. There is no such thing anyway.

4. Never worry about bad reviews or spiteful comments. Recognize that there are quite a number of stupid people out there who think they should be heard.

5. Every book – even a novel – is really a long newspaper article. That is where the word novel comes from – news. So the first task is to come up with a lede. Yes lede, for lead. Never mind why we put it like this. But once you have the opening thought, the rest follows. Moreover, every type of writing begins and ends with journalism – fact upon fact.

6. Drop the embellishments. Write the way you speak.

7. Do you like sex? If you are British or Jewish obviously you do not indulge. Otherwise, fear not, but write it as if you invented it.

8. Write your heart out. After that, cut it by half. You will be amazed to find that by subtracting you are adding.

9. Free yourself from worrying how your book will end. A book is smart. It knows when it is done.

10. Never approach your typing unwashed. Remember, writing is prayer; writing is holiness.

11. Consider yourself special, but also typical. Whatever hurts you, hurts the entire world. You embody the universe. Your job is to light up the place.

12. Yes, the world is tumbling all around us. Nothing makes sense. Remember, a simple candle brightens a darkened room. Be humble, but remember that in a world gone berserk, we need you. But never mind the answers. The questions you ask are more important.

13. Surprise yourself from one page to the next. If you can't surprise yourself, no way you can astonish your reader.

14. Write the outline to make your editor happy. Then discard.

15. Begin by approaching the mainstream (NY) publishers. After they have thanked you and rejected you, get it done by small press and/or digitally.

16. Read the classics. Then read the pulps. Read everything. Keep writing. Eventually you will find your own voice.

17. Study the movies. Screenplays show you how to condense.

18. Find the type of writing that suits you best. You are good at describing? Describe. You are good at dialogue? Do that.

19. Are you sure you want to write a novel? If nothing but dialogue keeps happening, maybe you wrote a screenplay.

20. Do not be a perfectionist. Perfection never comes. So why wait? The Liberty Bell is most famous for its crack.

21. Be kind to yourself as you write. Imagine your mother peering over your shoulder as you type – not your mother-in-law.

22. Grammar is important, but people forgot to tell William Faulkner and James Joyce about this and they did okay.

23. You will find that virtually every paragraph that runs five sentences or more can and should be cut to two.

24. If you write a sentence and must think it over more than three times, it is sending you a signal that it does not work. So give it a fresh start.

25. Actors should never be caught acting. Same goes for writers. Never get caught *writing*.

But the first rule to remember is that you stand on the shoulders of literary giants who came before you, but still, you are on your own.

Now shut up and write.

**More bonus essays
are included at the end of this
book, starting on page 215.**

Chapter 1

So it's four in the morning, Saturday night all over again, and I've got Zone 14. That's the worst there is, down there in the back, in the dark, where it's all pennies, nickels and quarters. It smells pretty bad, the stench of people who've sat in the same chairs all night long and haven't bathed since the last jackpot. I could use a shower myself.

They keep pumping in the coins like it's not real money. They think it's play money until they get home and can't pay the electric bill. They sit there delivering the slot machines their paychecks, their pension funds, their unemployment extensions, and they go at it like zombies, hypnotic, trance-like, panning for the gold. Someone told them this is "gaming," not gambling. The buses keep rolling in, pulling up, and more people keep spilling out. They dash for the same machine that was generous to them last time. This time of the night it's mostly the shadow people from Chinatown and Harlem. It never ends.

From the moment Atlantic City was given the okay to go round the clock, like Vegas and elsewhere, it never begins and it never ends.

Life itself has a beginning and an end. Only casinos live forever. Maybe they're onto something.

I've been working graveyard for more than a year. I'm a slot attendant. We are the ants. Everybody's your boss. I could have gone the Security route, become a guard, same pay, $8.25 an hour and more respectable, but that means elevators, checking doors and floors. I don't travel well in those, in elevators. Family tradition has it that my mother was stuck in an elevator while I was still in her belly, so that's my explanation. But even this job, slot attendant, wasn't easy to get. I was asked to fill in what category I fit and damn I couldn't remember what category I fit.

Maybe some of us don't fit, you know, categories.

I was also asked why I want this job. Why does anybody want a job? It's the economy, stupid. We need the money.

I was asked where I see myself in 10 years. Most likely dead, I told them.

I'm wearing the casino's official slot attendant uniform, black shoes, green pants, green shirt, green jacket. That, plus a tool and key belt, standard equipment. The key opens every slot machine in the place, the hoppers full of money, so in that sense we're special. Only we have those keys and, of course, our supervisors and shift managers. The shirt I'm wearing is wool and it itches. The pants, the jacket, these also itch. I use my official casino screwdriver to scratch my left shoulder blade, where all the itching seems to collect, and my wife, Melanie, always gasps when she beholds the welts, blisters and scabs. She says screwdrivers were not meant for that purpose. I usually scratch when I get upset, but I've been good about that and getting better. I'm learning to behave. You play the hand you're dealt. That's gambling. That's life.

The big glass doors keep opening and closing. There's a draft, there's a chill, I'm hot and I'm cold. I've been running from machine to machine. People hail me by snapping their fingers, by poking me in the ribs, by whistling, or by shouting, "Hey, you, slot attendant." I try to ignore the whistlers. They do bother me. The man who trained me, Suliman Veejay, told me, that time back, that he never responds to whistlers. That's too rude. There's got to be a limit. But what can you do, especially if a supervisor is watching?

Pini Cleopatrus spots me leaning against a pillar. She informs me that it's against the rules. Pini is so small that she has to stand on her toes to meet my gaze, but she is a supervisor. I think this may be the moment to drop my keys and tell her and the rest of them to take this job and shove it, but I think that every day, sometimes every moment, but it's a job, a paycheck, and above all, the Benefits! I try to remember what Philo said: "Be kind, for everyone you meet is fighting a great battle." I guess that includes Pini.

The supervisors started off as you did, as slot attendants, having only moved up a notch, but still, they are gods. To you they are god.

So I'm back to my rounds, but there is no catching up. I'm always behind. Slot machines are clumsy and keep breaking down. Coins get stuck in the comparators, a job that requires use of my tongue depressor, and bills get caught in the bill validators. If it's a real problem I use that special key to get inside. If it's something I can't fix, I have to call for a supervisor, and they hate that, being summoned. Around here, everything is an emergency. People don't like to be kept waiting, gamblers especially.

I'm proud of that key. I earned it after four weeks training with Suliman Veejay. The rest of them – it took them only two weeks to get the hang. Suliman said to relax, it's okay. But I was worried because I was on probation and people kept asking Suliman what was taking me so long to train up. Suliman told me not to worry, as he knew how to smooth-talk the supervisors and shift managers. He'd been at this 20 years. Kids, after all, learn faster. This is really a job for kids just getting started or for grownups just finishing up.

Pini Cleopatrus swoops down and snags me again for being so slow, and being so short and so thin she does have an advantage of being unnoticed until she's at your nose. Jackpots are ringing, zinging and buzzing all over the place, and the people want their money and they want it now. We all lead lives of quiet desperation all right, only here it's not so quiet.

Pini and I used to get along, there at the start, but, after a while, it goes sour. Slot attendants and supervisors seldom get along.

A black lady calls me over, and there's fury in her eyes. She's got those Sevens all across and she wants to know why no jackpot. I'm experienced. I know the problem. I knew it even before I scooted over. I explain that you have to insert the maximum amount of coins, three, otherwise poof, you're out of luck. She'd only tried one.

"You're all alike," she says. "You white people."

Pini strolls over and tries the polite routine, to no avail. The lady says it's all rigged against African Americans. (She is correct, in a sense, except that it's rigged against everybody.) Pini tells the lady to go to hell, if not in those words, and stomps off. Pini Cleopatrus is from Ethiopia. She is not African American. She is African. Africans, I've begun to notice, feel and express no kinship with African Americans. Anyhow, people are not at their best in this environment, no matter what color they go by. If you're going to become bigoted at this job, there's no single group to choose. They're all the same.

People are people, and that's no compliment.

"Hey, you, come here and do your job." I know who that is. That's a certain man named Howard Glass who's playing that same machine he always plays, the Wild Cherry, which is only a quarter game, and though the jackpot is ten thousand dollars if you get the cherries even and across, it is not a rich man's game, and Howard Glass is rich, rich, mean and spiteful. He's always at my zone, somehow, and he's got it in for me for some reason, as if I once did something to him, which I didn't. I don't know him and he doesn't know me, but he's assigned himself to be my bully.

Actually he does know me, that once I was somebody and did something big, which he'd probably read about in the papers, so now that I'm here, a slot attendant, which is quite a comedown, actually a crash, he loves to rub it in. He's an old man with a limp and watery eyes and saliva dripping from his crooked lips and it seems that he comes here, to the casino and to my zone, just to mock me. That's what he lives for. He knows that I can't talk back for the risk of losing my job.

Sometimes he just sits there at a machine and doesn't even play but just waits for me to pass by so that he can give me that scoffing grin. Usually, though, he makes a comment, like, "Too bad, huh?" Or, "What happened to you?" I just ignore this, but just once I would like to sock him, or at least tell him off. He's gotten under my skin, this Howard Glass. Sometimes he's with his wife who's a member of the Salvation Army or something and she is worse than he is and they do make quite a couple.

So he's calling me over, and I know there's nothing wrong with his machine, and I say, "Yes, Mr. Glass, what's the problem?"

He smiles that ugly, watery-eyed smile and says, "Just want to keep you on your toes. Make sure you're doing your job."

He stares at me, still smiling, waiting for a reaction, which is what he wants, his triumph, my defeat, but this I will not give.

"I'm doing my job."

"Just making sure," he says, and I move along as if nothing bothers me.

I stroll over to the Keno, which is where I'm not supposed to be because it's outside the territory, outside the ZONE where I'd been assigned, but I like that action, Keno. There's a man here who's always at the same machine, wears those shades and always has a book tucked in his lap. He is obviously a scholar, an intellectual (smart people also go for dumb luck) and he reads during the dry periods, when his numbers don't click.

Sometimes they do. Just now, in fact, he's hit six out of eight, and that means four hundred dollars. I shouldn't be here and the slot attendant whose zone this is should be here any second, indignant, so I'd better hurry with my question. I ask him, "What's your system?" He says he gets his numbers from upstairs. God gives him the numbers. He's into Kabbalah, which is all about the mysticism of numbers. "You ought to try it," he says.

Well, I have. I've tried it at the racetrack, for exactas and trifectas, but God keeps giving me the wrong numbers.

I'm back where I belong and I'm starting to get groggy and heavy in the legs. I'm getting light-headed and woozy. It's the hours, 10 p.m. to six a.m., wears you down. Real people weren't meant to work those hours. They've offered me daytime, but that's even worse since that would keep me from my writing and out of touch with New York. Six o'clock will soon be here, thank God, and soon I'll be trudging over to the train station. I don't trust the jitneys. They come late, or they don't come at all.

I'd better not fall asleep on the train and miss my stop. Except that usually that's the only sleep I get. Dave, the conductor who's become sort of a buddy, enough of a buddy that he's got an autographed copy of my book, doesn't always remember to wake me at my stop in Lindenwold.

More often than I'd care to remember I'd dozed off and ended up in Philadelphia, 30th Street Station, where the big trains, the real trains, come and go, and had to wait two hours, grungy and grimy, for a train back. That's the one good part, watching the big trains. That's quite a sight, watching them roar in, clanging, so huge, so powerful, like a leviathan on rails. My wife knows to wait it out and not to worry. My wife knows everything. Melanie knows the whole story.

Chapter 2

It's my day off and I'm up in my literary agent's office in New York. His name is Sylvio Morinaro, the hottest rep in the land. His office is near Grand Central Terminal, on the third floor. That's why I picked him. I can use the stairs. Actually, he picked me. Six years had passed since my Big Book, *The Ice King*, and nothing, nothing much, had happened since. *The Ice King* was a smash, a bestseller, and then turned into a Major Motion Picture. Everybody made money. We, my wife and I, made enough to square a generation of debts. That's how it is in the writing business. It's a labor of love for writer and reader, but otherwise it's not an occupation that commands a shingle and draws customers to your door. Editors aren't idling impatiently for you in the waiting room and they're not rushing for your services through the emergency entrance. Nobody cares.

We never got rich thanks to my Big Book, well – obviously.

So, six years since my last score. My last hit. Is that a long time? Is it like the old man who had gone eighty-four days now without taking a fish?

People tell me that I should have made enough money to live like Trump or Hefner. My agent at that time, Gloria Marlowe, admitted that she'd goofed. The contracts she'd had me sign for book and movie were not in my favor. I signed every paper put in front of me. What did I know?

She'd goofed all right, but I did have that Big Book, so I had fame, reputation, pedigree; bigger offers were sure to come. Life had other plans. Take it from me, when one door closes, another door closes.

So six years zipped by and I worked odd jobs, even driving a cab for six weeks until everybody realized that I had no sense of direction, especially the passengers. I usually gave them the grand tour but never on purpose. Too often I had to ask *them* for directions and anyway, soon the Somalis and the Afghans took over, one by one, every single cab. Nobody knew where those newcomers got the money but there was talk about a grand scheme. I was never big on politics, figuring, as I did, that none of it will ever get resolved, so why be troubled? But there was talk among the cabbies being bought out and forced out that Muslims were taking over this country stage by stage. Let it be. Life is too short to worry about everything. Finally (always when you least expect it) can it be? Yes, it's Sylvio Morinaro on the line and he asks what's happened to me? Yowzah!

I said that I'd been working on another Big Book. This was true. The name of it was *Smooth Operator* and what's new in the world of publishing is that they don't reject you so much anymore; they just don't respond. Ring Lardner advised writers never to add their return addresses along with their submissions so that publishers wouldn't know where to return manuscripts together with rejection slips. That was supposed to be a joke.

So when they wash you off like this, the question you have to ask yourself is this: Is it possible that I am right and the rest of the world is wrong?

Have you been kidding yourself all these years? Can you really be that mistaken?

Part of the trouble is that once you've sold a book to Hollywood, you're stamped as writing for the movies even though you're not; you're a serious novelist and Hollywood just happened. Whose fault is that? New York and Hollywood don't get along. New York is about words. Hollywood is about pictures. No wonder. Anyway, I got caught in the middle, and here comes that phone call from Sylvio.

I send him *Smooth Operator* and he likes it and says he'll sell it in a snap. That was some months ago. No snap.

So now I'm in the waiting room. There's another writer waiting with me, brimming with bright-eyed high voltage energy that they teach you in those 12-Step seminars, which are usually reserved for business go-getters, though artistic-types may monitor those classes to learn that failure is not an option, except when it is, which is something you learn after class. (Failure is an option. Despair isn't.)

Anyway, this guy, his hair is uncombed and he's dressed like a slob, but he's a writer, so it's legal. He's wearing jeans that Melanie, my wife and wardrobe terrorist, wouldn't even allow me to wear up to the 7/11. He tells me he's written a Big Book and that Random House has poured in an offer. It's all over but the signing. He says, "We all need that Big Book." He raises his arms and gestures quote marks with his fingers when he says Big Book. This is so annoying. People should not do this, writers especially. He says only "genre" books sell these days. What's my genre? I don't have one. I don't have a genre.

Writers, I have noticed, do not get along with other writers. Writers – all artists – are entirely self-absorbed.

Who cares? Nobody cares.

He's written a book, this writer, for the improvement of individuals and the world and I know that this genre sells – these are always at the top of the bestseller lists – but strangely, altruistic as this is, speaking as a slot attendant, I have not yet seen any improvements in most individuals or the world. Agents and editors have asked me to tackle this subject but it is not my style since I haven't the vaguest notion how to improve myself or the world. Even step one is beyond me.

Another writer steps in and he is in a hurry, only came in to deliver his manuscript. He is bald and rumpled and breathing fast as if he has other more important engagements. He tells the receptionist that Sylvio was expecting this. She asks his name. "Weiss," he says, "but I am not Jewish." She tells him to have a seat. I say, "Your name is Weiss?" He says, "Yes, but I am not Jewish." Finally Weiss gets to deliver his manuscript and is off again to remind people that his name is Weiss, but not Jewish.

Out comes Sylvio with another man and both are sipping champagne. The man is red in the face and neck from an abundance of joy and keeps shaking Sylvio's hand and thanking him. He backtracks out the door still bubbling his gratitude. Sylvio gives me a nod but the other writer, who was here first, gets ushered in and now it's me and Sylvio's assistant, Marci, a sweet-natured nearly-attractive blonde.

I like Marci because she's pleasant and also because she's been here longer than two weeks. Good help is hard to find and even harder to keep. Most "office managers" in the literary and entertainment world last until the nearest paycheck. They've all got bigger plans. So one day it's Susan, next day Carla, and then Cindy and suddenly it's Gabriella. You're always reintroducing yourself and starting from scratch.

But Marci is staying, I think. She says, as she's doing business at her desk and computer, "Your day will come."

I don't think she knows my name. In an agent's office, authors are as common as oranges to a grocer. You are not special.

I say it already did. My day already came.

"Came and went, huh?"

Then she apologizes. Didn't come out the way she meant it to. She saw the movie of my book, *The Ice King*, but hadn't read the book. She knows, though, that it was a wonderful novel and that the movie surely didn't do it justice. Wasn't the book number one on *The New York Times* bestseller list for quite some time? Wasn't the sexy cover splashed all over the place here and abroad?

What, asks Marci, was I doing these days, besides, of course, this new novel I've got going with Sylvio?

I tell her (in that mask of jubilation that I've managed to adopt) that I'm also doing journalism, which is true. I write for my hometown paper, *The Gazette*, for which I get paid $75 per opinion article. I do not tell her, naturally, that full-time – well, full-time I am a slot attendant in an Atlantic City casino. (She wouldn't believe me anyway. Nobody does. Even Melanie's mother cannot believe this and frankly even I do not believe this but it is true. It is true.)

She is also Sylvio's reader, so she's read my manuscript for *Smooth Operator* and likes it very much (especially the sex scenes) and it is sure to top *The Ice King*. Just hang in there, she says, "You know Sylvio has never lost a patient." She chuckles and I smile at the odd inference, at the thought that a writer is really a patient who needs to be cured; of, perhaps, this writing affliction. "No, I mean it," she goes on. "Sylvio sells everything, and for huge bucks."

I like hearing this.

"Six figures," she says.

I like six figures.

She starts giving me the names of some of those writers that Sylvio had turned into winners and I pretend to know them but I don't.

I don't care about them either and am beginning to get tired of hearing about other writers.

I do not care about other writers unless they are failures and the successful ones make me sick.

Finally, Sylvio steps out with that genre writer and they're not sipping champagne but they are happy. Sylvio asks me to give him a minute, so I'm still waiting. But I don't mind. I'm in New York, not Atlantic City, and I'm not wearing my green uniform. I'm in decent pants and jacket and one of those polo shirts without a collar that Melanie, my wife and, as I keep reminding her, my wardrobe tyrant, made me wear. She really is something, Melanie, when it comes to clothes. I am not color blind but I just don't know what matches. I think women want to keep on dressing you the way they kept on dressing dolls when they were girls. I think that's what it is, what it goes back to. They want to turn you into Barbie, or is it Ken? So, anyway, I'm in New York and we're talking books and writers and huge bucks.

I've done all this before, six years ago, and I was happy then, too. I love New York.

Marci asks where my ideas come from and I know that she's just making conversation but I start explaining anyway that ideas come from a parallel universe and as I'm really getting into it, just getting warmed up, talking about the mystery, the magic and even the miracle of creativity, a buzzer sounds and Marci says to go right in. She wasn't paying attention anyway. People pretend but nobody cares. This too I have noticed.

Sylvio is on the phone, that headset contraption they're all using these days to free their hands. I sit down, opposite him and his desk, and he's talking to a publisher, obviously, though from moment to moment I'm not sure if it's me he's addressing or the phone, and as he shoves a book in my direction I'm not sure whom he means when he asks, "Have you read it yet?"

"Me?" I whisper.

He nods.

The book is titled *Plaintiff* and no, I haven't read it and wonder why I'm being asked; I am here, I thought, to talk about *my* book, not someone else's.

"Robert Dunlap wrote it," he says.

Good for Robert Dunlap.

Sylvio has a soft voice for a big man. He's got a pink, baby-faced complexion and, especially when he's seated, his body is shaped like a pear. He is rather fat but not jolly. He is the hottest literary agent in New York, but his reputation is not spotless. *Time* and *Newsweek*, or some such magazines, have taken swipes at him for being "an ambulance chaser." When bad things happen to bad people, they go to Sylvio to turn their stories into books, the bad people do.

So Sylvio is on the phone between me and the party on the line, and I remain confused.

"We'll talk it over during lunch," he says and I shrug to ask if it's me and he shakes his head that it's not.

"But he's got a big name," Sylvio is saying to the phone, "so don't give me mid-list. We've been through all that and it's time to talk turkey."

Is it time for me to get excited?

"No," Sylvio is saying, "we've already passed the eight hundred thousand dollar figure." Sylvio wants a straight million. That figure makes headlines. After all, he says, "I'm not giving you some kid off the street. I'm giving you an established writer who turned out a prime-time book, never mind that movie." Then Sylvio pulls out the ace: "Look, I've already got a million dollar offer from another house, so let's stop playing games."

I did not know this, and yes, let's stop playing games.

"What do you think?" Sylvio says.

"Me?"

Yes, he's talking to me.

"A million bucks sound all right?"

"Sounds good to me."

Then it's back to the phone and Sylvio is listening and then smiling and then laughing and then it gets private and then it's over.

"He's a tough nut," Sylvio says, "but I'll bring him around."

That won't be necessary, I say. I will accept the $800,000.

Sylvio says, "Oh, that wasn't about you."

Oh. My mistake. (I keep wondering why agents are always talking about that OTHER writer.)

"That was for Robert Ivers. Ever read him?"

"No, sorry."

"You should. This new novel of his, sure to make it all the way to the top."

"That's great." (I'm thrilled.)

"I'll get you a copy."

"No rush."

So all of it – the sale, the million dollars – was for another writer, as you sat there, thinking, just once, Dear God, it was for you. Why not? Is good luck a limited commodity? Why so short the supply? There should be enough to go around. Why not make it bountiful so that we all get a turn? So you sit there and show no wound, no pain. To you it is life and death. To Sylvio it's another day at the office.

He leans back, then forward. "What can I say? Just this morning we got another rejection for Mister Smooth."

"You mean *Smooth Operator.*"

"Right, *Smooth Operator.* So what can I say? Your writing is so good, but they're not biting. We'll just keep plugging away."

"I'm grateful for your persistence."

(True, another agent would have given up on me. It's amazing how quickly they give up on you in this business – or maybe it's the same in any business.)

"Nobody wants good writing anymore," says Sylvio.

"There must be somebody."

"You have to learn to relax."

Yes, I will have to learn this.

I never considered patience to be much of a virtue.

He tells me it's all about salesmanship, that I must get myself a publicist, get out there, promote myself, do television, social media.

"It's never the book that sells," Sylvio says. "It's always the author."

Yes, I will have to make myself famous. But I do not want to be famous, only my books. Fame (as I have known it) is a bother.

Fame is only good if you are 21 and need it to get laid.

One time I did end up on TV but the host never read my book (or any book) and the commercial interruptions were driving me crazy. I still say that commercials – commercial interruptions – cause brain damage. It's impossible to focus when every five minutes the brain gets bonged. Also, I think I lost her, this host, when she tested me on Denis Johnson or some other writer she favored, or flavored, and I responded that I am not current and don't much go for the genius of the month.

She tried me on Saul Bellow and this didn't click either when I said, "That's not writing. That's kvetching." Same for Philip Roth.

When we got around to such novels as *Madame Bovary* and *Indecent Proposal*, novels about temptation, she quoted surely the most controversial (and misunderstood) observation I ever published: "As long as there are women, there's going to be trouble." This only works with people who have a sense of humor and we are losing them by the hour.

"Something's got to give," says Sylvio. "You've got too much talent."

Never mind talent. Luck is all we need. Luck is everything.

Sylvio seems to be reading my thoughts. Says he can't figure it out. I had such great success with *The Ice King*. Such a funny business, publishing. It's all so subjective. Besides, people aren't reading fiction these days, there is so much non-fiction going on around the world. Americans just want the headlines. Fiction is dead. Well, the experts said the same about radio, the movies and rock and roll. Also, I know more about the Civil War from Margaret Mitchell than from anything non-fiction. I don't tell him any of that because he'd just say – I'm only giving you the facts. He tells me, again, not to worry, it's still out there, being read. Anything can happen. How am I making out otherwise? How am I making a living? His phone is buzzing and he'll take the call. I take that as my cue and as I rise for the exit I say I'm doing fine. Just fine.

"We'll get there," he says, signing me off.

Where?

Chapter 3

Like everyone else, I get two 40-minute breaks, so that's where I am, on my break, up here in the employee cafeteria, smoking section, sitting by myself, doodling on my notepad or writing the great American novel. We may never know. I do have a title for my next novel. I'm always coming up with titles. This one, this new title, I think is my best, and it's *Boy Meets Girl*. That simple. I think it's good because it encompasses all Literature, just about. Boy meets girl. That's how it starts whether we're reading the Greeks or the Romans or any of them up to this minute. Even the Hebrews had it like that, though their inclination was more like, "Boy Meets God."

As for me and *Boy Meets Girl*, I can already see it plastered on a million book covers and hoisted upon ten thousand marquees.

Down on the casino floor I sometimes write entire novels, in my head of course, going from machine to machine, from hopper jam to jackpot. Up here in the employee cafeteria I do most of my daydreaming, even though it's at night. Unlike Elvis, slot attendants are not allowed to leave the building because we have that key, the key that opens every slot machine in the casino, each hopper containing anywhere from fifty to fifty thousand dollars. So that does set us apart. We may be lowest in rank, even lower than the maintenance people, but the keys do give us some status.

There is an occasional temptation to dip in and pocket some of that loot, but there's also that eye in the sky that sees everything. But something has been going on.

I think I know what it is. I think I even know who it is. Toledo Vasquez once asked me if I'd want to go partners.

I asked him for what? He said never mind. But I can't forget that smile. But I also like Toledo and don't believe he's capable of that kind of action.

Anyhow, there's already been a scandal from Coin Redemption where a whole group of them conspired for an amount in excess of $60,000. They got nabbed.

I don't mind sitting alone up here in the cafeteria. It's by choice. These are pretty good people, most of these employees, but they are not my people, whoever those people are; I still don't know. It gets quite cliquish. The table dealers (they make the good money) have their own crowd as do the slot attendants and the supervisors. Some of the dealers are up here wearing tuxes, which tells you that they deal high-limit, which could be $100 blackjack, but usually it means baccarat. They're supplied those uniforms from the Uniform Department, much like actors who get outfitted from Alliance Pictures' Wardrobe Department out there in Hollywood. That brings back memories, some good, some bad. But it did happen for me, for us, that one time and maybe that's all anybody's entitled to, one time. If one person got all the luck there wouldn't be enough for anybody else. But once I did; I did walk the red carpet. So let's keep that in mind. Let's remember that even as we sink lower and lower. My green uniform, here at the casino, comes from the Uniform Department, where they can never find your exact size. Those clerks in Uniform are always nasty. If you don't like the jacket they hand you, well screw you, that's all we got. I get along with one of them. I actually think she has a crush on me. Or maybe that's how it gets to feel when somebody smiles.

None of the uniforms ever fit, certainly not for me. The pants are too long and the jacket is too short. Sometimes the pants are too short and the jacket is too long.

Fortunately nobody cares enough to notice or notices enough to care.

So I'm sitting here minding my own business, munching on a cheeseburger, when an old-timer pulls up a chair, Russell Burger, the elder statesman among slot attendants. He has a story. We all do. We all have a story. I've heard his before, and I like it, about how he used to be a top engineer for Lockheed or Boeing or something, and blew it all on craps. Lost practically everything and was into the IRS for about $80,000, and they were coming after him.

So he got to them before they could get to him. He surrendered, plain surrendered, like in the old Wild West. He marches into the nearest IRS office, extends his arms for cuffing, and says, "Arrest me." They think he's nuts. They laugh and say, "Not so fast, not so easy. Work it off." So that's how you become a slot attendant. We all become equal under the same law of gravity which is now rendered as "default." We all return to our default position though some come at it free-fall and tumbling.

Whenever I get together with Russell Burger I think of that Depression song: "Once I built a railroad, now it's done, brother, can you spare a dime." But we are not about self-pity around here, I don't think. We're working, after all. We have a job, with Benefits, and we are not standing in any bread-line. Down on the casino floor Burger uses his own equipment, most famously that screwdriver from home, and that's against the rules, but the supervisors don't bother him about it because he'll soon be gone anyway, downsized, incapacitated or dead. That's the figuring, so they leave him alone, mostly.

Burger doesn't really walk when on duty; he shuffles along. One of the kids told me how she hated Burger for his "old man breath and his old man smell."

I explained that even young people grow old, so watch out!

"What's your story?" he asks as always.

"I have no story," I say as always.

"There are rumors about you," he laughs.

"Like what?"

"That you committed a crime or something."

"Wrong."

"Or that you failed at something."

"Wrong."

"Isn't that why we're all here? Because we failed?"

"I didn't fail. I'm just getting started."

"That's the spirit," he says.

He's gone but then I'm joined by Toledo Vasquez, who's been sitting with that group of kids, all slot attendants, all of them Patel Indians, Asians, some whites, some black kids from the hood, a virtual United Nations junior league. I get along with some of them, especially the Patels, but it was different at first. What's there to talk about with spanking new people? Most of them, the kids, are into hard rock and heavy metal and I still can't get over Patsy Cline.

Maybe, to be honest, I felt superior. Or maybe, to be more honest, I felt inferior. So I've kept my distance, though down on the casino floor there is no avoiding contact, and sometimes conflict, as our zones do overlap. It's good form to come to the aid of a fellow slot attendant when he's having trouble with a machine or a customer, but it's bad form to poach on his territory for a tip after someone's hit a jackpot.

So Toledo Vasquez joins me and I've begun to like him anyway. He's a chunky, muscular, bright eyed kid of about 22, American-born of Mexican parents. Or maybe Puerto Rican. They all call themselves "Spanish" regardless. He lives in a rough neighborhood and gets into many fights, mainly to preserve his girlfriend. He loves her with a passion that is clearly Spanish. They love for keeps. Toledo grew up tough in Camden, New Jersey. That's where every next day is a triumph.

I've given him tips on women (as if I've got it figured out) and even shown him some crafty moves in self-defense. He's tougher than me, largely on account of his youth and street experience, but I have fought in a war and earned a Black Belt from a secret (Russian) martial arts society. I'm big on boxing and once got knocked out. It's not so bad. It's like taking a sleeping pill, only this, a knockout, works much faster; makes you swoon. My jaw still relocates every now and then. I don't know how these boxers take it on the chin a thousand times a fight and still go on. I got hit that way but once and am still remembering.

Yes, I fought in a war. I was in combat. I do not talk about this. Once in a while, at home, it slips out when something about it, where I fought, is mentioned on the news, and I remember. I remember how it was and how the chaveireem fought so gallantly but still fell. I wrote a book about this. Some time ago this was. I sent it around. No bites, no takers, no hope. They loved the writing but I had picked the wrong side even though it was the right side and some day this would be the justice, but not today, not in this world, not in this lifetime.

Even Sylvio, back then, said it was too politically incorrect. One publisher said he would scoop it up in a minute if only I would switch the good guys to the bad guys.

Imagine!

That is when I learned something about the publishing business. Like everything else, it was the politics, not the writing. The politics.

You had to conform to a particular point of view.

Toledo says, "Man, they raked me."

"Who?"

He says the State Police and law enforcement members of the Casino Control Commission questioned him about theft, precisely a theft ring. Thousands of dollars keep coming up short each day from the hoppers, so it must be somebody, but why him, he wants to know? He's aiming for supervisor and got a girl he wants to marry. "Have they talked to you?" he asks.

"Why me?"

"They'll be talking to everybody."

"News to me."

He doesn't seem all that concerned. Or maybe he is. I really can't tell. Tough kids like Toledo know it's wise to walk through life with a shine and a snarl.

"Could be big," he says, lighting up another cigarette. "Big trouble. Everybody's under suspicion. They got the spotlight on all of us; eye in the sky. They got it special on us, grave-yard. Even the supervisors, man. You clean?" I'm glad he's not asking what I keep writing in my notepad. Others have asked that question. They think I'm maybe a spy, a plant, a spook. But Toledo and I are cool. We cool.

In this notepad of mine I keep writing sketches and one or two of them may lengthen out into a novel. The ideas keep coming and sometimes I just can't stop.

So I say, "I'm clean. You clean?"

"I'm clean," he says after a pause.

He asks me if I'd snitch if I knew who it was.

"Depends," I say.

He laughs, pats me on the shoulder, and goes back to his friends.

I gobble down my cheeseburger, drain it down with a swig of Pepsi, and down I go to the casino floor where it's buzzing with all that action, but it's amazing how, after a while, you see nothing. It's all the same. That first day you were dazzled but now it's a blur. True, you never step into the same casino twice, but it's still just a place of business, a place where you work and do your monotony.

They've got me in Zone 7 tonight, not a bad zone. Mostly dollar games and therefore mostly a dollar crowd. I know some of these people, these players. They're not bus people. They're regulars and back home, white collar types. From zone to zone, it's worlds apart. I settle in and wish them good luck and some turn from the machine action and say they're glad I'm around.

I'm in for a busy night and that's okay. It's better this way, otherwise I go on rewind and everything comes back. I try not to think of Melanie. She never complains about having to sleep alone all night and I try not to think about it too much. We have a deal that I won't pity her and she won't pity me and it's been working out. She is afraid of mice, though. They come in from somewhere outside, obviously, and a couple of times, actually more often than that, she's greeted me at the station with that bad news face, and when it turns out to be a mouse in the house, and nothing more, I'm quite relieved, though after that I have to go chasing it down. I know that sometimes she can't sleep at night because she hears sounds, the sounds of a mouse or maybe something worse, something bigger. She thinks there's something crawling between the walls. There probably is. She is terrified of spiders. But spiders are a blessing. A great king of long ago, David, was saved by a spider's web.

But the trick is not to think about that, or anything, and get with the flow of the action, and there is always plenty of action down on the casino floor.

Maggi Holt is my supervisor tonight. We get along. Maggi is a bit on the dumpy side but she's got a pleasant face and an upbeat personality. She's got romance problems and never hesitates to confide what's happening and what's not happening. She's a flake, but that's good. I thank her for getting me off Zone 14, and she says there's a price. "Oh, Maggi," I say, "I'm married. You know I'm married."

Maggi wants to get laid. It's really that simple.

Turning half-serious, she says when she does the schedule she always puts me in good zones, though she can't give me Zone 1, the coveted $100 high roller spot. That's reserved, usually for Marty Glick in his tux, and we all understand that some cash may be exchanged between certain slot attendants and certain supervisors to gain that plush assignment. Can't be sure. But it's a reasonable guess.

It's all about tips. The better the zone, the better the tips. Some of the guys in Zone 1, like Marty, can whisk home in a Mercedes after another thousand dollar night.

Imagine that – slot attendant as a CAREER.

In a neighboring zone, Zone 8, I spot a subterranean. We're supposed to report them to Security to have them escorted off the premises. They get free food, free rooms, free play, all on forged documents, until they're snagged, and even then they start all over again. So we're supposed to report them, but I just don't feel like it today. Everybody's got an angle and who are they hurting anyway? We're all trying to make it and so what if someone finds an edge?

We're all doing it in one form or another.

So Maggi, also ignoring what's going on nearby, says, with my looks I must have been something in my day. Sizing me up and down: "You still got it, you know."

"Come on, Maggi. Behave."

"That's no fun. Just once. I won't tell."

"But I'll know."

"I'll bet you were something. Oh don't give me that innocent shrug. You know you were something."

"That was another life."

"I know you fool around."

"No I don't."

"You lie."

I used to think she was kidding, but no, Maggi wants to get laid. She says if I continue to spurn her she'll start spreading those rumors about me.

"What rumors?"

"That you're a spy."

She's heard, she says, that I'm really a writer. That I was once very famous.

"So what am I doing here?" I ask.

"That's what I'd like to know. That's what we'd like to know."

"There is nothing to know, Maggi. I'm a slot attendant."

"Oh sure."

"What you see is what you get."

"You can't make me believe that someone like you likes doing this. Come on, Jay, fess up!"

"I never said I like doing this."

"I just wonder who you're spying for. Management? The Commission? Some newspaper for an expose?"

"Afraid it's not that glamorous."

"But you were once a famous author, right?"

"I'm a slot attendant, Maggi. That's what I am."

"Once I get you to bed, you'll spill."

I am beginning to think that Freud had it right. It is all about sex. Just weeks ago I made a connection with a movie producer who was there as a club owner in Greenwich

Village during the 1960s. My pitch was that his memoirs would make a terrific movie, all that idealism, the music, the counterculture. He said that he remembered none of that, only that he kept getting laid.

* * *

After a time you get used to the hours; even graveyard can get to be a habit. Ten p.m. when you first hit the floor you're spooked. You don't know what to expect and where to expect it from. But you're gonna get nailed, for sure, from a player, a supervisor, from another player, from another supervisor. Most gamblers are surly. It's not life and death, but it is about money, so maybe it is life and death.

A few hours later you're in control, at least you've managed and working off the rhythm of the place, and working from your adrenalin. When the clock runs down to about four in the morning, you run down as well, and the last thing you want to do is check your watch. The minute hand never moves when you keep checking and sometimes it seems six o'clock, punch out time, will never come around.

When the clock hits six, six a.m., it's like a miracle, like being born again.

Chapter 4

So this morning I overslept on the train and find myself in Philadelphia, 30th Street Station, where even breathing echoes all around.

I settle in for a Danish and a cup of coffee at the McDonald's and watch people come and go. They're all groomed for action, business. I'm unshaved, a refugee from graveyard.

I need two trains to get me over to Lindenwold.

Finally, I'm back. My wife, Melanie, has kept the car running. Melanie is the most beautiful woman in the world, according to a survey I took. When she saw me among the missing at the 7:50, she knew. As always, she tried to run up the platform to activate a search party, but too late. Dave, the conductor, shrugged his regrets as the train took off with me in deep slumber. First time this happened, Melanie was alarmed, but it's become routine. Happens about once a month.

"I should remember," she says laughing, "to wait on the platform."

We don't talk much on the drive home to Voorhees. We rent in a fine apartment building, all very suburban with grass and trees and an endless backyard, and have even adopted a cat that came from a huge litter, the cat, Beige, really quite a charmer and an animal of deep wisdom. But they're converting these apartments into condos, and when that happens we don't know what we'll do. Melanie knows I'm beat. Obviously, she has no news. If she has nothing to tell, I have nothing to ask. But, back home, I ask anyway.

"Any phone calls?"

"No, no phone calls."

The cliché "no news is good news" doesn't work in my business.

"Nothing from Sylvio."

"Nothing."

I step in for a quick shower and remind myself that *Smooth Operator* is still out there, being read. Anything can happen. Sylvio said so himself.

When I come out and start toweling off, she says, "One day that phone call will come."

Better come soon. I just heard Philip Roth say it again, that the novel will be dead in 20 years.

From one novel to the next it's a race to meet the deadline.

We hardly make love anymore, Melanie and I. It really doesn't matter. It'll pick up, we both know, when our luck turns.

We hardly do anything anymore. Melanie has family, parents, aunts, uncles, cousins, the works, and she's always talking about them and wanting to visit. That's not me. I have no time for her family, or for mine. Tolstoy said all happy families are alike, but Tolstoy ended up half-insane and in the end was found talking to himself at some railroad station, so what did he know? I do have family, but I don't know where, and I don't care.

It's past noon and in about five hours I'll have to be back on the train again, back to Atlantic City. Not much time for monkey-business and not much time for something even more important, sleep. I'm toilworn, practically staggering, but that doesn't mean sleep. No, sleep is a battle. Sleep is a fight. Daylight is meant for being awake. The bedroom, even with the shades drawn, is no sanctuary. Pigeons have taken over the eaves, top and bottom. Their gurgling drives me nuts.

We had an exterminator come around, and he sided with the pigeons; said it was their home thousands of years before it was ours. Moreover, it's against federal, state, county and local ordinances to touch these pigeons. (I'd had dreams of picking them off one by one with a shotgun.) So, they belong here; we don't. They were here first and this is their home, so we're only visiting. In fact, all animals and even pests were created before we were, so they'll surely outlast us as well. The mouse and the ant, and the pigeon, came before man.

Melanie shuts off the ringers on the phones, as if that does any good. There's still traffic, horns honking, people talking, kids playing, babies crying, school bells ringing, hard-hats drilling, sirens wailing, garbage trucks rumbling. I'm in bed, taken one Valium. Nothing doing. I ask Melanie to bring me another, which she does, with a glass of water. That sends me to the bathroom. I may be getting another urinary infection, I don't know. Haven't been to the doctor in years. I don't want to know, and if it's something, I don't want it to come with a name. Anyway, Dr. Kozansky, when I do go there, all we talk is politics and books. There's barely enough time for an examination.

He admires me, Dr. Kozansky. Says he can't image what it's like being a writer. Where do those ideas comes from...and then to put them down on paper! Wow!

Dr. Kozansky – he's the one who keeps saying it's getting late. Time for another success. You don't want to hear that from a doctor, that it's getting late.

Melanie says that's what happens when you let your system get run down (as if it's my fault); you become susceptible. You get urinary infections. Used to be, for sleep, one Valium did the trick. Now it takes two. Soon it will be three and then four, and then what? Sleeping pills, I'd tried those, but they get you up still sleeping. They're meant for a full night, not two hour naps, which is what I average on a good day. I wonder how long this can go on.

I don't want to know the time. That's the worst thing to know when you're struggling for some shuteye. Panic never helps. But I know it's about 2:30 when I finally drift off, and by 4:30 I'll be up and that'll be it, as usual. I shower again, and shave, and wonder what happened to my face. I have no color and my eyes are vacant. I need a haircut. I've been spoken to about that by my supervisors. No beards, either. There is a grooming code for slot attendants. Einstein would never make it as a slot attendant. Neither would Hemingway or Beethoven.

Never mind time, I don't know seasons. All I know is day, when I try to sleep, and night, when I work. Seasons come and seasons go without me knowing one from the other. But I think it's baseball over on the TV, if not live then some replay. I used to follow every pitch. I knew all the batting averages. Now I don't even know who's on first. Is it time to call it quits when you don't care for baseball anymore?

I get dressed in my all-green casino uniform; snap on the tag. It says, "Jay Leonard, slot attendant at your service."

Melanie draws a deep breath and sighs. "Why do you do that, I mean while you're still home?"

I explain that I hate to change at work. That means going to the uniform department, in one of those dressing rooms, where who knows what's been going on.

"I just can't stand you in that outfit," she says.

Melanie, Lit and Journalism graduate from NYU, is a freelance book reviewer so our home computer is her place of business. She does pretty well, brings in enough money to help pay most of our bills, though we are maxed out on most of our credit cards and the phone calls have begun. We can't afford a new car or even a used car. The car we do have we don't trust beyond the neighborhood. If it weren't for the train, I wouldn't have that job in Atlantic City. We're actually quite fortunate.

Benefits! That's the one plus of the casino job. Still, as we await that wonderful phone call from New York, Melanie thinks I should be canvassing for a job closer to home – and, even more important, 9 to 5. She keeps reading the Want Ads for me. I refuse. That is too depressing. There aren't any jobs for writers anyway, unless it's technical, and I don't do technical. I'd already done the advertising and public relations, as we all have.

I stopped reading the Want Ads a long time ago but Melanie keeps finding jobs for me in hospitals, nursing homes, or homes where people are terribly sick, God forbid, and "caregivers" are always in demand. The hours are good, the locations nearby, but the pay is bad, and...no Benefits! Anyway, I don't think I'd do well in those environments.

You're supposed to network, and I do have friends, even friends connected to the literary world, but I don't know. I just don't know.

Melanie stays cheerful. I don't know how she does it, but she does. They say a happy childhood lasts a lifetime and I guess that's what accounts for her upbeat disposition, though there's no escaping what's plain and obvious, even for her. So she's built a wall. She calls it a wall. Once in a while the wall comes tumbling down, as when the electric company sends a second shut off notice.

This happened just yesterday, and she'd kept it from me. "Suppose," she says, as a bad moment overtakes her, "that phone call from Sylvio never comes?"

She's made me something to eat as she says this. I don't know what I'm eating, but it is food. It's soup, I think.

I'll eat a bigger meal once I get to the casino. That's another big plus. Free food. I don't know what I'm eating there, either.

She's expecting checks from five newspapers and two literary websites and these checks are always slow in coming. People just don't want to pay.

"We'll manage," she says.

She hates to send me off gloomy.

"We always do, don't we?" she says.

"Yes we do," I agree.

Sometimes I feel guilty having married her. She could have done much better. Until recently, we used to reminisce about my hit with *The Ice King*, how glorious it all was, money coming in, people wanting interviews, autographs, and the stars we met in Hollywood, and the red carpet treatment we got at the opening. But we don't do that anymore. That's done.

We don't even watch the movie when it comes on TV. That used to be an occasion when *The Ice King* came on. No more.

No, it's time for something different and *Smooth Operator* is where we've got our hopes pinned.

This is where I've made my stand, all or nothing, live or die, on that novel. There is this, and no hereafter.

It's about a guy who starts off as a Good Samaritan and then...oh what's the difference.

I tell Melanie my joke, the joke about how I'm going to accept the Oscar. I'll say: "I am mostly indebted to my wife for seeing me through thin and thin."

Melanie doesn't like the joke, mostly because it isn't true. We've had fat city. We've had plenty of good times, good days. Sometimes we compare ourselves to people who really have it tough. Just read the newspapers – and there's always a phone call from some relative of hers who's come down with something really serious. So we compare ourselves to the rest of what's out there and find that we're not in such bad shape, after all. People have it worse. Talk like that, usually at McDonald's, puts us in good spirits, but only for about five minutes.

I do worry about this, if and when that good phone call does come along: Maybe there comes a point in life when even success comes too late.

The world is getting started on you, begins to appreciate you, but you're finished.

"It's very upsetting when you get dressed in that outfit," she says. "You're making a statement."

She means that I'm expressing defeat, which is not true. Mere convenience. No, I'm in the fight. I really am. One day I'll get even. That day will come!

Six years is not that long a time to be absent from your latest success. Look at J.D. Salinger. He's been gone nearly 60 years and people still talk about him.

"We'll be fine," Melanie says, as that hour is approaching and I am soon to be turned into a slot attendant.

"Of course."

I take two books with me for train reading – F. Scott Fitzgerald's *The Crack Up* and King Solomon's *Ecclesiastes* – both, centuries apart, on the question of futility and whether life is worth all the trouble. Fitzgerald, his career in freefall after a thousand failures and rejections swamped his early success, said that he'd continue on as a writer but stop being a person. He'd present himself good and polite but only as a front, keeping his bitterness in reserve.

Writers, novelists, generally don't make it till the end. Twain grew miserable. Hemingway grew suicidal.

Nathanael West wrote two fine books while clerking in a hotel. I'm a slot attendant.

"Get some sleep on the train," she says. Then she pats me gently along the cheeks and gives me a big warm smile.

Back at the start, when taking the train from Lindenwold to Atlantic City (and back) was still a novelty, I wanted to get to know my fellow passengers. Now I know them. This still amazes me, how many of these people read the Bible on the train. Some hide the Book within the centerfold of *Time* or *Newsweek*, afraid to be exposed as religious fanatics. Better to be caught with *Playboy* than Genesis.

I got to talking to one of these people, a young kid and not a religious type at all, but a big fan of the Psalms. I opened by saying I'm a big fan myself. He asked me what message I got from King David, and I said, faith of course, though am not sure what faith is, not really, except that it's maybe like trusting that your father won't let go until you know how to swim. What attracted me, since I seem such a skeptic? The poetry, the majestic precision of language, how incredible that after 3,000 years not a single word or thought is outdated...but also, shame. Shame? Yes, how odd that King David's greatest fear was about being put to shame. Almost every Psalm deals with that, the fear of being put to shame. (Who can't relate to that!)

This same kid asked me if I've ever delved into the Talmud. He's not Jewish but wants to become a lawyer and his professor suggested the Talmud as a means to develop an inquisitive and argumentative mind. That's why Jews make such good jurists. So yes, I have delved, and we got to talking about that passage where it's asked what you should do if you find a stamped and addressed envelope on the ground? Instinct says, the kind thing to do is mail it, BUT...suppose the letter contains a bill of divorce and the person changed his or her mind, and there you go ruining two lives?

Of course, generally I know better than to talk religion or politics with strangers, or even friends, or even relatives, or anybody.

For some reason there are a good number of Born Again Christians on this train route, also devout Jews. I don't know why. On the Paoli Local there is gambling going on, here, occasionally, proselytizing. A certain man, actually a kid, who said he was heir to a travel agency fortune, once, on the train, when I was half asleep, told me something really disturbing.

He said that people who die in wars and famines and other catastrophes pretty much have it coming. This weeds out the weak and leaves us with survival of the fittest. He cited the Holocaust as an example of nature, or God, saving the best for life. I got into it with this brat. I suggested – suppose the opposite is true? Suppose it's the good and the strong that go first, leaving us with the bad and the weak? Suppose, as I have come to believe, it is the unfit that make up most of the world?

Is there any doubt about this?

Before leaving for work, I try Sylvio again. Marci answers and says he can't come to the phone. He's all tied up. I know this isn't proper, hardly even ethical, but I ask her if she knows anything. She says if anything comes up Sylvio will be sure to let me know right away, but she really has to go, it's so busy around here, so many publishing contracts to study and sign, and the phones just won't stop ringing.

"You know how it is."

Yes, I know how it is.

Sometimes I feel like giving up. But then where do you go? Is there something like a used car lot for people – used people, broken people, discarded people, forgotten people, wasted people, defeated people? Melanie senses this mood of mine and suggests that I give Ann Shutt another try; this editor, at a major publishing house, who fell in love with *The Ice King* but has ignored me since. I don't remember why. It's been several years. Oh gawd no – I really do not want to start that business again.

"Go ahead," Melanie says. "What have you got to lose?"

Plenty. You can lose your self-confidence. You can lose hope. You can lose your faith in people. You certainly can lose faith in editors.

But I do dial the number and she does pick up. Yes, she remembers me, but the voice is cold. No, she's not interested. Why? "I've been following your writing and you're an excellent writer but we have no place for writers who objectify women as you do." I do? I objectify women? "I write it as straight as it comes." Now I remember. She once read a column of mine (a piece of humor that obviously "objectified" women) and had her assistant e-mail me this: GIVE HIM THE AX.

Yes, now I remember.

"I think you've got the wrong party," I say. "Bukowski objectified women."

"Bukowski was a beast. We never would have published Bukowski. This is your hero?"

"Any writer who gives himself up without fear and expresses himself honestly – those are my heroes. Like Henry Miller."

"I found him unreadable. Will that be all?"

"Don't you OBJECTIFY men? Seems to me that you do."

"As you wish."

How did it get to this? I had no intention of getting into a brawl.

"Some world," I say, "when novelists are forced to adhere to rules and regulations and the dogmas set down by editors. You're running a tyranny, a dictatorship."

"Too bad," she says – and click.

This was a mistake.

Melanie drives me to the station to catch the 5:50. That'll get me there 6:50, and to the casino around seven. My shift doesn't start until 10 p.m., but I need those hours to unwind, or rather to wind up, or rather to edge into the job. I can't just jump in. So I'll take the escalator and then the back stairs up to the employee cafeteria, eat, watch some TV with the rest of them, and doodle on my note pad, and make plans.

We wait for the train and say nothing. Melanie has already had her day – she's written a movie review, she's expanding into that – so she's already had her day. I'm just starting mine, my night, that is. So we sit waiting for the train, not saying much. There used to be so much to talk about. You never want to end up like one of those married couples, in restaurants, who sit there glumly and won't even gaze at each other, like they're simmering from grudges that go back days, weeks or even years. Between them, everything's been said and done and there is nothing more to say and do.

I hope that doesn't happen to us. I don't think it will. We have a dream. Sometimes on the Boardwalk you see old couples, people in their 80s, holding hands and snuggling up and whispering, as if they were still dancing on the night they were wed, and that is so blissful to behold and so sad. They survived it all as a couple. They lived it together and they will die together. Sometimes that's my only dream.

As the train pulls up, Melanie hands me a surprise; a chocolate bar, that Hershey's Special Dark that I like so much. We are both chocoholics.

Melanie posted a sign on our refrigerator door that says, Just Give Me Chocolate and Nobody Gets Hurt.

"I got it on sale," she says, "two for one at Rite Aid." She is smiling like it's Christmas. She knows she's given me a thrill, and this thrills her in return.

(Melanie clips all the coupons and goes for all the sales. She'll drive 10 miles for a 10 cent bargain, never mind the cost of gas.)

We're not asking for much, as we always say.

Just that, a bar of chocolate, and it's a different world.

Chapter 5

Omar is a supervisor I don't care for at all. He sticks me in Zone 12, second only to Zone 14 for claims to Slum City. It's mostly row after row of 25-cent video poker and it's almost all bus people. You won't find Bill Gates at these games. I walk the aisles, back and forth, as I'm supposed to, to be of service. It's not all that busy tonight. I sneak over to the table games, for a second, where it's so much more lively, and here's a man, at the craps and he's got more chips along his rack and more money on the table, waiting for the next roll, than most people have in the bank. This is a game of wild swings, ups and downs, but real gambling, old gambling, back room, before it got corporate. At the same table there's a man in Chasidic garb and a man in Islamic garb and they're cheering and rooting for the same toss of the dice, the same point. Maybe that's the solution to the whole thing.

I rush back to my zone, to the slots in Zone 12.

I notice a certain woman at one of the joker poker games and she's easy to notice because of a shock of flaming red hair that she wears tussled and curled all over her head and face so that there's hardly any face, though from a view up close there's craziness in those eyes. She's a regular. We've never talked. You do get to know the players, even make friends and even develop a following, something like a fan club.

But this redhead, for some reason we never got to talking. I'm told she works in one of the other casinos and comes here after hours and that's something nobody knows, that casino employees account for a good percentage of the drop when they go next door, as many of them so often do. It's tough not to gamble when it's all around, though it's even tougher taking the plunge knowing what you know, that most people get skinned. They don't build casinos to make you rich.

So this redhead is in the middle of a row of players and as I'm making my rounds, she calls me over.

You never know what to expect. To them, you're the casino, you're the House. They blame you for everything.

You don't see our president, Bob Foster, walking the floor. He's up in his office. He knows where it's safe.

So I dash over to this redhead and she says, "Why are you staring at me?"

I say I'm not.

"Yes you are. You're jinxing me."

"I'm only doing my job, making my rounds."

"Well stop staring at me."

"Sorry."

"You make me nervous."

Omar swoops down about an hour later. That's how they do it, the nasty ones; they come at you from behind, gotcha-style. He's got that flushed up fiery look in his eyes, which is about normal, but I know there's something. He's from one of those Middle Eastern countries where they're all so hot-tempered. He says there's been a complaint against me. What did I do? You're disturbing the players. Who? That's not for you to know, he says.

But he's not going to write me up. Have I ever been written up? he wants to know. No, I've been good. I've been a good slot attendant. I've never been written up. Okay, says

Omar, I'll let it go this time and won't ruin your record, but I do have to report it as a warning. I shrug and say, "Whatever." He doesn't like that (existential) answer and advises me not to be smart. He keeps staring at me. I know he wants to fire me. I think he wants to fire everybody.

He has no choice, Omar says, about the warning. But a warning is not as bad as a write-up. So he's doing me a favor, although it will be part of my record when it comes time for my performance evaluation. That's due pretty soon. They usually score you low anyway, the supervisors do, because if you score high they're compelled to give you a raise. Company policy. Generally speaking, there is nothing more humbling than a performance review. That, too, is company policy all over the place – Corporate Inquisition.

I think this will be my next novel, about performance evaluations, how they can ruin people and destroy friendships and create hostilities within the workplace. I once wrote a column about this and it was published in *The New York Times*, which is good but not good enough. This needs to be addressed on a larger scale. But will I ever find the time? This job as a slot attendant is so time-consuming and exhausting. Will I ever find the inspiration? No writing, no true writing can be done without that inner voice, or perhaps it is an outer voice and this too I have considered as being altogether divine and mystical.

"I caught that action," says Flint, dashing over from Zone 10, where he rules over the customers playing the Hot Sevens.

You need Flint Odesso at a time like this. Jovial Flint, from Da Bronx, is always good for comic relief. He's been at this business, as a slot attendant, for some 10 years, and nothing bothers him, nothing touches him, on the surface, on the inside, who knows, but outside, you'll never catch him without a big smile or a big laugh and sometimes even a hug.

"Oooooh," he says, doubling over as if someone sucker punched him in the ribs, "it's almost time for your evaluation, Jay. Omar knows if you've been naughty or nice."

"If it's Omar I'm sunk."

This cracks him up as if I were Jon Stewart.

He says, "I'll bet it is."

He passed his own evaluation with flying colors, he tells me, but he got lucky, he got Roger Price, a good guy, a dream supervisor.

"Now it's my wife's turn," says Flint, laughing so loud you can even hear him above all the clanking coins. "I evaluate my wife every six months, just like they do here."

For a second I think he's serious because Flint married the old-fashioned way. He is wed to a mail-order bride from Russia. He got her off some magazine or website or off the rack. Until Flint wised me on this, months back, during one of our breaks up in the employee cafeteria, I did not know such things were still done. I thought mail-order brides disappeared with the stagecoach.

Flint says, "What about you?"

"With me it's the other way round. I get evaluated every day. I'm married to an American girl, remember?"

We agree that foreign women are the best, especially when they come from countries where they're trained, from birth, to wash your feet.

This is Flint's second time, and he made the right choice. His first marriage was a bust (an American woman, of course), and she must have been a first-rate bitch to get on Flint's bad side. He's so easy-going, though it's true you never know how people are at home. But I'd be amazed if Flint had a secret personality. He does flare, now, when Omar spots him backsliding, and motions him back to where he belongs, in Zone 10, where jackpot bells are ringing. Flint says: "Free country? Says who? Eight hours a day you're chained to a job, rest of the time you're chained to a family. That Omar. Let's get him fired."

Franco DeLima is over at Zone 5, which is also low-rent, featuring Jackpot Party machines, and I amble on by now and then, when I'm all caught up in 12, and really, what I'm doing is trying to stay clear of that crazy redhead who thinks I'm giving her the kibosh. You really have to be crazy to believe that, or massively superstitious, which most gamblers are, overly superstitious. Some players cross themselves before each pull and some place crucifixes above the knobs, as if it's not them against the House, but them against the Lord God. Maybe they're right. Maybe it is. It is amazing why some people always seem to win and why others always seem to lose. There's one lady, sweet Mrs. Paula Mason, who's here every day and NEVER hits. What's more amazing is how it's usually the wrong people who hit the million dollar jackpots, bad people or people who are rich already.

So anyway, here comes Franco DeLima and I can tell he's got a beef, the way he's thumping the ground with those wrestler legs. He's a big double-sized kid of around 26, wide heavy features, the word bully stamped all over him. He accuses me of poaching his zone, of pocketing a tip that belongs to him. This is a serious charge. This kid's been on me before.

I explain that Omar asked me, ordered me to go over and help him out, over in Zone 5, because hopper jams and jackpots were happening all over the place, and he, Franco, was falling behind. I wasn't even around when the payoffs came for those jackpots and certainly never pocketed any tips; not to say that poaching doesn't happen. We all do it when the timing is right and I do it when Melanie says we've got to pay a certain bill at high noon or else, and that's when

I go on the warpath, so I'm not altogether clean, only in this instance I am.

"I was just helping out," I tell Franco. "No tips."

"I don't believe you."

Of course, moments like this I wonder how it's come to this. I wonder who it's going to be on Book Talk this coming Sunday. Won't be me. Hey, let's not start feeling sorry for ourselves, okay? Many people have it worse and this is not so bad, not really. It is a job, for crying out loud! I watch C-Span regularly, whenever I can, to hear what other writers are saying, the successful ones, and it is all quite sickening. Who is their god? I even watch it when an award show comes on, like the National Book Awards, and listen in as they profusely and "humbly" thank their agents and their publishers, so humble these frauds, though once in a while a good book may be the result if only one had the time to sort them out, one smug writer from another.

How ridiculous to speak this way, on my part. They probably sweat bitter tears as much as I do. But really, why parcel out the luck so miserly?

"It's the truth," I hear myself saying, trading schoolyard language. "Ask him. Ask Omar."

Franco stomps off.

I'm near the craps tables again and a guy, dressed as conservatively as an accountant, no high roller this, I'm thinking, asks me which table is hot and I say they're all cold, or if they're hot, they're hot for the House. He stands there distractedly, saying nothing, and then says he's down to his last thousand dollar chip. He calls me pal. He says, "Pal, except for people like Donald Trump and Bill Gates, life sucks." I don't know if he means his last thousand of the day or last thousand of his life.

Either way, he steps up to the nearest table, throws down his single and last thousand dollar chip and says, "Eleven."

The shooter throws the dice and they roll over to ten. I'm watching this. That's the thing about gambling, there's a beginning, a middle, and an end. Where else do we find this? Most of life is so vague. My pal turns and part resolutely, part nonchalantly walks toward the exit. Where is he going? Where do you go? Will I be reading about this in the papers?

People jump out of windows quite regularly in Atlantic City. Einstein (supposedly) said that God doesn't play dice with the universe. This, the casino, is a good place to find out whether this is true or not – does seem, though, that life teeters on the roll of the dice and that the tumble between a 10 and an 11, one digit, can make all the difference.

Around four in the morning it starts to taper off and it's almost me alone – it is a weekday – on this side of the casino floor, and so I make a quick dash to the candy and news shop in the lobby where I buy that hard red candy that bursts in your mouth and helps keep you up when you've got two more hours to kill, and while I'm there I browse around the magazine racks and check out *The New Yorker* just to see who's in, who's not, who's cold, who's hot, and then I happen to glance at the paperback shelves and behold, there's my book, *The Ice King*.

What?

I can't believe this. The hardcover is out of print, I know that, and the paperback is still in print but out of circulation, or so I thought, but here it is.

The royalties had stopped coming ages ago. I'm stumped, don't quite know how to take this in.

I'm tempted to rejoice, but doesn't this make it worse? Your novel – here in a place where you work as a slot attendant? Who would understand?

I tell the clerk, hey, that's my book. It's a spur of the moment thing. He has no idea what I'm talking about. He's Indian. Can't speak English.

I rush back to my zone before Omar has a chance to nail me, but he's probably upstairs goofing off himself. It's that part of the night. I edge over to Zone 14. That's also the bus entrance where I find my buddy, Mark Pleszak, posted on guard duty. He's carding a couple of late-arriving kids and sends them back out past those big glass doors.

"Hey, Mark."

"Hey, Jay."

Mark has been in casino security for some 20 years, right here, same place. He wears a snappy blue uniform that is impressive, though casino guards are not even rent-a-cops. They get a week's training, carry no firearms and have no authority to make arrests. When it comes to that they have to summon the real cops. But they are impressive and they don't get hassled much, except by their own supervisors.

"I just saw my book in the lobby."

He knows part of my story. I know part of his.

"Oh yeah?"

Mark used to be in business for himself, but then it fell apart. Long story, but something about a family rift that got real ugly. Mark's motto is – Trust Nobody.

"Which book," he says, "the one they made into a movie?"

"Aha."

"Way to go."

"Yup."

Despite it all, that family contretemps, Mark carries no chip on his shoulder, no grievance, unless you really get him talking. His job is to keep undesirables from getting in, including drunks, pickpockets and underage kids. Depending on the day's assignment, his unit is also responsible for checking doors, fire escapes, bathrooms and separating two women when they get to scuffling over the same machine. They know every inch of the casino, these guards do.

"Was it a thrill?"

"Like sex."

"But masturbating, huh?"

I'm wondering if I'll be here 20 years, like Mark, which is one trick, the other is to accept it with the same compliant disposition.

I envy Mark's surrender. It is admirable. He's made peace.

"When's your next movie coming out?"

People seldom ask about your next book. They ask about your next movie.

"In my dreams."

That's a pact we have, Mark and I, downplaying everything. He likes my motto – I am nothing. I like his – Trust nobody.

He's probably my best friend in the place. He's an intelligent man. Like me, he still makes $8.25 an hour, even after 20 years.

Mark is pretty much my Algonquin Roundtable. He understands what it means when I say that writers die early and often.

I tell him, "Maggi Holt hit on me again."

He smiles. "Can a woman be that horny?"

"I figure it's my charm."

"Guess what? She's hit on me, too."

I spot Omar, so I make a quick check of the floor, and anyhow, Omar has pretty much called it a shift.

"Got news," says Mark. "Big investigation going on."

That theft ring, if it is a ring and not just one person, is all the buzz.

"Have they called you in yet?"

"No," I say.

"Everybody who's got a key is under suspicion. Watch your back."

"I'm clean."

"But not everybody's your friend. Trust nobody."

We drift back to women. He and his wife aren't getting along. Nothing serious. They're just not getting along.

"Mind if I tell you something?"

"Shoot."

"Top secret."

"Oooh."

"You know that Clara?"

"That hot dealer?"

"That's the one," he says.

"The one what?"

"She's got the hots for me."

"Who can blame her."

"I'm not kidding."

"How do you know?"

"I can tell."

"How?"

"I don't know. You know how you know."

"I know how you know. How do you know?"

"She's always finding reasons to ask me questions, steps up real close, gives me that smile. Trust me, I know."

"You gonna do something?"

"Just might."

"Go for it," I say.

"Just might do that," he says.

This Clara is our Miss America.

I make another round of checks – the place is utterly deserted – and when I come back we resume our discussion that started when we first became friends, which is that he believes in reincarnation, and that he himself, personally, has been reincarnated. In another life, he used to be a man named George Bendix who helped Ford build an automobile. In short, Mark used to be George, an auto engineer, or mechanic.

"Why pick that?" I say. "Most people pick Napoleon."

He's never taken off stride with that jest. "I'm not kidding. I was an engineer in Detroit, and my name was George."

"Your name was George."

"I always turn my head and answer to that name. Ever wonder why?"

"Come to think of it, you're right, George."

"It's true."

"You really believe this."

"I really believe this. I've got a real aptitude for cars. Why? Where did that come from?"

"That would mean every car engineer, or mechanic, is a reincarnation."

"Weren't you once somebody else?"

"In told you. Napoleon."

"I thought it would be Hemingway."

We both spot Omar lurking. "I'd better go."

"I'm glad about your book. You'll be back."

"I'm nothing. Just remember that, Mark."

"Not true," he says and being a horse player he adds: "Back class is always dangerous."

Chapter 6

Melanie is especially silent as she's driving me home from the train. She is actually quite grim. I know something's coming. Bad news, of course. Sylvio called, right?

"That, too," she says.

"That, too? There's worse?"

The bad news, from Sylvio, is that two more rejections came in for *Smooth Operator*. Which means one to go. (Or maybe two. I'm never sure.)

But it gets worse, yes it does. Casino law enforcement investigators phoned to set up an appointment with me.

"What's this all about?" says Melanie.

I tell her it's nothing. Routine. There's been theft. There's always theft. We're talking casinos. That's where the money is.

I notice she got her hair cut, short, or shorter. She's a natural blonde and I like her hair longer, but short is okay, too. I've been neglectful. Been a while since I've checked her out. There's been so much going on or maybe I mean that nothing's been going on. We've been so busy giving purpose to our days that there hasn't been much time for, well, romance.

"It's just a process."

"But why do they want you?"

"They want everybody. They want anybody with a key."

"What key?"

I explain about the keys that only we have as slot attendants; keys that unlock all the machines and all that money in them.

Even when I mention the words "slot attendant" she shivers from a chill of disgust.

She says she sometimes wonders why I bring home such large tips. Sometimes I bring home a hundred dollars in quarters.

"Well they are tips, Mel."

"I know we're desperate and that you're disgusted with the whole thing, but..."

"I am not desperate."

"Neither am I," she says. "But you know what I mean."

"I'm resigned. That's different from desperate."

"Well don't get too resigned."

"I wish you hadn't said desperate."

"That's not what we're talking about," she says.

"I thought it was."

"We're talking about that phone call I got from some sergeant. He sounded so..."

"It's not me, Mel. It's not me."

"It's not your way of getting even?"

"With whom?"

"The casino."

"No. The casino is what's saving us."

"The world?"

"There's no getting even with the world. The world always wins."

"I don't like that attitude."

"What attitude?"

"The world always wins. That's defeatism. That's not us."

I think she's beginning to cry, and I don't like this.

"What about our motto?" she says.

Yes, our motto – we're right and the rest of the world is wrong.

"Not that I blame you," she says.

"You got your hair cut."

"I wouldn't blame you."

"You wouldn't blame me if I stole?"

"I don't think I would. It's against type, against character, but people change, or rather, conditions change. Yes, I would understand."

Then she says, "That green uniform, it's such a symbol of everything," and she does start to cry, and I feel like crying, too.

"Tell me about Sylvio," I say after we're both okay.

He'd asked for me, but she took the message. He does not know that I work all night, of course, or where I work, of course.

"You want the details?"

"Spare me."

I'd read enough rejections. I knew the drill. There is a format. When they start off good, they end badly. "Best wishes elsewhere." When they start off negatively, they sometimes end with an offer. I once got such a letter and was so insulted that I never read the last paragraph, and missed a big chance. I only read the last paragraph a year later, and by that time the editor, McCormick, had died.

"So is Sylvio giving up?" I ask.

"No, not at all. In fact, he was very encouraging."

"Well, that's good, isn't it, Mel?"

"Yes, that's very good."

"So he sounded encouraging."

"Yes he did."

"But he didn't say..."

"You know how quickly they get you off the phone."

"But he was encouraging."

"Yes."

"Did he use that word?"

She's thinking. "I don't think so."

"But something like that, right?"

"Maybe he did say encouraging."

"Maybe he's got a bite, I mean despite those two rejections."

"That may well be," she says.

"Maybe he's got an offer and we're just talking price."

"I wouldn't be surprised," she says.

I wonder if I should tell her about finding my book, *The Ice King*, in the casino's gift shop. This could go either way with her, bloom her up or gloom her down. Maybe it's a good sign. Though we've stopped believing in signs, or at least I have. I don't think it's wise to tell her. So I won't tell her. I find that most times it's best to say nothing and do nothing about certain things, let it slide, and when you do, it sorts itself out, most times. No, she'll take it darkly.

After a shower, I take my first Valium. This could be my first triple Valium day. I take a broom and smash it against the bedroom window to disperse the pigeons. I hear them flapping away. But they'll be back. Oh they'll be back all right. They're very intelligent. They're even getting immune to my banging. They know it's fake, that I can't back it up. They're on to me. Why they've picked on me, I don't know. But like the man said, they were here before us. I actually think they're laughing at me, the pigeons. They're taunting me.

Melanie draws the shades. She knows it's a lost cause between me and the pigeons. She reconciles it to nature.

I protest. We're also nature, aren't we? We're a species. We're part of the scheme.

I'm in bed and she gives me a tender backrub. I know I'm taking up her time. This is her workday at the computer.

She's got reviews to get out. She asks if I want the TV on or off. I say off. At least the sound. The mute button is the greatest invention since the wheel. I haven't listened to a commercial in five years. Don't they know that when they pay the networks a million dollars for a 20-second spot? Nobody's watching. For sure nobody is listening.

Melanie says, "When I think of all the crap that's being published and produced..."

She should know, being a book and now a movie reviewer as well.

"Maybe..."

"No! You're a fantastic writer. They just haven't caught up to you yet...and yes, I know what Hemingway said."

When he was told that he was far ahead of his time, Hemingway said he wouldn't mind if they caught up to him just a bit.

"We've done it before, we'll do it again," she whispers as a means to lullaby me to sleep. "Our luck is bound to change."

"For the better."

"Well of course."

Always be careful how you phrase your dreams and wishes. God can be crafty.

Melanie has a friend whose husband was in a terrible car crash. This friend prayed that her husband might live, and he did, as a vegetable.

So you've got to phrase it just right.

An hour later she hands me my third Valium. Maybe I'll get in an hour's sleep. I try the TV and it's about that hurricane in Florida. All non-essential personnel are ordered to evacuate immediately. Hey, that's me. Non-essential personnel. I take this as an epiphany. Writers are non-essential personnel. Evacuate immediately! Another epiphany is that slot attendants ARE essential personnel.

Where would the casinos and all those players be without us? We are essential personnel, slot attendants. Not so writers. One writer more, one writer less, and it's a sure bet that nobody will know the difference.

I am tempted to share this new-found wisdom with Melanie. Better not. Sleep is more important, more important than anything.

Chapter 7

They're all sitting together at the same table in the cafeteria, or standing around, all of it loud and mirthful; Toledo Vasquez, Mini Gonzalez, Bob Michaelson, Franco DeLima, Flint Odesso, Hitesh Patel, Rakish Panchal, Pini Cleopatrus, Omar, Maggi Holt, Carmella Sanchez – a mix of slot attendants and supervisors whooping it up. They're talking cars, how some cars are masculine, some feminine. It's gotten pretty raunchy.

I'm secluded at a separate table, ready for inspiration with my pen and notepad. I'm a recluse, which is tough to do before an audience. Maybe I'm just shy. Maybe I don't want any part of this. They don't know. I don't know. They keep checking on me. Someone, Carmella actually, yells out and asks what kind of car I drive. I say Toyota. In unison they ooh and aah, as if I said something outrageous.

Carmella, in that sultry Spanish tone of hers, declares, "That is a real feminine car." Do I make love to it? They're all laughing.

"Come on, join in," says Flint.

I move in and become part of the game. After all the goofing it gets serious and I find out that some of them are aiming for an executive career in the casino industry, some are saving up to finish college – there's even a fledgling doctor in the house – and some are just a year or so short of becoming lawyers, accountants and engineers. All this is news to me.

Back to cars, I submit that my Toyota failed to pass inspection. They all jump in with advice. They all know a particular gas station that'll pass anything on four wheels, even faulty emissions. It's a place in Ventnor. Hitesh even hands me a business card of that pliable service station. "You don't even need an appointment," says Toledo Vasquez. "Just drive in, drive out," adds Bob Michaelson, who does business on the side, perhaps shady.

"Just don't get stopped," says Bob, who's in training as a State Trooper. "They do spot checks."

"No they don't," says Flint.

"Yes they do," says Bob, who used to be a front desk clerk at the hotel next door.

I did not know this about Bob. The crew cut should have been a tip-off that he's angling to become a New Jersey State Trooper.

At least that's his plan, his dream. They all aspire. They all have a dream. All this time I thought I was the only one.

Carmella Sanchez is a world-class Spanish beauty. She keeps giving me the eye, or so it seems. No, I'm right. You can't be mistaken about something so obvious, the way she sparkles and tilts her head to a side when she's talking to me. She's got long pitch-black hair that's combed back aristocratically tight. She carries herself accessible but dignified. Down on the casino floor, after the break upstairs in the cafeteria, we find ourselves sharing zones side by side. She has Zone 6; I have Zone 5. Both are near the Coin Redemption Cages. That's what the signs say. Some only say "Redemption," which I once took to be a religious message.

We keep bumping into each other, and there's that one moment when we're together and she swivels her hips and gives me that naughty sideward glance.

I tell her that she's more beautiful than Jennifer Lopez.

"Oh," she says. "Are you flirting with me?"

"Are you?"

"Maybe," she says.

Our supervisor is horny Maggi Holt, who is so easy to maneuver. They're whispering, Maggi and Carmella, and I wonder if it's about me, and I wonder if I'm about to be brought up on charges of sexual harassment because it's a new world and you never know. They keep changing the rules and guys don't know what the rules are day to day; we can't keep up with the changes. You can get fired, even prosecuted, for making a fellow employee "uncomfortable." What used to be flirting, or a pass, or a compliment, or teasing, or stealing a kiss, is now harassment and punishable. Just the other day it was different. It was okay. We just can't keep up.

Carmella slips over to me and says she got permission for both of us to take 20 minutes together. She needs something from her purse in the cloak room (something feminine, I imagine) and doesn't like to move across the casino floor by herself. She's been frisked and manhandled by prowlers on the floor and there are no security guards available to provide escort.

"No elevator," I say.

So we take the back staircase, and she takes my hand as we walk up. There are three floors to go and she moves my hand lightly over her breasts and this is a surprise and no accident. In the cloak room she falls into my arms. "We must not kiss," she says. "This can't go on." I did not know anything was going on, but it turns out that she has a terribly jealous (and violent) husband who suspects us. "Who me? You and me?"

"You and everybody."

He works in the Banquet Department, or did, until he got fired for getting into a fight, a fist fight, with his supervisor.

"He never touched me."

"Who?"

"Bernard, the Banquet manager."

"So your husband is out of a job?"

"You did not know he worked here?" she says.

"I don't know you, Carmella."

Her eyes light up with a smile. "Oh, Jay," she says, "you know what I'm talking about."

My arms are limp and at my sides. She takes my right arm, lifts it, and presses it against her breasts. I help myself to a handful, grow with the sensation, and then reach down for more and there's action here in the coat room. (The editor who lorded me with the news that temptation in life and in literature only happens to people who are unhappily married had it all wrong. Temptation can happen anywhere, any time, to anyone.)

"That's what I'm talking about," she says, still radiating.

I say, "I guess I do."

"I look at you. You look at me. You know. People have eyes."

"Okay."

"But nothing has happened," she says, now gripping my palm for assurance. (Right. THAT didn't happen. Close – but no cigarette.)

"Of course not."

"He's very jealous. We must be careful."

"Sure."

"He has friends who watch for him." As she's saying all this, I'm not so sure she's all that worried. Her eyes keep telling a different story.

"We don't want to get caught," she says.

"Anything you say, Carmella."

"Oh?" she says, smiling a certain smile. "Anything?"

"I'm behaving. I always behave."

"Hmm. Is this fun – to behave?"

"Safe sex is no sex."

She laughs, but then turns sad.

I ask if he hits her. Her eyes turn moist.

"Only once."

"That's once too much."

"But he's my husband."

"That doesn't mean he owns you."

She gives me a look that seems to say I don't know what I'm talking about. "Where I come from," she says, "girls are property."

"If he touches you again, leave him."

"That's not how it works with my people."

I offer to protect her. She smiles, pats me sweetly on the cheek, and says there's nothing to do. This is her life. I wonder what she wants, or rather how far she wants this to go. I'm wondering the same thing about myself. I cannot get mixed up in this for a thousand reasons, and one reason in particular. She extends her lips for kissing but then changes her mind at the same time that I change mine, and it's as if we share the same thought, that someone, something, is always watching. If it's not your conscience it's that Eye In The Sky which follows you wherever you go. To know this you don't have to be religious; you only have to work in a casino.

She's right. There's nothing to do.

Back on the casino floor, one of my regulars, Mrs. Helen Donalson, calls me over from one of the high-limit territories, Zone 4. She's very nice. She's here almost every night and is always pleasant, win or lose. So she calls me over and says she's heard from someone, doesn't remember who, but someone in the know, that I'm really a famous author. So am I? Am I really an author and am I really famous? I answer no, I am really a famous slot attendant.

"I don't believe you," she says. "There's something different about you. I would love to know more."

Even with people who appear to be reasonable, coherent and intelligent, I prefer to skip the details. They turn off as soon as you begin. So why bother? Why make a nuisance of yourself? Most people are interested in themselves and even more people are fascinated about themselves. About you, nobody cares. So often when people find out you're a writer they say that's nice, but wait till you hear *my* story.

Then, as if to prove my point, she says, "This machine better pay off soon."

She's playing dollar Joker Poker.

"I'm already in two thousand dollars. It's bound to hit. My husband's going to kill me. Oh, well."

She plays the same machine every night. She has hit in the past. She used to be a professor of English before she retired, over at Rutgers.

"You can't fool me," she says as she keeps playing her machine. "You've got class." I like this. I like hearing this. She's reading the latest Roth at the moment. What do I think of him? What am I reading these days and what am I writing? I go stupid and do something I never do; confess that I wrote *The Ice King*. This doesn't stop her play at the machine but she does give it an, "Oh my. I loved the movie." Right, this is expected. "I wrote the book, the novel." She did not know, she says, that there was a novel. This too is expected. But wait! "I read your book," she says. "What a wonderful book."

Maybe she did read it and maybe she didn't and certainly I will not test her. This can only lead to vexation and right now this is good, too good to waste.

As this is going on between me and Mrs. Donalson, Omar walks over and, this is a surprise, he's coming at me with an executive from Las Vegas, a silky man. Our Vegas bosses come around now and then to check up on the operation, how it's going and why – why there's not enough money coming in. There's never enough. There's always talk about layoffs. There's even talk about the casino being sold. The name Carl Icahn keeps popping up. So here comes Omar with this guy and I know there's something Mr. Vegas wants to tell me but he won't since it's just not done, from his level to my level. So it's left to Omar and what he says, and quite loudly, is that my shoes are not shined well enough. They should sparkle. That's what they've come to tell me, and then turn abruptly and leave.

"Can't you make this machine wake up?" says Mrs. Donalson. "Rub it for me. You're good luck."

Chapter 8

Toledo Vasquez is a good kid. He's abundant in muscle and toughness, but around me, at least, he's got charm. He's always telling me about the fights he gets into to thwart those pugs competing for his girl. Just the other day, he says, he got into it and knocked some guy unconscious over a slight. I believe him. That's back in his Camden neighborhood where he gets into all those rumbles, but around the casino nobody messes with him, either. I've taught him a few martial arts moves and he's grateful. He's from one side of the world, I'm from the other, but we match. He's from one generation, I'm from another, but we still match.

We got it started months ago when we were alone in the cafeteria and he started talking about Maria, his girl, and I told him I knew the score.

Yes, as long as there are women, there's going to be trouble.

So we're pals and he was kind enough to trade off-days with me. I needed his Friday. "No problemo," he said.

So Friday morning Melanie drops me off at the Greyhound/Trailways bus station in Mount Laurel. I'm off to New York. I go in and buy my tickets, go back out and sit in the car with Mel, waiting for the bus. I leave my briefcase outside to secure my place in line. That's how it's done. It's very civilized here in Mount Laurel. We don't say much, but then she says, "I like it so much better, you off to New York."

"Yup."

I try not to get overly excited, but am touched by travel fever. On the other hand, I know too much. That's never good. I love New York but does New York love me?

We keep going back to find out. Big meeting coming up. Every trip has become Gog and Magog.

But this meeting is really big.

Melanie is trying to find the right words. "Go there, walk in, like you're somebody. Remember who you are."

She's trying to prop me up.

"You're somebody, remember?"

Right, that other motto, I am nothing, I am nobody, won't do today.

"I can't heeeear you," she says.

"Okay, I am somebody."

"This is war, right?"

"Right," I agree.

"You always say this is war."

"Yes I do, Mel."

"So go in there and take no prisoners."

"Right, no prisoners."

"Just go in and take control," she says. "Dominate! Dominate the meeting."

Matter of fact, my movie *The Ice King* was on TV just the other day (it does appear quite regularly) and despite the law in our home that we don't watch the movie anymore we did stay for the credits, the opening credits only, just to be sure that my name was still where it belonged, and it was. You never know. Someone might decide to delete you altogether, for whatever reason. Anyway, Rob Lowe, or someone like that, introduced the movie and mentioned the director and the screenwriter but not me, the author, the novelist who started the whole thing from scratch, wrote a 200 million dollar movie that made everybody else rich;

wrote it on the kitchen table. That was a bit of a downer. Actually, Melanie was outraged.

"Dominate," she says.

Yes, that's what I'll do. I'll dominate the meeting.

"I still can't heeeear you!"

"Yes, sweetheart, I'll dominate the meeting."

"Remember who you are."

Is that such a good thing? No, banish the thought. This isn't the time to go on rewind.

The New York bus pulls up and I get a slight case of the willies. The bus starts from Philly so it's three quarters full. But I've got my place in line.

I scoot out.

"I love you," she says.

"I love you." More than you'll ever know, I am thinking.

I'm in the middle of the boarding line, the driver taking tickets, and am stricken by a strange melancholy as I watch Melanie turn the car around and begin to drive off. It's as if I'll never be seeing her again, that kind of sadness. I read her lips before she vanishes: "Remember who you are." You'd never know I'd made this hour and a half trip a hundred times.

It's at moments like this that I remember how much I love her, how much...oh hell!

I've got an aisle seat. I prefer window but there's no scenery this part of New Jersey anyway. It's all flat and a mole hill is a mountain. The bus is full of suits, some artistic types as well. The suits know who they are. The artistic types, not so much. For an artist, life is one audition after another, one tryout after another. Suits are confident people. They've already won, or give that appearance. This is the 7 a.m. Wall Street Special. I'm starting to feel good, almost happy; reclusive writer from the sticks onto bright lights, big city.

There's nothing like New York, of course. It's even more of a toss of the dice than Atlantic City. If you're a gambler, New York is the place. In fact I behold New York from the point of view of a slot attendant. That it's a place for gambling (just like AC and Vegas) except that in New York the stakes are higher. More than money is being wagered; your place in the world, that's the bet. (You do not want to be put to shame.)

The bus turns left, left again up to Route 73, a half mile up the driver swings right and we're on the turnpike and that's when your heart begins to quicken.

The lady next to me, at the window seat, is from Philadelphia. I know this and everything else about her because she's on her cell phone the whole time, no secret left behind. She's fast-talking, in an executive outfit, not bad-looking, but all business for the world...the New Woman that was carved out of the 1970s. I know that her kids are late being picked up for school, the dishes weren't done by Max, the maid hasn't arrived, the garbage hasn't been taken out, the dentist never called back, Kathy's braces are coming loose, the decorator is in for a lawsuit, Lisa forgot to cancel the hairdresser, a check bounced, and what good is that lawyer if he can't settle out of court? She's cussing up a storm.

Wait a minute. I think I know who this is. Now she's talking about column inches, typos, editing, proofreading, and can it be?

I think this is Barbara Moser, top editor of that big newspaper across the river. I can't complain. She gave *The Ice King* a good review, well, her book reviewer did, though her movie reviewer was nasty, when the movie came out. I recognize her from the picture in the paper. She writes a column, Sundays, once a week. I can never make sense of what she writes, it's all so muddled. You never know where she stands, what position she takes between two competing arguments, because she takes both, or so it seems. You never know. I guess that's the trick.

I assume she's now scolding her Food writer, or editor, for using the TH sound for some Hebrew delicacy.

She's saying the TH sound is out – "You should know that for shit's sake, what's the matter with you?"

I reconsider introducing myself. This is some bitch.

Down a couple of rows I swear those are two writers exchanging gossip. The one says, "We don't ship off writers to Siberia. We exile them to the Internet." Other passengers are reading newspapers, tapping their laptops, on cell phones, or napping and some are actually snoring. All are pros, Mount Laurel to New York professionals. I do like this. A sensation of great things comes with a ticket to New York. You must be important to be on this bus. You're going to be making deals. You're going to dominate.

Where the New Jersey farm lands end, almost abruptly, that's where Industrial America kicks in and you pass along acres of criss-crossing railroad tracks, smoke stacks billowing from acres of refineries and you can even smell the chemicals. What a swift and dramatic change. Local and trans-national trains speed along in different directions and overhead planes and helicopters fly low, landing or taking off.

When you're backed up serpentine for miles but then enter the Lincoln Tunnel, that's when you know it's happening.

Step outside the bus station on 42nd and you're in the suburbs no more. It's dizzying before you start walking and make the adjustment.

So many people, and all so different, and everybody wants something. We are all so grasping, so NEEDY.

I'm way early, so I start walking just to be walking, but I do have a purpose, and that is getting my shoes shined, as there is nothing like a New York shine, and I know exactly where to go, where I always go, to those shoeshine guys outside the Grand Hyatt, right alongside Grand Central Terminal. If nothing else, I will have a terrific shoe shine. I get there, hop up, and the man gets to work and it's almost like surgery, he's so serious, and he puts his whole body into it when it comes to the buffing. It comes to three dollars and I give him a five to keep and he says, "Thank you, Sir." Who says New Yorkers aren't polite? Problem is, I can't see my reflection in my shoes. This shine will not make it into the hall of fame. I hope this isn't a sign.

I take in a movie but don't even know what movie I'm watching or even what theater I'm in, I'm so anxious about my appointment. I buy one of those giant containers of popcorn and gulp it all down so fast that I need burping. I wish Melanie were here with me. No, this I have to do alone. Then I stop in at some OTB and make a couple of bets. Then I stop in at a tobacco shop and find the perfect pipe. I ask the price, which tips them off, of course, and the snooty clerk mumbles something about $850. I'm tempted to demand that he put it aside. I'll be back.

I make my way slowly to Sylvio's office, taking in Manhattan, which has a beat, a rhythm, as no other. New skyscrapers keep popping up. Suddenly Reuters and suddenly Bertelsmann. They weren't here last time. Or were they? I like to watch the tourists at Radio City. You know they're not New Yorkers. So Midwest. So grassroots. So chatty and goo-goo eyed. They're not in Cincinnati anymore. I walk around the skating rink at Rockefeller Plaza and marvel at all those glitzy shops. Where does all this money come from? Same for Fifth Avenue, where limos are parked all along the sides. Where does all this money come from?

There's still time before my meeting and a few blocks later, here I am at the Waldorf-Astoria. I am a lobby specialist and this is one of the best, refined, plush and understated. The carpets are so thick that you're practically floating. Feels good being among people so rich and so tall. People, even the staff and even the guests, keep smiling at me as if they know me. Maybe they feel so good about themselves they'll smile at anybody. Maybe they remember me from the time my picture was all over the place after *The Ice King* came out. I made some of the talk shows and was featured, profiled, in quite a number of magazines, back then. Maybe I'm having a good hair day. Maybe it's the shine of my shoes, though not really a great shine but good enough. I really enjoy this lobby, but it is time to go.

I take the stairs up and Marci greets me without a smile. It's been so hectic, she finally submits; all those contracts to be mailed in and mailed out. You know how it is. Yes, I know how it is. Oh, Sylvio is not in. He's sorry. But he's not in. Something unexpected came up. Also, the lunch with Roe Morgan is off. He phoned just minutes ago, Roe Morgan did. "But he still said for you to go over. He can give you fifteen minutes."

"I thought..."

"It's been so hectic around here. I need a vacation."

I tell her I know how it is. I still don't think she knows my name.

I take the staircase back down and walk over to the big building on 59th and Madison where I now have 15 minutes, not lunch, with Roe Morgan. He was to be, or is to be, my publisher of last resort. He published my big novel, *The Ice King*, when he was still with Michael Fain Brothers & Company, a small house but prestigious, especially on fiction. Roe Morgan bought *The Ice King* while he was still at Fain's and it made much money for all of them, including the Fain company and Roe Morgan personally. In fact it made his career, or so I'm told.

Soon after, Roe Morgan moved on to this much larger house, a publishing empire. No, I can't say he got a bigger desk in a bigger office in a bigger company all on account of me and the merits of my novel. But it sure didn't hurt. So it was something of a surprise when he didn't invite me to move along with him, as it's usually done, and it was an even bigger surprise when he turned down *Smooth Operator*. Actually, he never phoned when the movie came out for *The Ice King* and never phoned when the movie topped all box office records for an April opening.

Sylvio had been against this meeting. Editors don't like to meet writers. It just doesn't work that way. It isn't done. Particularly they do not want to meet with an author they've already turned down. But Sylvio set it up anyway (as a lunch) since, after all, Roe Morgan and I have a history, a good history. I suppose I rubbed it in when, a bit on the emotional side, I blurted out, to Sylvio, these words: "I am not disposable."

Actually, editors don't like writers, period.

I knew he was up on the 17th floor, Roe Morgan was, and it's what had me distracted on the bus trip over.

I usually case the lobby in instances like this, checking out the elevators to see if they're fit for boarding. Are they big, small, fast, slow?

This fear of mine, it is breathtaking.

I do consider the stairs. Seventeen flights. So what? But there's a sign and it says...Emergency Only. Alarmed.

Alarmed, you bet.

I wish there were more escalators in this world. But they're so rare. I love escalators.

So I wait around the lobby to build up some steam. At this moment Roe Morgan is the last thing on my mind. First, the elevators. Then, Roe Morgan. Finally, a guy wearing some kind of uniform steps in, so that'll be my choice, and it gets even better when a FedEx guy rushes in with him. If it's good enough for them, it's good enough for me.

I'm just hoping these two squared away guys join me up to 17. The elevator does zoom, and I like that, but stops at eight, where the FedEx guy gets off, and then it stops at 12, where the other guy gets off, and then it's between me and the elevator. Up at 17, I'm in a sweat and take a deep breath, and hold it, and wait for the doors to open, but they never will, I just know, I just know this is it, and I'm already reaching for the red button, or should I try the Open button, but slowly, much too slowly, the doors do part.

Place is deserted. No receptionist, no secretary, no assistants in the lobby, only poster blowups along the velvet walls of all the bestsellers.

There are many and many are surely Roe Morgan's doing. Though I really don't know how well he's been doing since I left him or since he left me.

He never even phoned when *The Ice King* reached number one in *The New York Times*.

Or when it was nominated for a Pulitzer.

I did phone him once, somewhere between *The Ice King* and now this, *Smooth Operator*, which would be about three years back. So I did swallow some pride, picked up the phone just to congratulate him on his new position and hoping that maybe he'd ask what's next from me. He took the call and thanked me but said nothing else, except that all they're publishing, at this new company, are high concept bestsellers. But he never asked if...oh that's the past.

I say, "Hello? Anybody home?"

Here he comes and says, "Jay?"

"Yes."

"Hi, Roe Morgan."

We had met only once, face to face.

"Sorry," he says, "everybody's out to lunch. You know how it is."

Yes, I know how it is.

He does not offer a handshake, but leads me to his office the way they lead you to your table at the diner.

His features are generic, opaque. The face tells nothing. He is not fat but not thin either.

There is nothing about him that is pleasant or unpleasant. He is not polite or impolite. He certainly is not rude, and he certainly is not charming.

"So," he says as we settle in, "what brings you to New York?"

He doesn't know?

"You," I say.

I intend to be direct, but I also meant that as a joke, an ice-breaker.

"If it's about your novel," he says, "the decision's already been made."

(The passive we. "Mistakes were made.")

I say decisions change. He says not very often. I ask why the book was turned down so fast. He says it wasn't fast, and it wasn't turned down, it just isn't right for us. That's no knock on the book. The book was given serious considera-tion, especially given my past. After all, I'm one for one, batting a thousand. The trouble with it, is that – and about here I begin to tune out, I know it's over – that it's too long here, too short there, too much of this, not enough of that, "and at the end of the day, we decided to pass."

This cannot go anywhere with a man, an editor, who says "at the end of the day."

But...I must go on. Find an opening, any opening. Failure...okay, failure is not an option. Remember who you are. Yes I will, Melanie.

I will remember who I am.

I will dominate.

I must dominate.

"Why can't we work together and fix up what's wrong?"

"The decision's been made."

"Isn't that what editors are for?"

This does not score.

"I know my job," he says. "Anything else?"

Now he's walking me to the elevator. Neither of us is smiling.

"Good luck," he says. "You're a damn good writer. The door here is always open to you."

It is? That is unexpected and encouraging. It's something, or rather, I'll take anything. As the elevator approaches, I ask if there's one thing in particular that could use fixing. Give me, I say, a clue, something to go on. He says, "The ending. It's too down." I do a quick "search" and bring up, in my mind, all the novels, great and small, that have endured with down endings. What is so cheerful about *The Old Man and the Sea*, or...there's thousands. Virtually all of literature, from the Greeks onward, is tragedy from beginning to End. I am astonished by this critique since I do not remember *Smooth Operator* as ending down. Sure it is not neatly tied up at the finish, as no decent novel should be. But it is not down. It ends up vague, for the reader to imagine what's next. You never want to finish off a novel cute.

"You want happy endings?" I say to Roe Morgan.

"Yup."

"Like *Moby Dick*, *The Postman Always Rings Twice*..."

"That's old news."

"I wouldn't mind old news like that, would you?"

"High concept," he says. "It's policy. Bestsellers."

"I thought I once gave you one."

"I really have to go. Thanks for coming."

Then he says...this is what he says..."You live in New Jersey, right?"

That's what he says. He says: "You live in New Jersey, right?"

I get the drift.

New Jersey, of course, is not a flyover state. It's a drive-over state. It is a turnpike state.

What exit do you come from? That's the joke.

Who comes from New Jersey? Well, try Walt Whitman.

But I get the message.

You live in New Jersey, right?

One more shot.

"Suppose I rewrite the ending. Will you..."

"No thanks."

That's what he says as the elevator arrives for the next trauma. That's what he says, "No thanks."

No thanks means no thanks. That's what it means. No thanks.

On leaving the building, I find Manhattan to be different. It's not the same. It's all a blur, and I don't care to take a cab down to the Village.

I just want to go home. I make it a quick walk back to the buses and catch the 5:26 and everybody else seems wiped out as well. We are not dominating anymore. I'm wondering if anyone else is coming back with "no thanks" and I'm wondering, as we travel in the dark, how to break this to Melanie, how to give it a spin. Well, he did say the door is always open. That is something to bring home. Also, there are other publishers.

The worst part about bad news is having to split it with somebody, especially somebody you love.

So happens that on this bus I am seated next to an actress and I know this from a cell phone conversation she is having and after she hangs up we get to talking. She's excited about a part in a movie she may be getting. I offer her my best wishes. She's in her mid-thirties and says, yes, it's a tough business and she still has not succeeded but won't give up. She asks if I have just returned from that Book Fair at the Javits Center where all the famous authors were gathered with their publishers to push their books. She says, "You look like an author," and I say, no, I am a slot attendant and that ends the conversation.

I felt like saying that I am a recovering novelist but it was too late and I was too tired to get cute and besides, we would have begun exchanging artistic stories, her troubles and mine about making it, up against the odds, but I have covered this territory too many times. There is no more talking to do about this. We would only be commiserating and I am tired of this, too.

There is no comfort in the knowledge that we are all alike in suffering. So what!

Melanie is waiting in the car at Mount Laurel and she knows right away. I don't have to tell her. Women know, wives particularly, Melanie first of all. The smell of success this isn't. I shut my eyes as she drives us home to Voorhees, about 20 minutes away. I don't feel like spinning and there is not much spinning to do. She asks what I had for lunch and I tell her popcorn. No, I don't remember what movie I saw. Maybe later, it'll all come back later.

"So there was no lunch."

"There was no lunch."

"Those bastards."

Then there is this, and I am not sure whose news is worse, hers or mine – the drains in both showers are clogged up. The water won't go down, just stays. She had already tried some Drano and that made it even worse. Things come up and won't go down. So I try the plunger and it helps, but not much. We will have no choice but to get extravagant and get the plumber, if he'll come. He's a bit perturbed at Melanie. We had something like this before, some time ago, and when he phoned to confirm the appointment, Melanie was on the other line with an editor about one of her reviews. So she wasn't rude to the plumber, but she was somewhat abrupt, and for that, for that reason, he didn't show up, and when I asked him why, he said it was because my wife wasn't nice to him. That's something, a sensitive plumber. Meanwhile, we're going to have to get him again, and behave.

Back home, over dinner, I tell her everything.

"He actually said that – no thanks?"

"No thanks."

"How cruel. What did you say?"

"I said nothing. What's to say? Everything's been said. What could be more final?"

"I don't believe this," she says.

"Well, believe."

"No, I don't believe this is final."

"Of course it isn't final. Nothing is final, not until you're dead, and even then it's not final."

She says, "We're not giving up, are we?"

"Are you kidding?"

"We're not giving up, Jay."

"That's right. We're not giving up."

I sometimes wonder which arrives first, old age or bitterness. If you're lucky, it's old age. Then it's expected. I find this on the casino floor, how cranky and mean-spirited so many of them are, old people. It shows, that they've lived the life and are just fed up. They're not going to take it anymore. I see their impatience, bordering on rage, when they have to wait an extra ten minutes for a payoff, which means they've won, but after a certain point, after a certain age, they've had it up to here with everything and everybody. Everything is a bother. I am starting to know the feeling.

"Right, Jay?" Melanie says. "We're not giving up. Not us."

This is rhetorical but I know Melanie and I know that she needs a response – affirmative, of course.

She needs the assurance like checking my pulse as proof that I am still ticking.

"Right, Jay? We're not quitters."

"Right, Mel. Not us."

Chapter 9

Lately, I've become a regular member of the gang in the cafeteria. I am an outsider no more.

Toledo Vasquez and I spar out in the hallway and I continue to advise and consent when it comes to his Maria, and as for my Carmella, there is something going on, there are moments but only moments and I take it, accept it, as nothing more than a diversion, perhaps even a form of revenge against this job and the forces that put me here in this place. If Fate operates on whimsy then this is my response and if God operates on a Plan this is my answer to Him, that I am not happy. I could use a sign that there is more to life than futility, unless King Solomon had it right all along in which case we are really in trouble.

Bob Michaelson is using me as a reference for his entry into the State Police force, where they need your history minute by minute from the day you were born; an inquisition even more exhaustive, much more exhaustive, than the ones performed by the Casino Control Commission, which is likewise pretty intense when it comes to hiring, where they examine you upside down, inside and out, almost to the point of are you now or have you ever been. To be a New Jersey State Trooper the candidate must be near perfect.

I am flattered that Bob is using me for that reference and I am flattered that Hitesh Patel wants some academic names from me at Rutgers, where I still have some connections and where Hitesh wants to resume studies for a degree in communications, and I am flattered that wild and crazy Humberto Valdez wants some tips on writing proper resumes and proper reports so that he can move up to executive positions in the casino business.

"My wife had incense and candles all around the bathtub," says Bob Michaelson with a smirk. He goes on and tells the rest.

There is this about Bob Michaelson. I like him all right and he may be a good man to know if he ever does become a state trooper, but he's always talking about his wife and sometimes it gets quite personal. He talks about their various lovemaking episodes and techniques. I'm no prude, or maybe I am, but I find that odd, very strange, that a man should be so public about his wife. A wife is sacred.

I think it would be just fine if he spoke openly about his mistresses or one-night stands. That wouldn't bother me. In fact Bob Michaelson frequents Atlantic City's massage joints – AC's other claim to fame along its side streets – and mentions the differing techniques from one place to another, specifically the techniques as practiced by Asian women, and that's proper. That's different. That's okay. But not your wife.

Humberto says he is doing the right thing by starting as a slot attendant, isn't he?

"Just like Donald Trump."

I say, "Humberto, Donald Trump started with fifty million dollars."

"Of his dad's money," says Flint Odesso.

"Turned it into a fortune," pipes in Bob Michaelson.

"Where can I get a job like that?" says Toledo Vasquez.

"Get a father like that," says Humberto Valdez.

Amid all this frivolity who should walk in but Omar, his face a hot coal of indignation. Now what?

He's come for me, and what did I do? Nothing, directly.

"They want you in the Law Enforcement office."

As I shuffle down the stairs, Toledo catches up. He wants to know what I'm going to say.

"Nothing."

"You da man," he says, giving me a shadow box.

An officer named Detective Conrad Stevenson sits behind a vinyl desk short of any papers or any sign of work. What sort of investigative unit he belongs to is unclear, but he is solid, as they say, in bow tie and crew cut and erect posture. Handcuffs dangle from his belt (so he is the real deal) and a badge is tethered alongside his belt buckle. Uniformed officers parade in and out but he is in plain clothes. My guess is that these are temporary quarters, or that these are people from the outside. I'd never seen these guys before.

All of it not quite a gulag but intimidating just the same.

He opens by saying there's nothing to worry about, if there's nothing to worry about.

I say that's fine.

"Have you any idea what's going on?" he asks.

I say I hear the talk. There's thieving going on.

Am I aware that someone has fingered me?

I swallow hard.

"No. May I ask who?"

"You can ask, but I can't tell."

I run through a reckoning of my enemies and there must be plenty of those as you can't go through life without trespassing. You're always offending somebody, always walking on somebody's grass, whether you know it or not. Maybe you didn't say hello or maybe you didn't say goodbye. Maybe you forgot to tip the mailman at Christmas, or didn't tip him enough, so maybe that's why he's friendlier to the people next door. Never mind the adversaries I've made during my literary and film endeavors, but even the Asian couple that run the dry cleaners took down my autographed poster of *The Ice King* when I complained about a crease that was pressed lopsided.

I have sinned against Hollywood producers and New York publishers and newspaper editors, and their sins against me don't count because they have the power and the glory. Awake and asleep I have cursed the powers that placed obstacles at my feet and prayed that they be recompensed and smitten for their snobbery and arrogance and for all those books of mine that they have murdered before they could be born. I have prayed to have their curses turned into blessings but so far they are ahead. In my dreams I have named names.

David kept asking why the wicked keep ruling this good earth and that is still a good question.

I do have friends. Most of them are at the racetrack, but even there I get in trouble when it gets to politics.

So for sure I've made lifetime enemies and for sure I've made casino enemies. Top of that list is Omar, the supervisor who's got a camel up his ass. I'd also had spats with a shift manager or two. There are always fellow slot attendants you've crossed down there on the casino floor on purpose or by accident, as when you've arrived three minutes late to exchange breaks. I know one girl, Latisha Johnson, who has it in for me for some reason. Beats me what I did to her, but word is that she does voodoo.

So I've made enemies and that's life, even casino life, where it's all so animated. The casino is a universe all gathered within the space of a single floor...the good, the bad, the ugly, the profound, the profane. Down on the floor, especially on weekends, it is madness, it's a whirlwind, and there is sure to be friction. Gamblers are always on edge – it's about money after all – and there is always something you are doing or not doing. As a slot attendant, you get it from all sides, from the shift managers, from the supervisors, from the players, from your co-slot attendants and even the cleaning people can order you around. The cocktail servers also get ticked when you hail them for a customer who's thirsty and wants to know where those girls are with the drinks.

The girls, the cocktail girls, can afford some dignity and independence, which is beyond us, the slot attendants. They're union, so they do not have to snap to.

Unless it's for a big tipper.

So they can pace themselves and measure their steps.

We are not union.

"Well I'll tell you anyway," says Stevenson, upon the question of who fingered me. "One of your co-workers, goes by the name Franco DeLima."

That makes sense.

"He's wrong."

"We know that," says Stevenson. "We've had you under surveillance. That's not why you're here. Okay?"

"Okay."

"By the way. Why are you here?"

"Beg pardon?"

"We ran a check on you. Are you the same guy who wrote that movie?"

"I wrote the book."

"So you're a novelist."

"Of that I'm guilty."

"I thought you guys are rich and famous."

"I thought so, too."

"So what are you doing in a place like this – a slot attendant?"

"Can I plead the Fifth?"

"What happened?"

"Nothing. That's why I'm here."

"I hope you don't mind my asking."

"Not at all."

"It's just that my wife is a big reader, and she's read your book, and thinks it's great."

"Please thank her for me."

"Me," he says, half chuckling, "I always think of authors as being dead."

"You got that right."

There's a pause.

Back to business.

Am I friendly with a kid named Toledo Vasquez?

"I know him. I like him."

"Well he's under suspicion."

"Toledo?"

"You're not really surprised."

"Yes I am."

"What can you tell me about him?"

"He's Puerto Rican, or Mexican, I'm not sure. He's comes from a tough neighborhood. He's trying to move up. He's a good kid. He's no thief."

"How can you be sure?"

"Character."

"Well, we think he's doing it alone or as part of a ring."

"This is news to me."

"If you knew, would you tell?"

I have to think about this.

"I don't know."

"You could be charged with complicity."

"You've got the wrong guy."

"Toledo or you?"

"Both."

He gets up and starts walking me to the door.

"I want you to know how serious this is."

"I know."

"The drop comes up short five thousand dollars a day. That adds up."

"Could be anybody."

"Exactly. A distinguished author like you, how did you get mixed up with this element?"

"There is no element, Sir. There's only the job."

"I hope, for your sake, you'll see fit to inform us if you know anything."

He tells me that crime doesn't pay.

Does virtue?

Back on the casino floor I make hasty rounds for Franco. I don't know what zone he's in but he'd be easy to spot for his height and his bulk. The place is jumping and I know I better find him quick before some supervisor detains me. I find him by the nickels where he's on runner duty, carrying and doling cash to the winners and shouldering bags for hopper fills. Mark the guard, who thinks he's George the auto mechanic from another life, is pushing the cart and Franco keeps unloading bags of coins from hopper to hopper.

Mark greets me with his usual smile and appears surprised when I don't smile back. Mark's always ready for some snappy give and take.

"This is not about you," I whisper.

"I get the picture," Mark says, nodding toward Franco.

"Right."

I step up to Franco, who's just dumped one bag, locked the door and moving on. I approach, blocking his path.

"Franco, I'm remembering this."

"What you talking about, man?"

"You know what I'm talking about."

"Move. You're in my way."

"You know what I'm talking about."

"Move, man."

Mark doesn't interfere. He could. But he doesn't. He knows, or suspects, what's going on.

"I'm remembering this, man."

"You're full of shit."

"Watch your language," Mark cautions Franco. "Customers."

"I'm remembering this."

"Yeah, right."

Franco has the last word, for the moment.

After that I feel better but I don't feel big. I feel small. Maybe Detective Stevenson was right. There is an element.

But is it the element or is it Franco? No, it's Franco. I'm tired...I really am tired of being here and being asked what I'm doing here.

What the hell am I doing here! Aren't there books waiting to be written? But here I am, here I am.

I'm ready to take the escalator up to the supervisor's office to find out where they want me. I'd originally been assigned to Zone 14, as usual. Siberia. But they'd replaced me there with a substitute on account of this investigation business. So on my way to the escalator I catch Carmella in the Hot 7s section where she can't seem to get a slot door to open.

"My key isn't working."

The customer makes no secret of his impatience.

"You people," he says, shaking his head and rolling his eyes. "What a joint."

He wants us to know how disgusted he is. Right now, we're everybody who's dumped on him all his life.

I try my key and it's fixed. We walk away together, Carmella and I, and as we do so our hips meet and she whispers that she needs to talk to me. We check around to make sure no supervisors are in the vicinity and dash for the loading dock nearby. It's always freezing out there (or broiling in the summer) but there are several dark corners that are invitations to hide, and we hide.

I cannot help but notice how sensationally beautiful she is. Really, this is a waste, the job, the uniform that covers all that splendor, and the husband, a creep, half her size, that I finally met a couple of days ago. What a creep and what a waste! How someone like her fell for someone like that I'll never know. She does have it over Jennifer Lopez, except for luck.

"Promise you won't tell," she says.

This is like the fifth grade. More like the third grade.

"What?"

"Omar."

"Omar what?"

"He came on to me."

I admit that I am not surprised. Who wouldn't?

"You don't understand. He propositioned me."

"I'm still not surprised."

Occupational hazard, I'm figuring – for beautiful women.

"He touched me."

Now I'm surprised.

"How? Where?"

"Where do you think?"

She's smiling.

"I can only guess."

She's still smiling. She unbuttons her blouse, unhooks her bra and reveals the eighth wonder of the world. "This is so you won't have to guess." Then: "No man can touch me there except my husband – and you, now you. Okay?" Well, yes, okay, and here we go, and there seems no end to this sensation, though her heavy breathing is nearly alarming.

She undoes her slacks, slips out of her panties (what a sight!) and says, "Here, too." This should be a bridge too far. She says, "Only the fingers, okay?"

Okay.

"I like it fast and slow," she says, her eyelids flickering open and shut, mostly shut now – "fast and slow, fast and slow, yes, faster, slower, yes, faster, slower, yes, like that, just like that, now very fast. Please, very fast. Please. Come on. Come on. Come on. Now please faster, faster, harder, harder, deeper, deeper, like that, like that, yes, yes, yes." I think she's done, by the sounds of it, from the rhythm of her breathing, but she's not, not done. "Now the palm of your hand, please, the outside, gently, yes, like that, like that, now rub, keep rubbing, gently, very gently, like that, yes, oh yes, and inside, go inside with your fingers, deep, yes, like that, but fast, please, fast, faster, faster, please faster, fast, fast, fast – yes."

Then: "Can I kiss it?" she asks, pleadingly. She unzips me and unpacks me and goes to work, same method, fast, slow, faster, slower, faster, speed to the whirlwind.

She dresses herself back up except for the bra. Needs my help hooking it together. She plants me a big fat kiss.

"This was only foreplay," she says. "Who knows what can happen next time?"

I escort her back to her zone and think I'm in the clear but here I am at the Wild Cherries, just passing by and here's Howard Glass, as usual, and he's giving me the evil eye, with that grin. He nods me over. I keep to my pace, my eyes fixed toward destiny, but as I'm walking and picking up speed I hear him say, "You're not so terrific anymore, are you, big shot!" I am not the only one who hears this.

Much later, when it's mostly me and Mark on the floor down by the big glass doors, where only a few Asians remain half-awake waiting for the bus to Chinatown, I tell him first about a party I'm forced to attend at my wife's insistence, second about Franco, to which Mark says the usual, don't trust anybody. "I warned you."

Then, since we share practically everything, I confide about Carmella.

Mark says, "We're married. We're not neutered."

The only reason I consented to the party was because there was good news. Sylvio had phoned to say that there was another publisher he was looking into and, separately, he was having lunch with Roe Morgan and "we ain't dead yet." Roe Morgan was after a certain hot young writer in Sylvio's stable, so maybe some deal could be arranged, with me thrown into the bargain. Not the most flashy way to get published, but what the hell! Anyway, that's the good news. I'm easy. Doesn't take much to keep me going.

So I'm all set for the party that Melanie has browbeaten me into attending, a party of fellow book reviewers and literary types and artistic types gathering in Haddonfield. Melanie does not like the expression on my puss as we're getting dressed and as she keeps making me change outfits as green doesn't go with blue and blue doesn't go with orange and orange doesn't go with yellow and that whole business that turns her into a wardrobe terrorist. As for her, it's magical what she turns into when she gets all dolled up. She ought to be in pictures. She knows it, too. I did get lucky on this score. On this score, I did.

She doesn't like my attitude even as we're driving along. I cuss out every red light. She says it's not personal, red traffic lights. I say it is. It's a sign from God. She gasps when I gun the engine and proceed on yellows. She doesn't understand. That's the way we drive. She doesn't understand that every car on the road, every driver, is an enemy. They're all in the way. Anyhow, she doesn't like my attitude. "These are your people," she says about the people at the party.

"No they're not. They're frauds."

"They're not frauds."

"They're sensitive people."

"That they are and what's wrong with that?" she demands.

"I don't cotton to sensitive people."

"You're sensitive."

"No I'm not."

"I wish you'd stop this."

"I hate writers most of all. Is there anyone more self-centered?"

"Well you're not."

"Maybe that's why I'm a bust. I am non-essential personnel."

"You're what?" she says.

"Never mind."

"Oh stop this! What's gotten into you?"

"Don't pay attention to me."

"You prefer to be walking around in that green casino uniform?"

"Maybe I do."

"Please," she says.

"They're Starbucks people, these people of yours. I'm a Dunkin Donuts kind of guy."

"You just hate parties."

This becomes even more apparent at the party, hosted by Gladdy (Gladys) Parker, queen of Haddonfield Society. Haddonfield prides itself in its Americana quaintness, its Colonial and Quaker history, and in its lively devotion to the Arts. More than 60 percent of Haddonfield's adult residents are college graduates and about the same percentage are millionaires, old money mostly. The speed limit is 15 mph and pedestrians always have the right of way. Driving is considered rude. People promenade. Victorian and Colonial homes and Boutique shops and outdoor cafes charm the main roads and the side streets and there is no crime. No crime. No burglaries, no rapes, no murders. Zero. (Five minutes away is Camden, New Jersey, which is annually cited as the most UN-livable and dangerous city in America.)

Sheldon Parker, Gladdy's husband, made his wealth on Wall Street and brought it back here in a place that honors its actors (The Haddonfield Plays and Players), its musicians (The Haddonfield Symphony), its painters, its sculptors and even its writers. That's who's here this evening, illuminated by the romance of true 19th century candlelight, the whole crew of them gathered pell mell in Gladdy's parlor, the length of a football field starting at the 50-yard line, carpet so thick that short people are in peril. Here, in this Victorian palace on Tanner Street, off Kings Highway, where actual kings of Europe once traveled, everything that glitters IS gold.

A few business types are sipping martinis, but the rest are artists or from the artistic community.

The women, generally, are too rich and too thin, and the men, of artistic persuasion, walk around like Byron or Chopin.

Melanie is greeted, hug hug kiss kiss, like everybody's favorite, and I'm here, too. I'm not eyeing the exit, as Melanie threatened me against, but I am casing the joint for a quiet corner to camouflage myself. Melanie, though, has me mixing and mingling. I never know how to disengage, politely, once a conversation has run its course and turned back to the weather. This is always a problem, how to tell a person look, it's over, you're boring me and I'm boring you, so let's move on to other people so that we can get bored all over again.

(At the casino, you fix the lady's machine, and it's done.)

Melanie walks me, like a delinquent, from gathering to gathering, all of it artsy and literary, and whispers, "You ought to love this. Grouch."

"It's all about flirting and boozing."

"Oh shush."

"It's about mating up. It's about adultery."

I had just read something about the King James Bible, how it went through so many disreputable changes that one version, called the Wicked Bible, forgot one word in the command "Though shalt not commit adultery." The forgotten word was not. Apparently that was good enough for entire generations even up to this minute: Thou shalt commit adultery.

I do bring this up at one of the gatherings and am marked as witty. Witty is good, and Melanie is pleased. I'm behaving.

"You can be so charming," she whispers, "when you want."

I spy a bedroom with a TV set showing, oh my gawd, *Lawrence of Arabia*, and figure this to be my resting place for the night, but Gladdy intercepts and asks me what I'm working on these days. I say, "Nothing." She laughs. I am so witty. "No, seriously. Don't be coy. What's the new novel all about?"

"There is no new novel."

Melanie jumps in before this can get any worse.

"Oh, Jay. Stop being so modest. Jay is always at work on his next, Gladdy. In fact, his agent..."

"Will it be as big as..."

"Bigger," says Mel.

Gladdy never saw the movie, but she had read the book, *The Ice King*. This gives her points. I can never dislike her.

But it does get worse, for here comes Felix Grubner, novelist, essayist, literary man-about-town, escorted by a phalanx of his worshipers. I don't know how people get TWO Ph.Ds, but he's got them, both, and it's astonishing. He gets fellowships and gives lectures and some university has named a chair after him. The problem began when we were both reviewed in a single review in the *Philadelphia Journal* when *The Ice King* came out from me, and something else from him. So what it really amounted to was my novel against his, and I won, and he never forgave me, as if I had anything to do with the write-up.

I found out later that he actually contacted the *Journal* to have them do a check as to whether I was related to the reviewer.

Fortunately, for him, for Felix, he succeeded thereafter, or so he keeps reminding his many fans. Truly, he is a success, though his wife seems never to be at his side, and when she is, she comes with a sour expression, exasperated, as if she's heard it all before, everything he has to say. Maybe they get along, I don't know, but I do not envy him in that department.

"Well, well, well," he says, extending a handshake.

"Good to see you Felix."

"Where have you been?"

"Around."

"Here, there and everywhere, huh?"

"Most likely."

We get to talking about his latest essay in the *National* something-or-other, in which he claimed that America's great failure is that its people are so parochial, so local. "We have no cosmopolitan wits," he wrote in that article and repeats again now. We lack gravitas. I explain that it's exactly that, our love of silliness that makes us great.

"We don't do angst," I'm trying to say against his smugness.

"Maybe we should," he says smiling that academic smile.

"We don't do weltschmerz, Felix. They weltschmerz. We romp. They gave us Hitler and Mussolini. We came up with Bob Hope and Jack Benny."

"Oh," he laughs, "yes, we gave the world the hula hoop."

"Also, Felix, the cure for polio."

"I understand you have a secret project in the works," Felix says, quickly onto something else.

"He simply won't tell," says Gladdy.

"Very secret," I say.

I refuse to name a novel in progress, for the whammy, and for the fact that a novel in progress is not a novel. Talking a novel, a novel that hasn't been codified as yet, is bad manners unless, of course, it's part of a class. Besides, there is no sense talking about anything that hasn't happened yet. It is bad luck to congratulate a mere pregnancy.

"In development" is another word, or words, for hell.

"Oh, very secret," Felix says theatrically.

"The mark of a true artist," someone says, one of his people.

Funny, I never think of myself as an artist. A writer, okay. I just don't get artist. In my neighborhood they used to beat people up for less.

You did not want to be seen carrying a violin across the football field, in my neighborhood.

That's what artist means to me: A kid carrying a violin across a football field.

So now it's time for Felix to give us the scoop on what's been going on with him, the prizes he's won for his books and commentaries, the honorable mentions in *The New York Times*, the *New York Review of Books*, the praises from academics as near as Columbia and as far as Oxford. He still has that chair named for him some place.

There are more than a dozen of his devotees listening in, awestruck or merely tipsy.

Melanie is not liking this.

She makes it clear that my one book got itself translated into 26 different languages, that its moral dilemma has sparked academic papers in more than a hundred universities...

"Then came the movie," says Felix, and it is plain what he means.

"But you didn't write the screenplay," says Gladdy, addressing me and defending me.

"No he didn't," says Mel, further defending me, her husband the author.

"What if I did," I snap. "I liked the movie." (I did, even though the screenplay was quite ordinary, as was the screenwriter herself.)

"Over my head," says Felix.

What a prick!

Felix is Felix and there is nothing to be done. He has turned quite political and his commentaries appear in numerous scholarly magazines and web sites. I know where he's going in his politics and it is not my direction and I know that I would never be published, or posted, in his magazines or web sites because of my views. I keep changing my views on politics anyway, though politics seems to be our new culture, our rock and roll. Those are the books that are published and those are the books that sell. Anyway, as a slot attendant, politics is distant, something that happens far away, especially when you're working graveyard and all you want to do is sleep.

On C-Span you are warned that only non-fiction writers and viewers are wanted. If you're fiction, go away.

"Is one book enough to make a reputation?" someone says.

The one-book-wonder knock. I know the routine. I'm tired of it, but I do suggest that I'll take Salinger's one book over what's her name's 200. Literature, I go on, is not based on quantity. James Jones' reputation (though he wrote several) is based on one book and a fine reputation it is, and James Joyce's reputation is likewise based on one book, and go argue with James Joyce, and altogether, I'll take Brahms' four symphonies over Mozart's 280, or whatever Kirchel's final count.

"I seem to have a knack," says Felix, "for combining scholarship with commercial appeal."

Yes he does, people agree.

Says Melanie, and this is getting ridiculous, "You know, Jay's been favorably compared to Hemingway and I.B. Singer."

She is starting to sound more like my mother than my wife.

Someone – must be from my side of the aisle – says I write in the absurdist tradition of Beckett and Ionesco.

"Never cared much for Hemingway," says Felix.

"Possibly he wouldn't care much for you," is all I can add.

This leads someone to ask how writers like to be addressed...author, writer, novelist?

"I go by writer and commentator," says Felix.

"How about you?" says Gladdy.

"Me? I go by slot attendant."

Melanie spills her drink. "He's joking, you know."

"Seriously."

"I'm serious. Slot attendant."

"Jay, stop this," Melanie whispers.

"You mean," Gladdy says, "casinos?"

"Yes."

"Those people who run around..."

"That's me."

"He's only doing it for research," says Mel.

"Of course," says Gladdy.

"No. I'm a slot attendant."

"What about your next book?" asks Felix.

The worst part about Felix is that in a perfect world we would be friends. Meanwhile, though, there is no one to talk to, not about writing.

"There is no next book."

"Oh please," says Gladdy.

"Yes, oh please," says Melanie, "and please stop this."

But I am enjoying this. Because it is the truth and if the truth hurts, so be it.

"We'll probably be reading all about it in *The New Yorker*."

"I don't think so."

"Isn't he funny?" says Mel.

"No he isn't," says Felix.

Felix is like a dog. He can smell defeat. I have been sent to him for an offering. His time has come. My time has come and gone.

"What exactly does a slot attendant do?" asks Gladdy.

"Well..."

"Oh, Jay, stop pulling people's legs."

"I don't think he's pulling anyone's leg," says Felix, getting his comeuppance over that original sin.

People dance at your failure even more than they dance at their own success. This too I have learned.

"You probably are doing research," says Gladdy to smooth it all over.

"No I'm not."

"Yes he is."

"What we want to know," says Gladdy, "I mean after your big success, and you made us all so proud, you certainly made Melanie proud..."

"Yes he did."

"What we want to know is what's taking so long and what's coming next."

"Nothing."

"You're a slot attendant?"

"I'm a slot attendant. That's all I do. There's nothing next."

"They get the picture," says Mel. "They get the picture."

On the drive back home I'm in for the silent treatment. Finally, back home, she does say: "He is a buffoon."

"Thanks."

"But what can be said about you?"

"Okay, I was..."

"Yes you were. You were awful."

"Yes, I was."

"Who were you trying to hurt? Me? Yourself?"

"Let's talk more about Felix."

"No, that's done."

"That's agreed, right?"

"Felix is a buffoon but they're not all buffoons. They're good people."

"I agree."

"No you don't."

"Let's talk about Felix, about what kind of a buffoon he is. He doesn't listen. How can a writer not listen? How can he know what to write?"

"What were you trying to prove?"

"I honestly don't know."

"You kept rubbing it in, rubbing it in, rubbing..."

"I know. I'm sorry."

"Weren't you thinking about me? Just for a minute?"

"I got all wrapped up, I guess. Let's get back to Felix."

"You wouldn't stop. I couldn't get you to stop."

"He's such a fraud, Felix."

"Just because people don't work graveyard shift, that doesn't make them frauds."

"Now you're defending him?"

"I'm defending artists."

"You mean people who don't work."

"I mean people who work with their minds, their hearts and minds, like you."

"But I'm a slot attendant."

That's good for another hour's worth of silent treatment. She showers, then sits by the edge of the bed, then drying and combing out her hair.

She doesn't understand, and she never will. There is some pride in the work that I do. Weeks before I took her on a busman's holiday, I mean we went to another casino so she could play some slots and I could play some horses. As we're walking around there's a jam-up at a dollar machine and the slot attendant, I can tell he doesn't know what to do. So I give him some advice, as sometimes all it takes is opening and shutting the door, and it works.

I'm smiling. She asks why, and I explain that I'm proud of what I just did. I contributed something. I made a difference.

You're proud of that? she said. You're proud?

She will never understand.

"I like your new haircut," I say to make amends for the Haddonfield party I left, we left, in ruins.

That almost gets a smile.

"You have no idea how you humiliated me. How you humiliated yourself."

"That wasn't the plan."

"Right, it just worked out that way."

"They kept coming at me...your next book...your next book..."

"Well you do have a next book."

"You didn't bring it up, either."

"Who had the chance? You were so busy."

"Just trying to come clean."

"Did you forget that Sylvio still has things going?"

"Yes, I forgot."

"How could you forget? Our life depends on it," she says with terrible emphasis.

"I'm not so sure."

"What is that supposed to mean?"

How do I tell her that I'm not sure about anything anymore? How do I tell her that part of me is gone?

"It means that I am a slot attendant."

"Stop saying that, please!"

"But I am."

"You mean that's it, this is the end, this is all we have to look forward to?"

"I don't know. I swear I don't know."

"This can't be you talking. What's happened to our dreams?"

"They're dreams."

Later, we're in bed, together. This is a treat. Our hours keep us apart for bedroom business. I've taken three sick days from work. I've got two left.

So we're in bed together and I sense her pillow moistening up. I snuggle. She snuggles back.

I have got to figure a way to make her happy, at least get the panic out of our lives. Tomorrow, maybe, I'll go back to filling out that paperwork for all those grants. Everybody gets grants. Felix gets grants. People with money get grants. People with more money get more grants. I've tried a thousand. They're so specific. Sorry, we only provide funds for writers focused on tomato growing in Vermont, and only green tomatoes, not red. Like that.

"We do have dreams, don't we?" she says, still snuggled into her pillow.

"Yes," I say. "We do. We do have dreams."

Chapter 10

Figures to be a millionaire to win the million dollar jackpot. Those new $10 "Who Wants To Be A Hero?" machines had just been installed about three weeks ago with a jackpot worth a straight million and Mrs. Hazel Beckman decided that it was hers to win, and so she was at it from one shift to the next every day, practically non-stop. She had the clout, so when she had to take a breather, maybe a nap up in her room, she had the okay from any supervisor to close the machine down until she returned. She was not going to let anyone else get that million.

Not Hazel, a widow in her mid-70s who had inherited a fortune and a terrible disposition. People did snap to her, though she was no tipper...but she was a high roller and high rollers are "valued" customers. When she wanted something, she wanted it not now, BEFORE. She was a bitch. No cocktail server, no slot attendant, no supervisor, wanted to be anywhere near her. She'd already had three of us (slot attendants) fired, plus one supervisor and even one shift manager; the shift manager, Matilda Sheffi, long gone when she refused to take Hazel's word that she had played two hundred dollar coins instead of one, thus depriving Hazel of the full payout. Down goes Matilda.

When Hazel is unhappy, everyone's unhappy. In the case of Matilda, for example, when the difference was $20,000, Hazel went right to the top; got on the House phone, got connected straight to Bob Foster, our president, who came rushing down with effusive apologizes and the proper check. Hazel wanted the shift manager fired right on the spot, and Bob Foster, our president, did as ordered.

The casino drop cannot afford to lose her kind of business. Usually, about a dozen high rollers (losing of course) account for a casino's daily profit.

She's in Zone 5, where those new games were set up, when the bells go off around midnight. She's hit. Is she thrilled? They seldom are, the pros, Hazel in particular. She's a pro. She's hit hundreds of thousands in the past (lost an equal amount for sure, or maybe not) so this is another day at the office. She sits there, grim as ever, and wants her money fast. By check, of course. Toledo Vasquez is the slot attendant on duty.

He gets busy. There's much to do.

First, as is obligatory, he congratulates her. She tells him to forget all that, you jerk, just bring the money.

For that amount, it gets complicated. Everybody gets summoned; the slot host, the supervisor, the shift manager, the casino manager, the public relations vice president, surveillance, and even Bob Foster, the president of the whole shebang. They all have to get into the act and they all have a role. But Toledo's first task is to get Hazel's drivers' license, standard practice for any win $1,200 or more. The I.R.S. is watching.

So it's not just a formality, it's a legality. So Toledo is only doing his job when he asks for it, and Hazel...Hazel throws a fit. She's insulted. She's been coming here, to the same casino, for 20 years, and still has to prove whom she is? Her identity is in doubt? What is this? This is ridiculous!

But it's not the routine that has her riled, she knows it has to be done; it's that someone as lowly as a slot attendant has the gumption. The slot host arrives and apologizes. The shift manager arrives and apologizes. The casino manager arrives and apologizes. They all congratulate her and apologize as meanwhile, Toledo does his job, writes up the jackpot, then, only then, steps aside.

As she waits for her check she leans over to play the next machine and hits for $10,000, peanuts, but a whole new procedure.

Toledo writes this up and she says, "Aren't you supposed to congratulate me?"

Forty minutes later both checks arrive, minus state and federal taxes. For a hit like this, a slot attendant should expect a $200 reward, minimum. There have been winners of far less who've tipped a thousand dollars. Marty Glick, over at Zone 1, knows all about this. They tip him even before they sit down, some do.

Toledo makes himself scarce because you don't want to be obvious.

Hazel Beckman nods him over and hands him a five dollar bill.

I'm watching all this from an adjoining zone and it is laughable. That's life. That's all you can say. That's people. That's all. Toledo strolls over to me and he is laughing.

"What the hell," he says. I warn him not to spend it all in one place.

"Forget about it," he says, and then asks how it went over with those investigators. I tell him nothing happened. There was nothing to say.

"I need to talk to you," he says.

"Any time, Toledo. But about what?"

His girl, again? Maria?

"About something."

The way he says it, it's not so simple, not about Maria. You get to know in advance what people have on their minds, especially when it's money, and this is money, I just know, I can tell, and it's not good money, I mean kosher money, I can tell that, too. I can't be sure. But it is a hunch and that is always the best bet, the hunch. He would not be whispering or taking me aside, next to Coin Redemption, if it were about girls. We talk women all the time, openly.

So I am wary and am not sure I want this to go the next step.

"Can it wait?"

"I don't know. I think you're the only one I can talk to about this."

I give him a hard look. "Do I really have to know?"

"You're the only one I can trust."

"I don't think I want to know, Toledo. I think it best you keep it to yourself."

"You don't want to know?"

"I really don't."

"We're friends, right?" he says pathetically.

"That's the point."

But, he says, it's something I should know.

"Some things," I tell him, "are best left unsaid, especially between friends."

"I think you know what it is," he says.

"No I don't."

No I don't know that it's about theft and whether he is or he isn't part of that trade.

He informs me that Hazel did shower some of the others. She passed around hundred dollar bills, even slipped the cocktail server a crisp hundred, and even Mark the guard walked off with the same. As she did so, going in secret from palm to palm, she said something like this, according to what Toledo could pick up: "Nothing for that Puerto Rican scum."

I shrug when Toledo confides this. Takes all kinds. He's been around, I've been around. We know the score.

104

Roger Price, the supervisor on duty, easygoing and one of our favorites, ambles over and asks Toledo what he got. Toledo shows him.

"That bitch," says Roger. Then he says: "We're the foot soldiers and the generals upstairs don't even know we're fighting a war."

Then he says, "I shouldn't be surprised."

Roger is college educated (Temple) but he got his learning on the casino floor. He's been at this 14 years and just wants to be left alone. You don't bother me, I don't bother you. That's his motto. So we don't bother him. He started off a nice guy (you can just tell) and he's still a nice guy, but the human condition, whatever that is, finally got to him. He walks around with a scowl.

He's seen everything and it's disgusting.

That's pretty much a trick we all adopt, those of us who serve the public. Keep that scowl and people stay clear.

Roger asks Toledo if Bob Foster, our president, said anything after he came rushing down from his suite of offices.

"Nothing to me," says Toledo.

"Figures."

Our director of marketing, Shelly King, did she?

"Nada."

Roger pats Toledo on the shoulder. "Don't take it too hard."

"I'm okay, man."

This leaves me standing uncomfortably with Toledo, as Roger moves on.

"Maybe you're right," he says. "Better you stay cool."

"That's the smart thing."

I wonder if I'm being too *adult*. That's been my ticket, acting neither high nor low, but just right, or just straight, yes, straight. No airs about being a bit older. Not airs, certainly no airs, about being an author. I'm one of the guys.

That's been the ticket, and no act, either. It's all come about naturally and routinely.

I'd hate to admit this to Melanie (though I already have), but I feel more comfortable around this crowd than her crowd, and more at ease, and more desired and desirable, down here around Toledo and Mark Pleszak, certainly Mark, and Maggi Holt and Bob Michaelson and Roger Price and Hitesh and Flint Odesso, certainly Flint, and Carmella, certainly Carmella, than I do around Roe Morgan and the rest of that highfalutin gang.

These are real people. They are not all good. But they are real. Actually they are pretty good.

Hobnobbing among the elite is never safe. You wonder, later, if you've said something stupid, and you probably have. You're always being judged, or so it seems, or even worse, or perhaps just the same, you're not being given a second thought. You are disposable, non-essential personnel. Nobody cares.

This is not the case on the floor, down here on the floor. It can be terrible but it is always authentic.

Toledo is neglecting his zone, but there's more on his mind.

"Something's really bugging me," he says. "It's really bugging me."

I know what it is. I'm pretty sure.

"We all have our secrets."

"Mine is too big to carry alone," he says.

What a strange thing to say! Almost biblical. Mine is too big to carry alone.

"Tell your girl, tell Maria," I advise.

"Are you kidding?"

Chapter 11

Melanie is relieved that it isn't me, or probably isn't me.

"Maybe," she says, "it's something else he wanted to talk about."

"I know what he wanted to talk about."

"You're sure."

"No."

"Instinct?"

"Look, I know."

I've taken another sick day. That won't favor me when it comes to my performance evaluation. But I've got to get regular and I've got to get some sleep, real sleep. I've been reading stories about how dangerous it is otherwise. People need sleep. Anything less than eight hours a night, said the article, is dangerous. Eight hours a night? Are you kidding? For more than a year I've been subsisting on one hour a day. I am going to kill those pigeons. One night, or one day, I will kill all those pigeons. I will try to sleep without a pill. We shall see.

But here's the good part about being up by night and in a fog by day. You hardly read a newspaper and hardly watch TV, the news. You don't know what's going on.

That's a blessing.

In the world of publishing, Judith Regan of Regan Books, says that she's had "amazing sex," but it wasn't with me, so what do I care.

So I'm not current.

When I was in newspapering I was current to the minute. I needed the news and the news needed me.

Well that's how it is anyway, when you're on graveyard. There is no news. Nothing is happening. No wars, no politics, nothing.

You've missed everything and you've missed nothing.

(Up in the cafeteria the TV is all sports or sitcoms and when there's news, it's Spanish.)

Rumor has it that there's a recession going on. Slot attendants, like me, keep paying jackpots and fixing hopper jams. The place is full. How come? What recession?

Melanie is at the computer fiddling with a book review. She's biting her nails. She's reluctant to write something bad about a bad book. Her mind has been preoccupied with her father in Cincinnati, who's had a bypass. He's recuperating all right, and her mother insists that everything is fine, but Melanie thinks we should make the trip, which we cannot afford to do, by car or by plane, and anyway, by the time we got there we'd be ready to head back. I cannot keep taking sick days and...we are saving my vacation days for New York, when it's time to celebrate the signing of a book contract.

Day to day we are prepared to celebrate, not me so much, but Melanie, who's the optimist, still the optimist.

Lucky we're one of each as I'd hate to imagine two pessimists in the same family.

"I think," she says, "you did wisely."

We're onto Toledo and what I'm not supposed to know about him but I do. That maybe he is a thief. "You never want to become an informer," she says.

I'm glad she agrees, but then she adds:

"I just keep wondering what you're doing in that world anyway."

Like it or not, I say, it is my world.

Melanie has given up on the computer. She leans back and sighs, rubs her eyes.

"I can't write a bad review," she says.

"So write a good one."

"Can't do that, either."

We drive over to the McDonald's. It's that or meatloaf. So it's McDonald's. They don't heat these places. I think I know why. They want you in and out.

We find a table that's clean except for two crumbs. No table at McDonald's is ever totally clean. There's always two crumbs.

She brings me a double cheeseburger, medium fries and a coke. She's having the chicken sandwich and a diet coke.

She doesn't need to diet, but she does. Not really, but she is temperate. She is temperate in food and in everything else. She does not have mood swings. Though lately...

"The fries are cold."

"Cold," she asks, "or just not hot enough?"

"Not hot enough."

"Should I take them back?"

"Never mind."

We sit there and munch. I stare out the window when I'm done. I'm a quick eater. I gulp it down. She's still eating. I wish there was something good to say.

Things could be worse, or, as my Russian self-defense master, Boris, keeps saying, things should never be better. That's considered a blessing where he comes from. Things should never be better. That's how you bless someone. You have to think about this before it sinks in. So we're sitting here and enjoying that roundtable up a few rows where the old-timers have gathered. All McDonald's are alike except that each table is its own universe. They're always here, a group of old men, retirees and most probably widowers, at the same table, gabbing away, swapping tales, usually about the wars they've fought in and how everything has changed, and this usually starts an argument, some saying that it was better before and others insisting that now is the best time of all, and how special it is just to be alive. They're always here from visit to visit and it's all very pleasant – although, given that these are mostly World War Two vets, and Korea, there's usually one of them missing, never to be seen again – another empty chair.

Melanie always smiles just to be watching them.

She brings back chocolate chip cookies from the counter, which is an extravagance but always a treat and more than that, somehow comforting, a signal that everything's going to be all right. She reminds me that there is still hope from Sylvio. Much hope. I don't tell her that you can't live off hope and can't live off the next phone call that may not even come. But she knows what I'm thinking.

"I think it's time to phone Lindy," she says.

Lindy is my sister, older by a few years, and it's a long story about her, but the short of it is that she is still quite gorgeous but refused to trade that in for acting and went for song writing instead, that, plus developing new shows for TV, the stage, and the movies. She's always had more creativity and talent than she knew what to do with, but it all went kaput when she came up with an idea for a children's show, and it got ripped off. They bought the project, except that they never gave her the money, or the credit, and the show became the biggest thing on the air...and still is. Walking in, she knew nothing about agents or lawyers and how to protect herself.

So after all that, and cured of ambition, she moved back to Montreal and became religious, though with ties to no particular religion...and not hypocritically pious. She has recovered and become quite strong. Now she teaches. She teaches Inspiration and Motivation and has quite a following.

When she calls, or when I phone her, she always tells me to bless everything.

"I think I will call her," I tell Melanie over another cup of coffee along with the chocolate chip cookies.

"I think you should," says Melanie. "You need a good pep talk."

We glance over at the kid who mops the floor and tidies up here at McDonald's. He's disabled, and severely so, walks on one good leg and there is something wrong with his face. He never talks to anyone and no one talks to him. Melanie always tips him two dollars. We watch him, Melanie and I, and we don't have to say what we're thinking, but I wonder if he is blessed, or thinks he's blessed.

I see blessings and curses every day in the casino.

She says, "You are doing the right thing, aren't you? About that kid."

"Toledo? Of course."

She says she's worried. "Suppose you were forced to talk?"

"I'd have nothing to say."

"But you know what he did. You know it's him."

"I'd never talk, Melanie. That's the first rule of the schoolyard."

"But this isn't the schoolyard. You were talking to a real detective."

"I'm no snitch, Mel."

"Listen to your language. You're starting to talk just like them."

"Snitch?"

"Isn't that how they talk?"

"Well, it certainly ain't how Felix Grubner talks with his two Ph.Ds. Anyway, you're so big on multiculturalism."

"Not when you bring it home," she says smiling, because she knows how I tease her about being such a flaming liberal. I can be a liberal, too, but I once got in trouble with her group in Haddonfield when, after another suicide bombing in that other part of the world, I said, "Can you be called a bigot if by their words and deeds they turn you into one?" That is no way to make friends and influence people; not in Haddonfield.

"Do you know how serious this is?" she says as we're finishing up here at McDonald's where, for some reason, I feel a sense of comfort. There's a part of me that's afraid to go home. Home is where the pigeons live. I particularly like Melanie's dad, a true, red-blooded Cincinnatian. I love his story about how the pigeons took over Fountain Square and, once a year, the citizens were allowed, even invited, to shoot them. I am not that kind of person, but about pigeons, yes. Anyway, I think pigeon shooting has been stopped in Cincinnati. Because of her dad, I root for the Reds, and he has plenty of stories about them, too, as he goes back to the days of Wally Post, Gus Bell, and most of all, Big Klu. A part of Cincinnati is hillbilly country, as it sits next door to Kentucky, and her dad always tells the joke about the hillbilly who refused to marry a virgin "cause if she ain't good enough for her own kin, she ain't good enough for me." This cracks him up, and me, too. I am also afraid of home because that's where the bills come, and the phone calls.

"So do you?" Melanie says. "Do you realize how serious this is?"

"I've been told. The detective told me."

"But you still wouldn't...snitch."

"Come on, Mel. Would you want me to?"

She's thinking.

"No, I guess not," she says. "No, that wouldn't be right."

I explain that, besides the ethics, I am a hero to Toledo Vasquez. As I am no hero to Roe Morgan and the rest of them, I am a hero to Toledo Vasquez. That counts.

"But what if it's a choice between you and him?"

"One step at a time."

"Could you go to jail? My God!"

"But you're with me on this."

"Yes. I guess."

"You guess."

She thinks I'm being awfully flippant about this business. But, I explain, there is nothing worse than an informer, or hardly anything.

"How bad can this get?" she asks.

"Pretty bad."

"Aren't you afraid?"

"No. Maybe."

She is still suspicious that I may be involved, considering all those tips I bring home. Are they really tips?

How is it that when she sends me off saying we need a hundred and fifty dollars for the phone bill, the next morning I bring home a hundred and fifty dollars?

Chapter 12

We drive back from McDonald's and as I pull up to the house I tell her I'm going for a drive. I need to air out. She understands and says she's sorry for being so tough on me, and lately, doesn't it seem, she says, that we're always quarrelling? Not exactly quarrelling, but at odds. It has been difficult, I agree, but, she says, we do love each other, don't we? Of course we do.

Because without that...

I know...

She sends me off saying, "Pleasant thoughts. Think about Sylvio and what he said."

Yes, he said we're alive, still alive. There's another publisher, and even Roe Morgan. Even Roe Morgan is still alive.

As I drive off I'm remembering what he said – No Thanks. You will always remember that, from Roe Morgan or from anybody. I have been rejected a thousand times, as every writer has, but I've never had No Thanks. That's heavy, near unforgivable. But forget I will, if it comes to that, for that's life. Better a live dog than a dead lion. I always hated that expression. But I was young. So, maybe Sylvio can still turn it around, hot agent that he is; never loses a patient, right? So will I forgive? No, never. But I will take the money. Integrity is a fine thing, but it comes in second to the rent.

For some reason I think back to my three minutes of fame on the *Today* show when *The Ice King* was so hot. That's all I got, three minutes, and it was a blur then and it's still a blur. A limo picked me up five in the morning from The Four Seasons in Beverly Hills, dropped me off at the studio, someone put some make-up on me, and I was on, though I couldn't see Matt Lauer, though he could see me, and so could the rest of America. That's a bit of a disadvantage when you can't see who you're talking to, how he's reacting. I was told by my publicist to smile and keep on smiling, which I did, and that was stupid. I'll never do that again. You look so stupid when you just keep on smiling. So I'm asked a few questions, and I answer, I guess, but it doesn't seem to come out right, from my side, and I wish I had more time, but this is television and there are commercials and other guests to do. Television is not a writer's medium, certainly no place for a novelist, as novelists do not think in sentences or sound bites. Novelists think in paragraphs.

Writers should not be out there selling their books, anyway. That's why God invented salesmen. Your job is to write and shut up.

I wonder, as I drive, if my marriage is in jeopardy. We said we love each other. We hardly ever say that because it is so understood. So why now? I know about me, my weaknesses, my temptations, but not about Melanie's, though I have had a suspicion or two. There'd been those late lunches with Harold Fermont, the writer, and once she'd even confessed to a schoolgirl crush – "who wouldn't?" Yes, the ladies of Haddonfield swoon for Harold Fermont – "who wouldn't?" I don't know if anything happened. I don't want to know. Maybe I do, but better I don't. No, we are happily married.

Or maybe I've been jealous and continue to be jealous because he's successful and I'm not. I used to be, but not anymore.

(At the outset she wanted to do the "let's have no secrets between us" thing – where couples confide about everything from the first crush onward. I was opposed to this. This, I argued, is an album better left closed. She finally agreed, though she is big on masturbation, admits to indulging for the release and the therapy. I never ask how often she does it, or who she has in mind when she does it, but I imagine it's quite frequent and would rather not know the rest, like who's the guy in the picture. She claims that "everybody does it" and this is true. Masters and Johnson, and others, did the research and even without all that research it is still true.)

Poverty does strange things. We're not poor. Together we're sort of, almost, making it, enough, even, to fake it, but we barely rate as middle class, except for the public face we put on, largely through her doing, and she is so good at it that for all appearances we're hugely successful. But six years now without a novel, yes, is it about the same as going 84 days without taking a fish? The thought of losing her never occurred to me, until she said she loved me.

I only hope Toledo has stopped doing what he's doing. I did not want to scare her, but this is very serious. Something has got to give. There is going to be trouble. They did not bring in those guys, those outside guys, for nothing. They are on to Toledo and who else? Who knows? Are they onto me for something?

If it really is Toledo, can you blame him? Of course you can, except that he's got a girl he wants to marry, a house she wants him to buy, a snazzy car she wants him to lease – and all that at $8.25 an hour? No can do. In the old days, the Vegas days, they took you out back, broke your legs or chopped off your hands.

They don't do that now, but maybe what they do is even worse. I know what they do. I'd seen it done. What they do is parade you out in handcuffs. They do it for show, as a warning to others. See, this is what happens when you cheat and get caught. Take note. That's the message – and everybody gets caught. There's that eye in the sky. God is watching.

The problem for Melanie – I think I know what it is. Suppose I get nabbed, for being directly or indirectly responsible, and suppose it hits the papers and makes a scandal? How will this go over in Haddonfield? Nothing wrong with a big scandal, a literary spat, like Truman Capote vs. Jack Kerouac ("that's not writing, that's typing") or Mailer knifing his wife, or Mailer, John Irving and John Updike ganging up on Tom Wolfe (that's not literature, that's entertainment); or even a journalistic scandal will do, like reporter Jayson Blair who nearly brought down the House That Ochs Built. Big scandals are good. People write books about them, and become even more in demand, even more popular.

But a puny scandal is not good. Slot attendant scandals do not translate into television or into movies.

Maybe it's time to go for a job that pays really big. I met this guy in the casino who made a fortune dubbing voices for the movies (looping), when they switch to TV and the F-word has to be replaced. He got rich changing F-You to Forget You. But he had the right voice. I don't. Amazing how people get rich. Like the hula-hoop, the pet rock, the intermittent windshield wiper. Amazing.

I'm driving and I know where I'm going, but I'm a bit lost. There used to be small farms around here, horses, cows. I used to drive past a place near our house that always had a horse tethered out front, grazing away. The sight of that horse made me feel good, still country. But all that's changed or changing and fast. The horse is gone and so is the farm. So are most of the farms. It's all being developed. Mostly condos (as what's happening to our apartment) and strip malls. When Starbucks comes, horses go.

I pull into the Wal-Mart strip mall and park in front of the sign that reads, "Boris Russian Martial Arts Center." I know Boris, but it's been a while. He's got a third degree Black Belt. Mine is second degree. Boris used to be part of the Russian Mob that came to America after the Soviet Union became simply Russia. He quit. He quit the mob, went straight and opened this business, martial arts, of which he'd been the leading expert in Moscow. People came to him from all over to learn his secrets, and still do. He taught the Soviet Army, which is not necessarily a high compliment, considering what we know these days, but he also taught the Israeli Army, and that is a high compliment.

"Jay," he says, repeating my name three times. He is something of a mystic and a thrice repeated name means something, I don't know what, but it does.

Boris also once taught me something that nearly amounts to a curse, or that will stop any adversary in his tracks. Goes like this: "I see ten feet under you."

That is supposed to freeze anyone in your path.

"So?" he says.

I bring him up to date on practically everything. He is a wise man. He says not to worry. There is a time for everything. If it is meant for me to be published, again, so it will be. If not, it simply was not meant to be, but there will be other lives, here, and in the hereafter. I am not so sure about the hereafter. Oh, he says with that big Russian laugh, there is. Trust me. Suppose I don't want to wait that long? He laughs again.

About my being a slot attendant, he says it is work, and all work is honorable. About Melanie, she will adjust, he assures me, if that is the end of my path.

She will come around. I am lucky, he says, to have such a wife. Yes, I am lucky. Even if that is all the luck I have, he says, it is enough.

We had it planned differently, I tell Boris...Melanie and I. We had planned on me becoming a great and famous writer.

Ah yes, says Boris, Man plans, God laughs.

We had planned on a literary life, not a slot attendant life. Melanie, at the outset, had pictured herself as hostess of a SALON, as in Proust.

Tell her, he says, that you have made peace. I do not tell him that would be a separate peace, in her language, surrender.

He asks if I am sure, really sure, that I want to make it big again, as I did that time before with the *The Ice King*. I say of course. That is my cut. But he's not so sure. He says maybe that world is closed to me (for the time being) because I want it closed, yes, subconsciously. He says we only fail when we want to fail. No, I want to succeed. I wrote *Smooth Operator* to succeed, not to fail.

"So it will succeed," he says, slapping my back and then collecting me in an affectionate bear hug.

But maybe, he says, I actually enjoy the casino life, even down in the squalor. That is where I feel accepted.

"To feel accepted," he says, "is everything. Like love."

No, not love. I do not feel love. In fact, I explain, this is why I'm here, to sharpen up. Bad things are coming. I tell him the story of Toledo Vasquez and my involvement and this upsets Boris, that it has taken this turn. I should be no party to this, and if anyone is familiar with corruption, first-hand, it is Boris. That is never good, theft, corruption. It soils the spirit. Boris is very spiritual. He was even spiritual when he was corrupt. There is nothing as spiritual as a spiritual Russian. They see ten feet under you.

Boris is now an American, very patriotic.

I tell him the story of Franco DeLima, how he informed on me. Boris says, "Aha." Boris knows the type.

Franco is probably behind Toledo's miseries as well.

"I think so," says Boris.

He even describes Franco to me. He knows how old he is, how tall he is, how wide he is and even was sort of family he comes from. Yes, he knows the type.

"There is evil," says Boris. "People say there is no good, there is no evil. We are all the same. I say no. I say yes. There is evil."

There is evil, and there is no root cause for it, either. No excuses. Some people are just plain rotten. Boris knows. Oh he knows.

What was Stalin's root cause? What was Stalin's excuse?

Boris's father had been sent to Stalin's gulag. There he died.

Boris has a last name but it can't be spelled or pronounced since it is so long and full of consonants, so he bought a vowel and made it Stone, Boris Stone. Boris has a dream. One day he will have these martial arts centers in every strip mall from coast to coast, and why not? This is America. Boris wants me to write his book on martial arts. He's got 280 moves that nobody else knows about. There are as many different self-defense techniques, actually in the thousands, as there are different steps for dance and different positions for sex. He used to pursue me for that book until he understood that everybody approaches me to write a book, just as everybody I meet has a niece or nephew who works for Disney in Hollywood.

We step onto his mat, his private mat, Black Belts only, and there are so few of us, but before getting started he nods to the next room where a class is in session, rape prevention. "Women," he says, "they're all over." He laughs that big Russian laugh. Women – they're everywhere! But it is serious. Martial arts is for women as much as it is for men. Men don't get raped, usually.

We go through the paces, Boris and I, up to defense against gun and knife, and Boris is pleased.

"You haven't lost much. You're ready for anything, almost."

But not Melanie.

She's changed her mind.

Maybe I should get it out in the open with Toledo, and maybe I should sing like a canary.

"Out of the question."

"Why?"

"Because I would hate myself in the morning and so would you."

"But your reputation!"

"What reputation?"

"You do have a reputation, you know. You're mentioned twelve thousand times on Google. I just checked."

"That's for the movie."

"But also about you."

"As a slot attendant?"

"Oh you're so funny. No, Jay, as an author. The author of the smash hit *The Ice King*. Come, see."

"I don't want to see."

"No, you want to wallow."

"Wallow. Good."

"There's also mention of *Smooth Operator*."

"That's embarrassing."

"No, they predict..."

"Who predicts?"

"One of those websites, yes, a literary review on the web. Take a look. It's very flattering."

"Never mind. I'm not informing, Melanie. Please don't! I am not an informer. There is nothing worse."

There is even a Biblical curse – May there be no hope for informers.

Later, when she's content that she's turned in a well-reasoned book review, she cuddles up and says I'm right.

No, my position, she agrees, is virtuous.

We kiss and make up, and it gets even better. That's Sylvio on the phone, actually on the phone, really on the phone, returning my call, and here's what it is; that other publisher is very high on my writing, big fan of *The Ice King*, the book, my book, not the movie, their movie. Very big fan, and he's halfway through *Smooth Operator* and it's clicking for him, resonating. Yes, resonating. You want that; you want resonating, always.

There's more! That lunch Sylvio had with Roe Morgan? It's over and done, and went well. No, it wasn't about me, about me especially, but my name came up. The lunch was about that other writer that Roe Morgan wants so badly and that Sylvio is saving as his ace in the hole. But my name did come up and there's promise, since Roe Morgan may be forced into a two-way deal, me and that other writer who, apparently, is from America and not from New Jersey.

"It ain't over till it's over," says Sylvio. "Now I gotta run."

There really is no talking to them in New York or Hollywood. They always gotta run.

So...good news.

"Great news, isn't it?" says Melanie.

No, great is when something has already happened. Good is when it may happen. Frankly, I don't even call it good. I call it nothing.

Hemingway taught us never to mistake activity for action. I'm pretty sure it was Hemingway. I should go back to reading him. It's been so long I've forgotten if he's really as good as I thought he was. I'm not sure I want to know. I do know that about five years back I checked in at *The Sun Also Rises* and was miffed at all those pages taken up with description. Half the book is description, and who cares about the roads and the hills and the valleys and the trees? Who remembers, who cares? He also could have used some editing. People like Jake Barnes are always nodding their heads. What else do you nod?

But who am I to knock Hemingway? He was our master, our king. But he really wasn't the first. Twain beat him to it as did that guy who wrote *The Red Badge of Courage* and whose name I forget, which has been happening to me a lot lately. Names just slip my mind, even names of authors, authors I grew up with and admired. Stephen Crane, right. Yes. Well Stephen Crane wrote just like that, hard-boiled, as did a slew of those mystery and detective writers, Hammett and Chandler and certainly James. M. Cain, the best of them all. But for declarative and hard-boiled you really have to go back, way back to the Bible. They all borrowed from the Bible, so far as style, simple but majestic. Even the titles, even that they borrowed, like *The Sun Also Rises*, and surely Melville had Jonah in mind when he wrote *Moby Dick*.

"And King David was old and stricken in years and could get no heat." That was written some 3,000 years ago, before Hemingway and the rest of us.

James M. Cain is not highly regarded within the smart set. Cain distilled Hemingway as Bukowski distilled Cain. Cain writes too plainly, nothing fancy, hardly any embellishments or descriptions, exactly what I like about him and they don't. He is not LITERARY and I have yet to find anyone who can tell me what literary is, as opposed to commercial. Literary must be when nobody knows what the hell the writer is talking about, so it must be literary. Some writers have to die before they're accepted as literary. That's something to look forward to.

"Yes, Mel, good news, pretty good."

We kiss and make up all over again.

Chapter 13

Two in the morning – I'm in Zone 14 schmoozing with Mark the security guard who thinks he's George from another life – so it's two in the morning when Omar swoops down and tells me to be ready. For what? For my performance evaluation. Half an hour. Two thirty. Sharp. Prompt. Is there anything I need to bring? No, just yourself. (Truly, what an asshole!)

The place is empty, except for the machines that have already done their jobs, taking in millions for the House a penny, a nickel, a quarter, a half dollar, a dollar at a time. They stand there, these machines, row by row, mounted upon their high places like idols awaiting the next round of worshipers, Big Bertha along the main aisle the biggest god of them all, and there is an attitude about them, according to size and jackpot. Big Bertha keeps watch over her lesser gods, Double Diamond, Triple Diamond, Wild Cherry, Slingo, Betty Boop, Jeopardy, Pink Panther, Keno, Joker Poker, Deuces Wild...just waiting but knowing that the sacrifices will come and hurl themselves at them to claim JACKPOTS GALORE.

Some machines talk back. One machine, which mostly the Asians play for some reason, says "phenomenal" each time there's a payoff, and I have a feeling that's been researched, that word "phenomenal." Must mean something beyond the obvious and trigger a subliminal message, just to keep you playing and keep you thinking that you're a winner, when in fact the payoff is usually less than what you've put in. The machine makers study these things and it's all quite psychological. I once read an article in one of these industry magazines, *Casino World* or something like that, and the message, in fact the headline, was about "perceived" value.

About the only player still in action, at this crazy hour, is my nemesis, my bully, Howard Glass. He's seldom here this late, but here he is with his usual scorn. He's over by the dollars and nods me over with that derisive grin. I clench my fists against my sides and against what I know is coming, and it does. He says, "Yeah, I've read all about you. You're a flash in the pan, a one shot wonder."

"Do you need any help, Mr. Glass?"

"I'm terrific. How about you?"

"Likewise."

"Oh, yeah?"

"I've got to run."

"Where? Doesn't look busy."

"Thank you."

"Just do your job."

Just do my job, he says.

But he's not finished. "How does it feel to be a reject?"

The trouble is, he's right. No argument from me.

I move on. I make a tour of the joint to rid myself of the creeps. I'll be all right. Just need to bounce myself back.

Anyhow, I've got bigger worries, like this evaluation process – performance evaluation.

"Why," I ask Mark, "should I be nervous about this?"

"You shouldn't."

"I mean is this fair? Isn't this like they do in North Korea or something?"

"Exactly."

125

"Is this really democracy?"

"It's ridiculous."

"Like they own you."

"They do."

"People shouldn't be allowed to EVALUATE people."

"Right. Corporate America is just like communism."

"Exactly, Mark. Do they EVALUATE you guys, too?"

"Oh sure. But it's real relaxed, unless you broke a rule or something."

"There you go, rules. They own us, Mark."

"Just like communism."

"This isn't free enterprise, not for us."

"Right, Jay. Not for us. Only for them upstairs."

"I'm so pissed about this."

"Hurry up with that book of yours, Jay, and get the hell out of here," says Mark.

"Only it's not much different in publishing."

"I guess it isn't."

"It's the same everywhere, Mark my man. Can't escape. Run but can't hide."

"I keep telling you," says Mark, "every workplace is a dictatorship."

"Corporations."

"They keep getting bigger," says Mark, "and soon we won't have any rights at all. They keep chipping away. Why should I have to wear a seat belt? Why shouldn't I smoke where I want? They keep making new rules and you'll see, one day they'll knock on your door to see what books you're reading, what movies you're watching. I've been telling you this."

Yes he has.

Mark has told me about all this new technology that's coming up for better snooping, that now there's more than an eye in the sky, but also an ear, so how far are we from a mind in the sky, meaning that soon, if not already, they'll be able to read your thoughts and come after you with the Thought Police as only Orwell could have imagined. Mark believes that it's all connected to telephone wires and cables, that the phone company is behind it all, along with the government, even though there is no more Ma Bell, no more monopoly there, that's all been broken up... but those wires and cables are still up there, and there is still a government, and that is still a monopoly and has not been broken up. So now it's the cable companies, like Comcast, that rule over us, along with the feds and the corporations, and the casinos, with some aliens thrown in. He probably is a conspiracy nut, Mark, my man Mark, but strange things do keep happening.

"But these performance evaluations, that's the worst," is what I say. "That's the worst snooping. That's the worst indignity."

"They have no right."

"Except they do."

"That's right. They do."

Mark suggests that I write a book about politics. But writers are as ignorant about politics as are politicians.

"Good luck," says Mark as I take off for my inquisition.

So I'm up there, in the tiny untidy room that's supervisor headquarters, for the time being. It keeps changing. They keep changing rooms on us. The casino is always in flux.

There are two of them for this performance evaluation.

I'm surprised. There's usually only one. But I've got Omar, bad cop, and Roger Price, good cop. I don't know why and who cares.

So, I'm sitting there across from them and they've got papers in front of them, on the desk; for sure my history.

There's an entire list to run down, and they take turns, and of course Roger is his customary casual self and Omar is Omar.

The points run from one to five...one the lowest, five the highest. Very few get fives. If you run out of there with a three average you've done okay.

No raise, but okay.

If you score a two you could get disciplined or fired, depending on how badly they need slot attendants at the moment.

Okay...show time!

How do I carry myself in uniform, neat and tidy or sloppy?

Omar, frowning, or maybe he's smiling, gives it a two.

"I thought I dress pretty well," I say meekly, for we shall inherit the earth.

"Two," says Omar resolutely.

Roger shrugs, as if to say it's really Omar in charge.

Is my hair short enough?

"Two," says Omar.

On this I have no dispute. I need a haircut. I always need a haircut. I am an arteest, when the meter is down.

"Your shoes could always use a shine, I've noticed," says Omar.

"If people would quit stepping on me."

"Let's move on," says Roger, giving me a wink of caution.

Am I well-shaved?

"Two," says Omar. He loves that number.

"I'd give him a three," says Roger. "I really think he's well groomed."

"I think so, too," I say.

Omar submits, I guess. He's writing something down. I guess three.

How do I relate to customers?

"Three," says Omar.

"I really disagree," I say. "I can give you testimonials."

"He is well-liked," says Roger.

Omar writes something down. Either three or four, or maybe two, back to two.

How do I get along with fellow employees?

"Generally," says Omar, "I think you do pretty well."

"I think he does, too."

"Thank you."

"But you've had some run-ins," says Omar.

"We all do. You know what it's like downstairs, Omar."

Omar himself has gotten into tantrums with slot attendants, and customers. He could have gotten fired a dozen times.

"Well," says Omar, "we've had complaints from Latisha Johnson and Franco DeLima."

"I've got complaints against them."

"That's a different story."

"We don't want to go into that," says Roger.

"There was an incident with Franco," says Omar. "Didn't you threaten him?"

We go back and forth as to whether I legitimately threatened Franco DeLima. When he informed on me for theft, I said something like – I'm remembering this.

Omar considers that a threat.

"That's not for now," Roger tells Omar.

"I'll give you a three," says Omar.

"That's not fair, Omar."

"That's for us to decide," says Omar.

Roger gives me another shrug.

How do I relate to my superiors?

Omar laughs. He shakes his head.

"Pretty near insubordinate," he says.

"You do have a mind of your own," even Roger agrees.

"I'll try harder," I say.

"To do what?" asks Omar.

"To not have a mind of my own. Isn't that the point?"

"Some initiative is okay," says Roger.

"I already tried that once," I say, "and got in trouble."

"I think you could do better," says Omar. "Your general attitude has been noticed."

Ach zo.

Omar scribbles something and I'm sure it's a two, maybe a one.

Do I extend myself beyond the call of duty?

"He sure does," says Roger.

Omar nods. I think I'm getting a four on that, maybe a five. No, they never give you a five. There is always room for improvement.

How well-versed am I with the mechanics of the job?

"You've had trouble with some machines," says Omar.

"Everybody has."

"That's true," says Roger.

"The keys don't always work, you know."

"They do for everybody else," says Omar.

"No they don't."

"Let's not be here all day," says Roger.

I'm getting a three for mechanics.

Am I fast, slow or medium moving from customer to customer?

"There's faster, there's slower," says Omar, and gives me a three.

Am I trying to improve myself?

Omar laughs again.

"I don't think you are. You wouldn't accept supervisor even if it were offered, would you?"

That I can't deny. They want you to be ambitious, but not overly ambitious. You really don't know what they want.

I figure I'm getting a two on this.

Am I easily distracted?

"I think you're always distracted," says Omar.

Roger can't disagree and neither can I. I imagine that gets me a two. Distracted, that's me. I'm usually someplace else, sometimes in another country altogether.

Do I present a positive image before the public? I thought we'd covered this already. But it means do I make people want to come back for more.

"I'd give him a four for that," says Roger.

I figure that's what I'm getting.

Am I approachable, friendly?

"I don't think so," says Omar.

Omar is the most unfriendly person in the world, the least approachable. Nobody wants to get near him, employee or customer.

Oh he'll smile, for shift manager or above.

"I think I'm friendly."

"That's what you think," says Omar.

"That's what I just said. That's what I think."

"Now you see, Jay," says Omar, "you're being argumentative and I scored you pretty good on your relations with supervisors. Do I take that back?"

"Do we not show...may we not show spine?"

"What you talking about?"

"Am I supposed to roll over?"

Roger moves in quick. "Jay, just relax and let's just get this done."

"But this isn't a kennel."

"What's he talking about?" says Omar.

"Jay, be cool."

This is that bad moment when you want to tell people who you are. Do you know who I am? But that is so uncool. That is so gauche. Melanie does it too often. She not only reminds me who I am, she reminds others. When our movie first came out and the line was a mile back, she asked for the manager, and she told the manager who I am. She said that this movie, *The Ice King*, that is packing them in, that is doing all this business, all this box office, right here in Marlton, was written by this man, right here, my husband. So may we please get a seat, to watch our own movie, this movie that my husband wrote, that is doing all this box office. The manager said this: Get in back of the line. Get in back of the line.

But it is tempting to tell Omar who I am. Does he know? Does he read? Does he care? Would it make a difference? Get in back of the line.

"I certainly am approachable," I say.

"I think some customers are afraid of you," says Omar.

"Afraid?"

"I've talked to a few customers."

"I think you're wrong, Omar," says Roger.

I'm getting a three.

Attendance?

"That's a joke," says Omar.

"I only take sick days coming to me," I say.

"You're at the limit."

"So?"

"I wouldn't call that dependable."

That's a two.

Do I walk my zones properly?

"You know," says Omar. "I talked to Pini about this. She caught you leaning against a post several times. She even warned you."

"That's four in the morning, Omar. There's nobody in the place and I'm dead tired."

"She warned you once, she warned you twice. You're not allowed to lean."

"I've seen others lean."

"Who?"

"I won't mention names. You know I won't."

Pini has her favorites. They all do.

"Leaning is an infraction. Rules."

"But he does walk his zone pretty regularly," says Roger.

"But he was caught leaning. I can't go against regulation."

"Come on, Omar," says Roger.

I figure I'm getting a three.

Do I display temper? That's some question from a guy who walks around with a snarl on his lips and fire in his eyes.

"I think he's pretty even-tempered," says Roger.

"I've never lost my temper."

"Not with a customer he hasn't," says Roger.

"But what about Franco, and there've been other instances."

"That was at the beginning," says Roger, "when he didn't know his way around."

"I was uncomfortable, not temperamental."

"Okay."

I may be getting a four.

How am I in emergencies?

"I think he's pretty good," says Roger.

"Down on the floor every minute is an emergency, you know that, Omar."

That's probably worth a four.

Am I well-spoken? Do I understand the language? This is most strange since English is the least spoken language anywhere in Atlantic City. I do not understand Hindi, Urdu, Jamaican, Spanish, Russian, Polish, Flemish, French, Italian, Hebrew, Arabic...English, yes, but to what good? Some Blackese escapes me, too, but I am starting to catch on. Even picking up some Spanish. How can you not?

I expect a four on this.

Am I respectful to minorities?

"I treat everyone alike."

"That's the trouble," says Roger, meaning it as a joke.

This isn't the place to say that in good times you hate them all, black, white, whatever. This is war. They're the enemy.

Blast them all, the long, the short and the tall.

I think my score on that is three.

Am I respectful to the elderly, the disabled?

"I think he is," says Roger.

"I've never seen him trip anyone," says Omar.

I say, "Not on purpose."

Maybe a four.

Have I ever been caught sleeping on the job?

"I never caught him."

Even Omar has to admit that he's never caught me snoozing, except at the beginning, when I was just getting the hang of graveyard. Tough adjustment.

"But you have been caught reading," says Omar.

That's when I was really getting into Henry Miller.

"Pini caught you."

"Again, that was four in the morning, the place was empty..."

"But you were caught reading."

"Regulations, right?"

"You can make fun all you want, but yes, regulations."

"He's a writer," says Roger.

"I don't care what he is."

"It was four in the morning," says Roger.

"I don't care."

"I think we can make an exception, and it was only once."

It was much more than once, but I only got caught once.

"You're always supposed to be ready for a customer," says Omar. "That's why we're here. We're not here to read."

"He was only caught once, Omar."

"We can't make an exception, Roger. If he gets away with it, anybody else can start reading."

"You mean it could lead to reading."

"You don't get my point?"

"This is all yours, Omar."

So it is. Usually I favor Roger's insouciance. But I could have used more help.

My final score is three. Pretty good and pretty much as I expected. As I'm leaving, Roger catches up.

"Sorry about that," he says.

"Nothing's wrong," I say. "I'm fine."

But I know how I really feel. I feel shamed.

Roger confides that he's so fed up with this whole business, he can't wait to call it quits.

Thirteen more years to go, and then there's his wife, Charlotte, who works here as a cocktail server, and she's not so happy, either, in her job, all that running, it's given her leg and foot problems, for which she may need surgery, and as for him, he may need triple bypass.

"So I won't be around for a while."

"When did this happen?"

"I've had heart problems for years."

"I didn't know."

"I'll be going on disability."

"The stress of the job?"

"They don't know."

"I'm sorry about this, Roger. I really am."

"Thanks."

Bad luck and it's true that bad things happen to good people. You do start caring. You seldom think of them as having a life outside the job. You forget that there's more to them than the one dimension you get to view of them those 40 hours a week and you forget that after they punch in and punch out, just as you do, they go home to start another day, another life, just as you do.

Roger gives me an easy zone, Zone 8, to finish off the night. He knows it's been rough with Omar. I'm thinking of Omar and I'm thinking of Roe Morgan and they become one, and soon they become everybody along with the pigeons. That's bleak! Taking it all together, the trick is to renounce bitterness. Outrage is okay, but not bitterness. Must not let that happen. BUT – it does seem that all the wrong people are in charge, all over.

Chapter 14

This is the worst of it, the worst part, 9:50 p.m. and the waiting outside the supervisor's office for your assignment and your key. You don't know where they'll send you, to a place where it is civilized and the tips are bountiful, or to a place where it is cold and full of the buses, Zones 12 and 14, usually reserved for me, depending on the supervisor. You have as much say over your destiny as a leaf in the wind.

But that's not the worst part, not yet. The worst part is just waiting in line with about 20 of them, all of them younger than you, except for one or two and sometimes three, but most of them younger and full of gusto and plugged into hip-hop, like Humberto Valdez, who is tall and thin and restless and full of mindless wisecracks, and I think I dislike him the most, for all that, and I think I dislike them all, right now, right here, when I find myself so different and so out of place, so wrong.

They're rapping and you don't even have the same memories as they do. We are all in uniform. We are an army of slot attendants.

So this night I'm waiting with the rest of them and am in a hurry to get this over with, get the assignment, get the key, and get downstairs and lose myself in the job, and then start liking these people, these kids, all over again, when we're all in the same boat – but it's never that quick, this part. There's always dithering among the supervisors, confusion as to who made up the schedule and who marked an assignment for a slot attendant who's on his day off.

I'm trying to think of something, something else, as that's the trick, for now, think of something else, be in another place, and what comes to mind is F. Scott Fitzgerald saying, "No one is reading me; what's the point of all this writing?" When I turn the corner into the office I trade some patter with Flint Odesso and Bob Michaelson, we're about the same age and we speak English, and I'm glad it's Maggi Holt on duty, Horny Maggi.

She says, oh, there is no assignment for me, no key and just when I think it's over, I've been fired, and begin calculating what unemployment benefits are due me, and worse, the loss of Medical Benefits, when you're sure to need root canal, Maggi says that there's a message for me from the Executive Offices. Someone in Marketing wants me. In fact, the Director of Marketing wants me, Shelly King.

"Whoa," says Gabe. "Big time!"

Maggi asks if I know what this is all about.

"I don't know. Do you?"

"I'm only a supervisor," Maggi says. "We're nothing to them. They don't tell us a thing."

She doesn't even know where the Executive Offices are located. That's another world. That's where they start at $100,000 a year.

That's where they have real offices, with carpeting and secretaries.

Maggi is impressed.

"Is this the start of something?"

"I swear I don't know."

Can't be trouble. That's another department and I've already been there, and will probably be there again.

No, this is different, and quite astonishing.

"She wants you right away," says Maggi.

The secretary, Shelly King's secretary, asked what shift I was in, and was surprised that it was graveyard. But anyway, Shelly King was staying late just for me.

I take the staircase down to the casino floor and haven't a clue where to begin, where the plush offices begin. I pass by Zone 10, the Hot 7s, and here's Carmella, busy, at a machine, some customer complaining about the coins, dollars, that keep getting stuck. "Nothing works around here. I'm never coming back." Carmella asks for my help, but I have no belt, no equipment, so we both tell the player she'll have to wait for a supervisor. "Oh you people," says another satisfied customer.

"I need to talk to you," says Carmella.

I explain I have to be someplace. She doesn't know anything about Marketing, but she knows it's something big.

"Good luck," she says. "Gaucho."

"What does Gaucho mean?"

"Means handsome," she says.

"Carmella, you're such a tease."

"Oh? Are you sure I'm teasing?"

Mark the guard is standing post by the mid-escalators, and I ask him if he can accompany me to Marketing. The guards know every inch of the place.

"Sure."

He calls in for permission and when his replacement arrives he says, "Let's go."

We snake our way to the northern edge of the casino, enter a storage room, then a suite of secretarial offices, and then take an elevator up to nine. Before he drops me off he says he knows my fear of elevators – must be something from a previous life. Yes, Napoleon. "Weren't you once a war hero or something?" Mark says.

"Yes, but most wars take place on the ground floor."

139

He's thinking of making his move on Clara, that hot dealer who's got the hots for him.

"Don't tarry. If not you, somebody else."

"That's right," he says. "There's always somebody else. See ya."

Now I'm all alone up here and follow the sign that says Marketing. It's quiet, as you'd expect this time of night. There's no graveyard for executives, unless there's a banquet or some other function. Or they're up there on the top floor in the Golden Player Lounge. That's where Bob Foster, our president, hangs out when he stays late, schmoozing up the premium crowd.

So I'm walking the long, thick-carpeted hallway and remember that some time back I walked an even longer hallway to meet the president of Alliance Pictures. Then I knew what it was, and I knew that it was good, but now I don't, I don't know what it is. Must be good, though. Or maybe not. You never know what they want. You never know what you did. At some point in life, you don't want anything, not bad news, certainly, but not even good news. You've had it to the brim.

Years before, Melanie's mom was upset when Melanie phoned her to give her the news that Alliance Pictures was buying and coming up with big money for the *The Ice King*. Melanie said, "Mom, I've got good news." Her mother said, "What's wrong?" Even after Melanie straightened it out, and expected congratulations, her mom was still upset and begged her not to startle her like this again. She had reached that stage where she simply didn't want any news. That's how it gets and now even I usually answer the phone with, "What's wrong?"

Usually nothing is wrong, but sometimes it is, and it's always about health, someone's health. We are defective units. We were created with so many parts that can go bad, like used cars. Never mind what's waiting for us on the outside, but our very own bodies keep trying to kill us. Usually it's someone from Melanie's side of the family, or Melanie's friends from high school or college. Some, still relatively young, have come down with serious defects, and one or two have even died. I've quit responding to my friends, so they've quit bothering, most of them, though I do get e-mails from friends I made in the newspaper business, the horseracing business and the boxing business. Boxers and jockeys and thoroughbred horse trainers are the finest people around. I respond to them. Boxers are very gentle people, outside the ring. I have few friends in the movie or literary world. That's fair, on both sides.

But Sharon Glazer was okay, Sharon, president of the Motion Picture Unit for Alliance Pictures, said – that time in Hollywood, "We're making this picture for YOU!"

She said that I had written a fabulous novel. *The Ice King* will be sensational as a movie and will do boffo box office. (Which it did.) She was so effusive, when we first met and during the filming, that I thought she loved me and wanted to have sex and that before you know it, we'd be an item. The slight matter of being married, from both ends – well, that's show biz. That's Hollywood.

But someone else was going to write the screenplay, and this was perfectly acceptable. I am no screenwriter. That's a different skill. What do I know from angles?

Strangely, though, people keep referring to me as a screenwriter, the screenwriter for *The Ice King*.

Out there, a book is but a precursor to a movie. No wonder Salinger said no to Hollywood. "Holden wouldn't approve," he said.

Kathy Lynn Boyer wrote the screenplay and I didn't mind it when in all those interviews she never once referred to the novel.

I didn't mind because I got the check and when you sell to Hollywood, well, it's sold, gone with the wind. It's not yours anymore. That's a different medium. So I didn't mind when the director, Monty Rogers, and Kathy Lynn Boyer, kept the concept and kept much of my dialogue, but combined to change the locale of my novel and even the ages (younger) of my characters because you cannot insert one art form into another. Beethoven would not dare tell Picasso how to paint his Third Symphony.

Even the ethnics in my novel were changed to yuppie white breads.

So I was okay with all that because it's nothing personal, it's beezness, and with or without a movie, a novel breathes and lives onward upon its own two feet.

Maybe I would have appreciated a mention or two when all of them got on TV and the host raved about the movie and about the concept and the audience kept on applauding each time another clip was shown. The actors and the director and Sharon Glazer herself forgot to mention where it all came from, and the screenwriter, taking bows, kept forgetting to name her source. Melanie, slamming the refrigerator door much too hard as all this is going on over the TV, and refusing to watch the rest of the show, and later vacuuming four times around the house as she does when she has bad energy to burn, asked me if I'm surprised at being omitted and I said no I'm not surprised, my name's in the credits, they even spelled it right, and the check cleared, didn't it?

The second time I met Sharon Glazer, over in Hollywood, it was different, a different hello and a different goodbye. *The Ice King* had already made all that money and I was here, this time, at my own expense, to pitch a concept, also high, as high, I thought, as the first. That first time, all expenses were paid to bring us on the set; we were given First Class

Tickets and set up at The Four Seasons. Room service is especially satisfying when it's on the studio tab. "This is heaven," said Melanie, so radiant that she outshone even the movie stars on the set.

The concept that brought me to Hollywood again, now without fanfare, was simple: Joe saves Marty's life. It's a highway accident and Joe reacted swiftly and heroically. Marty is grateful, but how much does he owe this Joe, this man who saved his life? For Joe has been coming around making demands. He wants more and more in payment. He even wants Marty's job, then even his wife. He wants everything. Joe, this one-time Good Samaritan, has turned into a monster, inflicting holy terror upon Marty and his family. So, when someone saves your life, how much do you owe that person? That's the WHAT IF...the High Concept.

Sure, towards the end there are Stephen King elements here, but still, high concept, and original, I thought – and still think.

So the second time I went out there to meet Sharon Glazer, it was on my money and second class. Her assistant, Sandy, a guy, was pleasant, but not quite as before, and said it would be awhile as Sharon is on the phone, and who could miss that, for all the shouting, no, absolute hysteria. Sounded like a relative she was talking to, possibly a daughter. But Sharon Glazer was in there, in a room with thick walls, going berserk and using R-rated language. This lasted for about an hour. I asked Sandy if my timing was bad, and he said no, be patient.

There was no choice but to assume that this was routine, normal behavior, as here, in the outer office, among the five administrative assistants, no one winced. I had not seen, or rather heard, this side of Sharon Glazer during the filming of *The Ice King* so maybe things were not going so well since then. Back then it had been all flattery and charm.

This time, when I went in, when she was ready for her close-up, Sharon greeted me warmly (as if there had been no tantrum a moment earlier), but then seated herself atop something like a throne. I was sunk into a sofa with deep cushions and kept sinking lower and lower, near to drowning and gulping for air. She was up, I was down, she was big, I was small.

She is a big woman, tall, broad at the shoulders, and lucky for her, she's brunette, not blonde, as blonde wouldn't go for someone so formidable.

I gave the pitch and she said it would have to go through the system. She sent me to another part of the building where I pitched a man I still call Dr. No.

Actually, I don't call him anything, not anymore. You get the hint.

Dr. No just sits there at the far end of the Admin Building and listens politely, never adds, never subtracts. He's here to listen and say no, and it does not impress him that once you built a railroad, that once you built a movie that most likely is still paying his salary. You are starting from scratch. Every concept is not quite right for us, or has already been done. We want something that is original...but also derivative. A good story? Yes, we're always after a good story, but we're after demographics. That's the story. The young. The kids. But (I protest) we still have old people. Yes, but the young make Box Office. Our Focus Groups can't be wrong. Light, crazy comedies, you know, where guys make love to pies, and where guys get their penises caught in the zippers of their pants...I wonder, though, if he's so smart, how come there've been so many flops from Alliance, straight to DVD?

Lately, they arrive at a trend when it's already over. Alliance released *Spoiled Brats* after four other studios had already cleaned up with their versions of *American High*.

But I have no regrets about the whole thing. It really was great when *The Ice King* was happening. I don't get it when writers gripe about The Industry. Hooray for Hollywood. Nobody has it good there or anywhere, so what's the complaint? We lunched and dined with movie stars, and that is enough. The sentry manning the famous gateway to Alliance Pictures recognized our names without checking his clipboard, and that is enough. Melanie had that operation and recovered just in time to fully enjoy the opulence of the premiere, and that is enough.

The director of the *The Ice King*, Monty Rogers, was eccentric, a Brit. He walked out on his own premiere. He is temperamental. Well, he's an artist. Well, I am also an arteest.

We crossed paths several times on the set, or rather we didn't, directly. We kept to ourselves, actually avoided any sort of contact. The first time I showed up on the set he asked the script girl who this was, and she told him, and he gave me a snort and a nod. I've never figured that out. The last person they want on the set is the writer. They want no part of him. I understand.

Actually, Sharon Glazer wasn't all that warm the second time around. The warmth lasted for about eight seconds when she remembered that *The Ice King* brought in half a billion dollars for Alliance Pictures and made her personally very rich. Then she forgot and she was up on her throne and down to business. "Okay," she said, "show me what you got."

I had been warned, by more than one producer, how swiftly she flashes from hot to cold. Snap she's on, and snap, she's off. She was doing me a favor, she said, by hearing me out, for as president, now, she only takes pitches from producers, but in my case, she was making an exception.

So I made the pitch but pitching is an art, but not for me, and I knew that I was bombing because I felt as if I were lip-syncing. I did bomb.

The entire meeting with Sharon Glazer lasted maybe ten minutes. I thought we'd do lunch.

* * *

But is it any wonder that so much wife-swapping goes on once people get together to make a movie? That's no surprise. There is so much (fake or real) effusiveness going around that you are bound to get sucked in. Happens all the time. It happened on the set of *Basic Instinct* and it still requires a scorecard to remember who ended up with whom. Strangers are thrown in together and snap, they're family. Love happens, and of course it usually fizzles once it's a wrap and it's onto another set and another family. I saw up close how easily you can get seduced, and it wasn't just Sharon Glazer.

In proselytizing circles that's called love-bombing where, to snare you to convert, they overwhelm you with adoration.

I keep thinking that one day I'll do a novel or a screen-play based on what happened to Edmund Purdom who starred in *The Egyptian* back in the 1950s and was ready for above-the-title billing. I think it was Edmund Purdom who shared a garage with his wife who worked cleaning houses as he made the rounds. He finally hit stardom and did what comes naturally; left his wife for someone who doesn't do windows. The public got a hold of this, back when scandal was bad, and finished him off.

That's what I think I will do, one day, I mean write a novel or a screenplay about a down-and-out screenwriter, a near hick from the Midwest, who finally gets to principal photography and dumps his loyal wife in favor of the starlet, who has promised him love everlasting. This lasts until the next movie. She moves on and there he is, humbled and alone, and what a sucker!

Something like this was already done in the Kevin Bacon flick *The Big Picture*, but there's always room for more, and they're always making remakes anyway, and there is no such thing in the movie business as plagiarism; it's homage, pronounced French as in frommage. We're always borrowing from something past. The concept for *Planet of the Apes* had to come from Kafka's *A Report to an Academy*. Though what I've got, I'm pretty sure, is original, and derivative.

* * *

So how do I approach this, this meeting with Shelly King, director of Marketing up here on the casino's ninth floor, me in my green slot attendant uniform? Suddenly, I agree with Melanie. It is disgraceful walking around in this when not on duty. It is degrading and disgraceful, makes you like a soldier in the wrong army. So...what does this woman want?

Shall I dominate? In this outfit?

Strange, you fought in a war, combat house to house, hand to hand, and NOW you get the heebie jeebies?

The door is open and I hear someone talking, on the phone obviously. I knock but no one answers. I step in, and it's Shelly King, and she is on the phone, and now I recognize her. I'd seen her on the casino floor, usually with Bob Foster, our president. I thought she was his secretary or something. But she does have that title – Vice President of Marketing, or Director. She is important.

She motions for me to have a seat. She sits behind a semi-circular half-moon shaped butcher wood block oak desk. She's actually tucked in, as if she's been here forever and will remain forever. I admire such nesting. To the side are vinyl desks with advertising posters scattered all over, even along the floor and around her desk. Busy, busy, busy. "Get Hot With Our Slots," is our current campaign. Bob Foster has made the claim that our slots pay off at a higher rate than any other casino in Atlantic City.

Business has picked up, especially among the nickel players. I'd be among the first to notice.

Shelly offers a smile as she's still on the phone, a business smile. I smile back, same kind, business, neutral and neutered.

There's a photo of some family on her desk, but I don't think it's hers. I think it's her sister's, for some reason, and for some reason I don't think she's married, not anymore. There is something joyless about her. You spot that right off. She was once quite okay, that too is obvious, and I measure her as being in her mid-thirties and as a girl who was runner-up for Prom Queen and runner-up for everything else, always coming in second. She's still not bad, but the legs are a bit on the chubby side, though she has not let herself go. You can't if you're a woman and want a career in business. You sure can't flaunt it and come on sexy. You can hint but you must not flaunt, and Shelly King doesn't, doesn't flaunt. You can tell she's made it a habit to connect with her male side. She's done the work, probably beginning in college, where she probably took Marketing, or Business Administration.

I'll bet, early on, she probably also took some Lit, and maybe even wrote some poetry, love poems. That's all over. That's done. Down to business.

"So you're Jay Leonard," she says after she's finished on the phone. "What a pleasure to meet you." We shake hands, firmly.

I am not surprised when she says she never saw me before. They don't see your face when you're down there on the casino floor. One green uniform is the same as another. Then again, all players, all customers, are alike to us as well. We can hardly tell one from another and when someone says, "Don't you remember me, you paid me my last jackpot," you say you do, but you don't. It all blurs.

Well, she says, she did not know – WE did not know – that we had a celebrity in our midst.

"Why didn't you tell us?"

Nothing to tell.

"You're a famous author."

"I'm a slot attendant."

"Oh," she says.

She doesn't even know what that is. I have to explain. She explains that everything that's done in the casino falls under Marketing.

"Oh," I say.

She sits there unsure of what to do with me, or with my attitude, for I am not being forthcoming. I feel resentful but don't know why. Is it that I know she can fire me in a snap? Is it that we both know this? We are both uncomfortable. I seem to have her frozen. So, she can have me fired, at a whim, or, she can move me up. Up or down, she can do whatever she wants with me, and this possibly is what I resent.

She shifts uneasily in her chair and says, "I won't ask all the reasons that brought you here, I mean as a slot attendant."

I thank her.

Now she gets up and plants herself on the sofa and as she does this, her skirt moves up; up, up and up until her legs are on full display.

Do women know that practically everything they do is a turn-on? We (men) are all such horn-dogs.

"Though it is strange."

"I agree."

She lets that sit for a while. I am not about to volunteer. You never want to answer questions that are not asked.

"Frankly," she says, "I'm baffled."

"Sorry."

"No, I didn't mean it that way. I mean...we've never had an author. You understand?"

"First time for everything."

"Never a famous author."

"I'm not so famous."

"You had a very big hit, didn't you?"

"Six years ago."

She shakes her head. She's beginning to understand.

"That's not so long for an author."

"It's still six years."

"We do have great Benefits," she says reflectively.

"Yes you do."

She smiles, and this time a real smile, actually a defensive smile, and says, "You know, one of our lawyers is quite nervous about you."

"Huh?"

"Phil Kraut. He's suggested that you may be a plant."

"Not so."

"Some sort of spy."

"Not me."

"Well you know lawyers."

"I know Phil Kraut."

He came down once and chewed me out. I didn't know who he was except for a suit. This was one of those rare nights when I had Zone 1 (Marty Glick was out sick) and some nasty high roller hit a jackpot for twenty thousand and so I did what I'm supposed to do, I congratulated him, him and his lovely daughter, except that it wasn't his daughter, it was his wife, and this offended this man. He went ballistic on me. I apologized, but that wasn't enough. I said it was a compliment; his wife so attractive and youthful as to be mistaken for his daughter, and this made it worse. He called for my supervisor. Roger Price came over and backed me up and then it got ugly. The man wanted Bob Foster, our president, who wasn't in, and the closest thing available was Phil Kraut, the casino's top lawyer. Kraut said that I was just a slot attendant, that I was nothing, and not to be taken seriously. Kraut asked the man if he wanted me fired. He'd be happy to do so, Kraut would. Right here on the spot. My insult was unforgivable. These slot attendants must be taught a lesson. The man said, no, not to go that far. He was okay now, now that a lawyer, such a high authority, had stepped in. Kraut took me aside and I thought he was going to say something nice, something like, you know I had to do this, you know, to cover your ass and my ass, otherwise it would get straight to Bob Foster, so I'm sorry for all those things I said about you. But that's not what he said. This is what he said: "Watch yourself, boy. Watch yourself."

So yes, I know Phil Kraut.

She leans back and she's wearing a sweater and it's getting tight on her and I'm wondering, the way you wonder. We always wonder. Do women know this?

"So what do we do with you?"

"We go on," I say.

Obviously, that is not the right answer.

"You want to go on? How much do you make an hour?"

She knows, of course. She's got my total history in front of her. Today, especially, it's impossible to obscure yourself, what with Google and Search a touch away.

"Well I've been giving this some thought," she says.

Would I care to advance up to slot host? I immediately say no. I half expected this.

"No?"

They wear suits and ties but boot-lick even more than slot attendants...and work mostly off commission. They practically shanghai high rollers from one casino to another and even backstab within the same establishment. They're babysitters and I've heard them on the phones begging Mr. and Mrs. Smith to please come down for the weekend, we've got a fabulous room waiting for you and have already booked you into our Steak House. They keep a list of every birthday, every anniversary and even every funeral. All they do is suck up and they're always on call. If a high roller steps in, no matter the hour, they have to get dressed and rush on over, like a doctor. No, even doctors don't do this.

At least in my job, rough as it is on graveyard, once your eight hours are over, it's over, unless you volunteer for overtime.

"I'll pass," I say.

She is not surprised.

Well, she says, she's been talking to Bob Foster, our president – and she straightens up when she says this, when she mentions his name – so she's been talking to Bob Foster and he, Bob Foster, favors offering me a special designation; celebrity greeter. She pauses for my reaction. I do not react. She goes on. All I have to do is stand around and greet, or walk around and greet.

"Will people know who I am?"

"Of course."

I laugh. "I'll wear a sign?"

"Sure."

Not exactly a sign, but a tag with my name on it, my name plus this: Author of *The Ice King*.

That's how I'd walk around greeting people, and Joe Louis flashes through my mind. Isn't that how he ended up, only it was Vegas...and Willie Mays, here in Atlantic City?

Landing without a parachute.

I'm also thinking of *Requiem for a Heavyweight*, with Jack Palance, that terrific TV play written ages ago by Rod Serling. I always thought it was Paddy Cheyefsy, or Ben Hecht. But no, I just found out it was Rod Serling. But a terrific play, about a heavyweight champ and how he's reduced to a laughable wrestler when his boxing career is done. He has to take it, he has no choice, but it does destroy him, as I recall. What a terrific drama. Rod Serling, prolific as hell, went on to write maybe 200 more plays or episodes, but nothing like this. Who cares? All it takes is one. Arthur Miller could have stopped with *Death of a Salesman*, and perhaps he should have because he never topped himself, never even equaled himself, but that, *Death of a Salesman* is the finest piece of literature of the 20th century, or right up there with anybody.

Salinger knew when to stop.

"Let's go upstairs," she says. "Bob Foster is expecting us."

This catches me off guard.

"Upstairs?"

"He really wants to meet you. He'd be honored."

So up we go to Floor 19 – I'm okay in this elevator as it's got somebody at the controls – and step into the Golden Player Lounge, busy with loud alcoholic voices. This is the limo/butler set. Limos and butlers are always at the ready for them. Some gamble as much as $100,000 a night...some much higher. It is a lounge but more plush than the usual, and all drinks and snacks are free, of course. There's no entrance to the room, or even to the floor, without a key, and the key is that you must be a whale. Bob Foster comes over and introduces himself and says it's an honor. I say, likewise.

He's average height, average build, much younger and much less imposing than a casino president ought to be. He's pleasant and has a kindly face and easy smile.

He's the only one in here who isn't drunk or loud.

We sit down, the three of us, and Bob Foster starts it all over again, about what a surprise it was to find me, someone like me, working for him.

He doesn't mention my specific job, even though I am still in my green uniform. But that subject seems to be put aside.

We are not talking about that anymore. Decisions have been made. I can tell. I can tell much talking has been done about me, what to do with me.

"I admire writers and I just don't know how you guys do it," he says.

He graduated from Loyola and took Lit as a minor. His favorite author is Faulkner but he's also a big fan of Elmore Leonard.

Faulkner is okay, if you have the time to follow him, but on Elmore Leonard I totally agree.

Obviously, stereotyping is out, as far as getting judgmental about what a casino boss should be like. They were not like this in the old days, in Vegas.

"I think," he says, "you should give this serious consideration."

There'd be more than just greeting the high rollers. There'd also be book parties for my books, book signings and much publicity in the media.

"We do it all the time for singers like Tony Bennett and we just had that guy in from the old Sopranos. We've never promoted a writer. But wouldn't that be new and different?"

He says that the casinos could use some class, some culture, and why not start here and now. I quite agree. I remember, I tell him, when to be called a gambler was to be called a degenerate and that now something like 47 states have lotteries and casinos so that we're a nation of degenerates. He laughs about the rap, and how it still needs changing. I also remind him that in my religion, when it was practiced to the full, a gambler's testimony was unaccepted in court just for his being a gambler, and that whereas only about a generation ago virtually all gamblers were men, at the racetrack or in smoke-filled backrooms, now more than half of this nation's gamblers are women, at the slots. Bob Foster laughs and agrees. That's even more reason to instill class and culture.

Shelly asks how many books have I written.

I do the math. "Published? Five. Written? Twenty."

Bob Foster catches on. He likes me. I think I like him.

"I think book parties sound like a terrific idea," says Shelly King.

"Give the man some time," Bob Foster says slowly, offering me a wink. "Writers think carefully."

"Nobody comes to book signings," is what I say.

I know this from experience. People don't show up, unless it's Dan Brown. At one Barnes & Noble, in King of Prussia, after two hours of me sitting there at that table and no sales, the store manager urged his clerks to buy some copies (this was before *The Ice King* caught on) so that I wouldn't be fully humiliated and perhaps kill myself. Hemingway killed himself. Writers are known for this.

Some people do stop by and flip through the pages of your book, set it down, and go on browsing in the Self-Help section.

Does anybody really get helped?

"I'm thinking," says Shelly, "that we might do something else as well."

She's thinking we might form a class for employees, teaching English, me the instructor, given all the foreign people we have working for us.

"Hey," says Bob Foster. "What do you think?"

"Something to think about," I agree.

"I've been approached by people, especially our Indian employees, who'd love something like that," says Shelly King.

Our Indian employees, my buddy slot attendants, many of whom move on quickly to become dealers, are motivated, educated, and cultured. They are clannish, but aren't we all. Though I have become part of their group. I once complained to a roundtable of them that when they speak their language I don't know what they're talking about and that makes me think, sometimes, that they're talking about me. They were very upset about this, that I felt that way, and apologized, and it never happened again. At least they stop it as soon as I join them and learn from them as they learn from me. They're very cultured. I've discussed their history with them, that is, their British history, and it is a sore topic. I have also discussed the shame of Indian bride burning and that is also a sore topic.

"I think this would work," says Bob Foster about my teaching English, "in addition to Plan A."

"He makes a good appearance," Shelly informs Bob Foster, speaking about me. I make a good appearance.

"You do look like an author," he says.

"He has the look," says Shelly.

"What look?" I ask.

"Distracted," says Shelly.

"Well writers are always thinking, aren't you guys?"

"Yes we are."

"Always coming up with something," he says, and then asks Shelly if she's read my Big Book. She's flustered.

"Not yet, but I'll get it out of the library."

"Writers don't like that," says Bob Foster. "Writers need sales. Am I right?"

"You're right," I say.

Bob Foster leans back and I take it to be over. It's back to downstairs – but I've been made an offer, and surely a raise in pay is in the offing.

But I do not ask.

"You have a lot to think about," says Bob Foster.

"I know."

"Do you like this?" he asks, pointing to my green uniform.

"It's a job."

"Right," says Bob Foster. "Every job here is important, but…"

"It's a paycheck," I add, "and Benefits."

"We're the best in town when it comes to Benefits," says Bob Foster.

"That's what attracted me."

"I really like that book party idea," says Shelly King. "I'd love to get started on a campaign, the AC Press, *Philly Inquirer*, radio, TV."

"You can dress as you like, you know," says Bob Foster. "I mean on the floor. Wouldn't have to wear a suit. Writers don't wear suits, right?"

True, a writer in a suit and tie is a loser. He's obviously not writing or getting published, no, he's job hunting.

"But I'd wear that badge?"

"Oh yes, people would have to know who you are."

"So I'd be walking around with a sign that says I'm an author."

"Sure, the author of *The Ice King*. Everybody saw the movie. I see this as great for our business and a terrific boost for you. A real career move."

"No downside," says Shelly. "Win win."

"You'll have to talk with Carl Giddings."

"Who's that?" I ask.

"Advertising," says Shelly.

"We could start a whole campaign around you," says Bob Foster.

"Advertising, PR, could be so exciting," says Shelly.

"What do you say?" asks Bob Foster.

"I'm overwhelmed."

"Are you happy?" he asks.

"It's something to think about."

Shelly doesn't care for my drift.

"Does your book have sex?"

"Only where necessary."

"Of course it has sex," says Bob Foster. "You gotta have sex."

"Sex sells," says Shelly.

I could say yes right now. But I can't. I just can't. I only want to escape, get down there at my zone. I don't know why. I don't know what's the matter with me. Something's wrong. I'm like the cheap thoroughbred who wants no part of the starting gate, unseats the rider, and makes a dash back to his barn where it's nothing much but it's familiar and he knows it's where he'll be fed.

Hey, I've been discovered, like Lana Turner at Schwabs, or Alain Delon at Cannes. So this is good. But it isn't. It is not quite the same.

"So what do you think?" says Bob Foster.

"I don't think you have a choice," says Shelly. "You don't belong..."

"Listen, can I think about this?

"Sure," says Bob Foster. "Sure. Think about it and let us know."

"By the way," says Shelly, "you'd be answerable directly to me. You wouldn't have to go through anyone else."

"Sounds good, doesn't it?" says Bob Foster.

"That's a real plus," I say.

"You'll let us know, right?"
"Yes, Mr. Foster."
"Call me Bob."

Chapter 15

I did not know, until recently, that the eye in the sky also has ears. Mark the Guard had warned me about this but I had not quite believed him.

"What were you two talking about?"

That's Detective Conrad Stevenson again, and they'd been listening in when Toledo Vasquez approached me that day. That was the day when he got a five dollar tip off a million dollar win and the timing seemed right for him to open up. There are 60 surveillance monitors up there, each scanning a particular spot. There are about a hundred surveillance authorities up there and their job is to nab theft and stop larceny among players and employees and they're well trained and good, very good at their job. They had only picked up snatches of my halting conversation with Toledo for all that casino ruckus; coins make heavy noise. For visual, they can zoom in for close-ups so magnified that they can catch it if your teeth need flossing, but the sound system of those cameras are not yet cutting edge.

So mostly what they heard was that he wanted to talk. Which is no crime, as yet. Mark the guard would say that's next. The one remark of Toledo's that caught their attention and had them going "Aha" was when he made that quite Biblical remark about his vexation: "Mine is too big to carry alone." I thought it beautifully quotable, and so did they, those guys up there in the sky.

"What did he mean by that?" asks Stevenson.

"I have no idea."

Which I don't, technically.

"No idea, huh?"

"No idea."

"You talk to a guy but you have no idea what you're talking about."

"It's hectic down there," is my only comeback.

"You two were sure going back and forth."

I explain about that million dollar win and that five dollar tip. That's something to talk about, but not much to remember.

"I know about that," he says.

He even knew about the tip. Upstairs, the cameras picked that up. One of our supervisors got fired for taking a tip, against company rules. He hid it fast, but not fast enough.

"So you know everything."

"Not quite," he says.

I am in for a grilling. This isn't like last time, when it was almost civil. Once they get a grip, these guys, they don't let go.

"I really have nothing to add."

"We think you do."

It goes back and forth like this and yes, Stevenson has dropped the good cop routine. He's near unpleasant.

I recall that his wife read my book. Makes no difference. I forget if she liked it or not. I don't remember. I think she liked it, yes.

Some people say they've read your book, period. They say nothing else. They say, "Hey, I read your book."

Some saw the movie but THINK they've read your book and begin to take your book apart for all the movie's flaws.

Stevenson informs me that if I know and don't tell I could be charged and detained for complicity. I think he threatened me with that before.

Now he changes his approach and appeals to me as one educated man to another. "You're not like them," he says.

Maybe it didn't start like that, but now I am like them, I think. I'm pretty sure I am. Anyway, what's wrong with THEM?

I've gotten to like them, most of them.

They're people like everybody else. I'll take Gabe and Mark and even Toledo over Roe Morgan any day, and where is Roe Morgan?

I do this often. In the middle of one conversation I find myself abstracted into another, into something else, altogether.

Where is Roe Morgan? Is Sylvio still talking to him? Is that door still open?

"There are no secrets," Stevenson says. "You're a smart guy and you know there are no secrets. We know everything."

George Orwell said it about the same way. Back in 1985, when I was quite young and working through a first novel by means of doing PR for the phone company, the department head came over to my desk to tell me, smugly, how wrong Orwell was about *1984*. He said, "See, nothing like this has happened." Meanwhile, monitors scanned every work station and every desk.

"Know what I mean?"

"Of course."

"I'm not nuts about it myself," he says. "The shadow knows. Technology has us by the balls. Every minute of every life is watched, recorded, documented, sealed. We're bar-coded like lemons at the supermarket. We're bar-coded and stamped from cradle to grave and even beyond. You can't even die without them bringing you up again. Our DNA tells everything about us and makes us everlasting. Really, immortal."

He's right. You're not even allowed to die. There's all that, and then there's DVD where everybody comes back.

A couple of officers step in to talk some business with Stevenson. It's not about me but I wonder if it's for show. They've got those weapons and handcuffs at their sides. These guys, they don't do anything that isn't calculated. When I was doing martial arts regularly with Boris, he also had a crew of municipal cops and even State Troopers in there brushing up on moves, especially defense against gun, and lately more and more defense against knife for the new brand of domestic violence that was developing out there, and I got to know some of them, even sparred with them, and when I earned their trust they told me how calculated it all was.

They're always watching, even when you don't know they're watching. It's all profiling, racial and otherwise. They can tell what kind of person you are by what kind of car you drive, how you drive it, how you stand, how you sit, how you walk, even how you move your eyes. That's all profiling.

When the others leave, Stevenson turns back to me as if he forgot what page we were on.

"Where were we?"

"How you know everything."

"How everybody knows everything, right?"

"Right."

He makes a joke. "Your mother-in-law has the goods on you every day when she checks the computer."

"Probably."

"I understand you're married to a very beautiful wife."

"I hope this doesn't get personal, Sir."

He knows he's stepped over a line and switches back. "I underestimated you," he says with a roughhouse smile. "The camera picked that up, too."

I didn't have to ask. I knew what he was getting at, that brawl I had with Franco DeLima out on the loading dock. It was a mistake, it was juvenile, it was schoolyard – but it had to be done! Franco had youth and size on me, but I had the speed and the tricks, and the indignation, so he was no match. I took care of business. I also used Boris' line: "I see ten feet under you," and it worked.

Stevenson says, "For all we know, you're part of this ring."

Why else, he adds, would I be so evasive?

"So catch me if you can."

"That's a wise answer."

"Well I'm resenting this – this Third Degree."

"Resenting? You're wasting my time, and you're resenting?"

"I've done nothing wrong."

"Maybe. But we know that kid has, and we're going to nail him."

"He's a good kid, Toledo. He's getting married."

"So?"

"The last thing he'd want is a stain."

"Or maybe he's desperate. We know all about Maria. She wants a house, a car. You can't get that at eight bucks an hour."

"I'm not an informer, Mr. Stevenson."

"You think you're being honorable?"

"It's all we've got."

"No, freedom is all we've got. Staying out of prison is all we've got."

"I'm not going to jail."

"Let's hope so."

"I suggest you find somebody else to do your snitching."

"I think you'll come around."

"Don't hold your breath."

It's getting ugly. "Really, I was hoping you'd be different. I thought you were different."

"I once thought so, too."

"You're all the same."

I can't resist. "So are you."

He agrees that a wall of silence exists among his elites as well. It's the same all over. Then the phone rings and he turns soft, obviously a child, his son, he's talking to, and a loving father he is, or seems to be. He's a father now, Dad, and likable. I remark, to myself, as I'm listening in, how different we are in the different places of our lives. In another place, this man and I could be friends. We would not be talking about informing, about going to jail. I would not be on the hot seat, my freedom at risk.

We'd be talking sports. Those Eagles, those Phillies. I know he's originally from Philadelphia.

He's telling his kid, as kindly as he can, that there is nothing he can do. He can't just go over there and do that, especially in his position as a cop.

After he hangs up, he confides that his kid is having trouble in school, with a bully. He's taught his kid, of course, some of the tricks of fighting, but this bully is big, and won't let up. As a father, there is nothing he can do, and as a cop, there's especially nothing he can do, except report it all to the principal, again. These days all the rules protect the bullies, he says. All the laws protect the bullies.

He's lost in thought. Then: "It's getting worse out there for the rest of us. The courts..."

I know what he's talking about.

So he resumes, after he hangs up – he resumes that soft, or softer, approach. He wants to talk Literature.

He loves Hemingway.

Yes, I agree, Hemingway taught writers not to be afraid of writing.

Somebody pokes a head in and says he's needed outside. There's new information on something. Stevenson excuses himself and steps out.

I'm wondering about this new information, as I sit here, just a touch concerned. How would this play in Haddonfield?

Sure to make the papers, if this goes on. Me, I don't care, but Melanie! That would be devastating.

I really do not give a damn what they do to me, as if they haven't done it already, and the casino is the least of it all.

New information, huh? Well, maybe it's about me and maybe it isn't. What did I do? Something wrong? Maybe.

I know I once parked in a handicap spot at the 7/11, and didn't even park, just ran in for a carton of milk Melanie forgot, and I kept the car running. But I've done worse. Plenty.

But jail, may just be the career move I need. They publish sinners. Sylvio made his bones on O.J. type tell-alls. Confess, repent, and you're on TV. Crime pays. Crime publishes. They love scoundrels. They love it when you done bad and then repent. America loves rehab.

Detective Stevenson steps back in and keeps on eyeing me and shaking his head. I'm waiting for my rights to be read, and the handcuffs.

"You can go for now."

"Thanks."

He keeps eyeing me as I go for the door.

"This isn't over," he says.

"I'm sure."

"But you can go."

"Thanks."

"But don't go too far."

Chapter 16

Sylvio has heard from the other publisher. Hey, says Sylvio as I'm in his office after inviting myself over.

Hey, says Sylvio, not bad.

This publisher likes *Smooth Operator*. Are we talking contract? Not so fast. All he wants, this publisher, are a few changes, and then yes, we can talk. Nothing major, nothing drastic, nothing that departs from my "vision." The publisher wants the man, the hero, turned into a woman. Just a suggestion. He wants the locale switched from Cincinnati to New York.

"That should be no big deal, right?" says Sylvio as he's on the phone with someone else but still talking to me as well.

The publisher wants more description, less dialogue. Wait. Maybe it's the other way round. The publisher wants more dialogue and less description. After all, show, don't tell. We'll find out, if we get that far. Wait. The publisher wants less of both or more of both, yes, more description, less dialogue. Sylvio is quite positive. Also – less interior dialogue.

"He wants the weather," says Sylvio.

That means more interior dialogue.

What else?

He wants a new beginning, a new ending, a happy ending. I can do new beginnings, but endings are tough. I had my ending pretty much as it should be, vague.

A novel, really, should never END. It should go on, as unwritten.

As for a new opening I had this in mind, "Call me Ishmael," but that's been taken.

What else?

He wants the ages of my characters reduced by 10 years, make it more hip, more accessible to younger readers.

You really can't identify with anyone over 25, according to the publisher. Beyond a certain demographic (I think it's age 41) Americans are as good as dead. On the other hand, the publisher also wants more old people, as the young don't read. Only old people read. So he wants my young people younger and my old people older. He also wants more people in the middle, as this generation still reads, though some don't.

He wants more sex. He wants two or three more female characters, since only women buy books. Only women read. Men watch football.

What else?

I mention a second marriage but nothing about the first, how and why they got divorced. The publisher says I must explain. No I mustn't. This isn't a biography. This is a novel. If I go into the first marriage and the divorce it will throw the entire novel off its rhythm and take it into new territory that has nothing to do with the story. It will bring up things that don't belong.

"You're the writer," says Sylvio.

Also, I say they fell in love, but why...the publisher wants to know what made them fall in love.

"I don't know," I tell Sylvio.

"What do you mean?"

"How do I know what makes people fall in love? There's no REASON. People fall in love, period. There doesn't have to be a reason. There shouldn't be a reason."

"I'm just telling you what the publisher wants."

What else?

He wants no religious or ethnic references. No Jews, no Arabs, no Christians. He does want an African American, as that's how it is these days.

Above all, he wants a yarn.

"Can you do all or some of that?" says Sylvio. "If you can, we maybe got a sale."

"I can give more sex."

"I know you can. You're good at sex."

That is true. I am very good at sex. One reader once told me that *The Ice King* was the best sex she ever had.

"I don't know if I can change Cincinnati into New York. The locale is one of the characters."

"I'm not sure I know what you mean."

"People in the Midwest think and act differently from people in New York. It's miles apart in more ways than traffic."

"He thinks nobody cares about Cincinnati."

"Faulkner wrote about a county that never really existed and what about Atlanta? Did anybody care about Atlanta until Margaret Mitchell came along?"

"Actually, nobody even cared about the South," Sylvio agrees.

"So there," I say.

"What about changing the man into a woman?"

"Are you kidding?"

"I was afraid you'd say that," says Sylvio.

"Question. What's this about a yarn? What is a yarn?"

"A yarn is a yarn."

"I really don't know what a yarn is, Sylvio."

"A yarn is a story..."

"That says nothing."

"You're trying to say something."

"Yes. I'm not trying to teach or to preach, but yeah, I'm trying to say something."

"Like what?"

"That's for the reader to figure out. The writer is the last two know."

"Well, he wants a yarn."

"I don't do yarns, Sylvio. *The Ice King* wasn't a yarn, either, and it did all right."

As of right now, this publisher sees the movie, not the book. It is photographic, too photographic.

Meanwhile, Sylvio has submitted *Smooth Operator* around Hollywood and the word back is that they see the book but not the movie, not photographic enough.

New York says my book is perfect for Hollywood. Hollywood says my book is perfect for New York.

So we're back to Roe Morgan, our last chance, again. But that's the business, one last chance to the next.

I have begun to get nauseous at the very name Roe Morgan, the very name. Maybe it's from the moment he said No Thanks. That probably did it for me. But Sylvio assures that the door is still open with Roe Morgan. He, Sylvio, is selling me as part of a package deal along with that other writer Roe Morgan has the hots for. I am the loss leader in this deal. Roe Morgan is not asking for changes. That's something. Sylvio, who seldom gets personal, tells me not to despair. We are still very much in the hunt.

Sylvio says, "Have you thought about golf?"

"Golf?"

"Those books sell. Golf is big."

"Golf?"

"Give it some thought."

But for perhaps the first time I think Melanie is despairing. "What happens if that falls through?"

We're having donuts and coffee after she's picked me up from the bus station at Mount Laurel. I had fallen asleep on the bus and am still drowsy. We're at the Dunkin Donuts in Cherry Hill, where Melanie had just gone for her regular medical check-up. I love those glazed donuts and that coffee.

I hate it when Melanie starts despairing. I'm always tottering myself and without her spiritedness, who knows? She does snap back awfully fast, though, and that's good for both of us. I wonder sometimes if I'm manic depressive. I think I would like that, as it would be something to talk about and wear around at parties. I don't drink or take drugs, and these are flaws if you're an artist. I do smoke, a pipe, of course, but that's not serious enough unless you light up around non-smokers, which is practically everybody these days. People need you to be recovering from something. I'm not manic depressive, either. If I am, one good phone call, and I'm cured.

When Melanie is down, it's like an affliction that I've caused by my failure to produce, and that's a guilt nobody needs.

She says, as she begins to brighten, that we should take in a movie at the Loews while we're here, it's been so long, so long since we've taken in a movie, or done anything, what with my hours being what they are and me being so tired even on my days off. We don't do anything, go anywhere. "You want a date, huh?"

"What's wrong with that?" she says.

"Nothing."

"You used to be so romantic."

"When?"

"When you were courting me."

"I was courting you?"

"You sure were."

"Didn't we go to bed that first date?"

"Second date. You're thinking of someone else, or all of them."

"No I'm not."

"Second date," she insists.

"So that's not courting. Courting is when you've got chaperones and all that business."

"You were romantic."

"First date."

"Second date, Jay. I wasn't that easy."

"Second date is playing hard to get these days, right?"

"I think so. That's our culture. Our parents never KISSED until the fourth date."

We sit there, and we're enjoying ourselves, and trying to remember the last movie we saw together.

"Was it *The Ice King*?" she says. "Our movie?"

"That far back?"

"I think it was," she says.

"Can't be."

"I know," she says. "I'm sure we've gone out since. Can't be that far back."

Melanie's connection to the movies dates back even before our movie. She was named after what's-her-name in *Gone with the Wind*.

Well, of course we've seen other movies. I usually pick the ones that got the worst reviews, upon my conviction that the world and everything in it is upside-down. I use the same method of handicapping in choosing what books to read and what horses to bet. I don't always win but I make my point. I have read reviews of movies, say Woody Allen movies, where the critic says I'll be rolling in the aisle, and this has never happened. I have never rolled in the aisle.

"So the publisher can see the movie but not the book, and the producers can see the book but not the movie. Ridiculous," she says.

Same thing happened with *The Ice King*. First New York saw it as a movie and Hollywood saw it as a book. Finally, after many tries, someone saw the book as a book and someone saw the book as a movie, and both turned out to be winners. Until then they were all wrong. Maybe they're wrong again.

I give her my mantra. "Is it possible that I am right and everybody else is wrong?" Again!

"That's more like it," Melanie says. "That's the talk I like to hear."

Yes, maybe I am right and the rest of the world is wrong. This happens.

Golf?

We drive over to the Loews multiplex to see something with Tom Hanks, and maybe catch a double-feature, which everybody does, I think, by sneaking into the neighboring plex. I like Tom Hanks most times. I did not like him in *Saving Private Ryan*. I think he was miscast by Spielberg. Should have been an unknown. I always knew it was Tom Hanks, an actor, and not a real soldier. Anyway, we buy the oversized popcorn and a Pepsi and walk over to the usher to get our tickets ripped up, and the usher is a kid, well, around 22, and he gives me the up and down and practically gasps.

He says, "I know you. You're the author."

Melanie starts beaming. But I am sure he is thinking of someone else. Been years since I made the papers, certainly television, and certainly any new book cover. For sure, I'm guessing, he thinks I'm Tom Wolfe, though I am not wearing a white suit and am not nearly that age. I know that Melanie is in for a huge letdown and am already kicking myself for letting her talk me into this.

"You're Jay Leonard," he says.

He says he reads me all the time, on the Internet, and knows *The Ice King*, movie, and book. He asks for my autograph.

I do that and he says, "Thank you."

"No," I say, "thank YOU."

As we're walking into the theater, Melanie, smiling high and wide, says, "See!"

"See what?"

"Tell me you're not pleased."

I'm thinking F. Scott Fitzgerald and that movie about him, of his later years, from the story by his lover Sheila Graham, *Beloved Infidel*. Gregory Peck plays Scott and Deborah Kerr is Sheila in this movie that nobody thinks is all that terrific except me, particularly that scene where they find out that a play has been adapted from one of his novels and is being produced off Hollywood, and out they go, Scott in his tux, Sheila in her evening gown, and Scott, of course, has been forgotten and unpublished for years, so this is a big moment, and Sheila is so determined to make him happy, and when they get there, instead of arriving at a major theater, the place is a basement of some sort, and it's all a bunch of kids who are doing the play. Sheila asks a group of them if they know F. Scott Fitzgerald and they giggle and someone says, "I thought he was dead." I can watch that scene a hundred times, and probably have.

"Go ahead," says Melanie. "Tell me you're not pleased."

"I'm pleased, Mel. I'm pleased."

"Remember, it's only the moments that count. This was a moment."

Chapter 17

Knock it all you want, there is nothing like working for a big company. Those Benefits! They've got you covered. Need root canal? Ten dollars. From dentist to dentist, from doctor to doctor, from hospital to hospital, just whip out that card and it's magic. That time when I was attacked by migraines, I whipped out that card, at the hospital, and I was in. I am a hypochondriac, but only about money, and since getting coverage I don't worry about getting sick. I can get sick as much as I please.

That's what attracted me, an ad in the Courier Post after Melanie said we're not making it, even close. The phone calls were cluttering up our answering machine. We had one bill collector say, "American Express is bigger than you and bigger than me. Do you know what they can do to you?" So, I'll have to find a job. The timing for this is always the same, always when I've just finished another novel, when in walks Melanie, into the den, sits down and says she's happy that I've finished up, but that I'll need to get a job. Writing a novel is wonderful, but you still need a job.

Right after you've finished a novel it's time to pack and off to Europe. That's what they do, what successful writers do, off to Europe. Or, some vacation, anywhere, if Europe is in the dog house for the moment. France used to be the place. You were bound to run into Hemingway, Joyce,

175

Picasso, James Jones, Henry Miller. They didn't fly. They sailed, on the Queen Mary.

But if Europe is in disgrace, Paris especially, and even Sweden, there's always Mexico. We'll always have Mexico. So that's what I'm thinking. I'm done, done the novel, and I'm pleased. There is nothing as pleasing as finishing up a novel. You've done the rewrite, 20 times, and feel a sense of soaring achievement.

That's when Melanie steps in and sits down, her expression, heavy. It's full of love, but heavy. I show her the pages I've just printed out. She shows me the bill that just arrived. Where shall we go, Monaco, Cancun? No, up the street to the newsstand, that's where we shall go, for the Want Ads.

"Our Benefits Package Is Like No Other," says the ad under casinos in the Courier Post.

Luckily, there's a train stop right near where we live, the Lindenwold Station. Next day I'm in the personnel office. I'm sitting at one of those school desks. There are six rows of them, here in human resources, all busy with people filling out applications, me right in the middle. There are only three other guys my age, the rest are kids. We're all on our best behavior. We don't want to be sent to the principal's office. We want to fit. We want to get hired. Times are tough.

I am the only one wearing a suit and tie. In my business that means you've lost, you're starting over again with a smile and a shine.

The ad was for slot attendants. I did not know what that was. I thought it was something like a slot host, though I did not know what that was either, though from my visits to the casino, I knew there were people walking around with suits and badges who back-slapped the customers, and that didn't seem so bad. Humbling, but not bad.

But it is good to be humbled. Samuel Beckett died in a nursing home, alone, forgotten.

Actually, it had been years since I'd been nailed to a regular job. My freelance journalism, together with Melanie's book review operation, kept us going. My end dried up when I wholeheartedly joined the literary racket. We were also kept afloat from sales of *The Ice King*. I keep forgetting that part, it was so long ago.

That first check was a whopper, for us, and then other monies followed, from domestic sales, from overseas transactions, from Hollywood.

We thought bigger things were sure to follow, bigger books, bigger contracts, bigger checks.

So I'm filling out my application for slot attendant and don't know what to write, what to say about myself that will make any sense, for it makes no sense, one from the other, one from a background such as mine, to this. Job applications are meant for people who move from job to job, not book to book, or book to movie – and how to explain the fall and decline!

The Ice King, for the moment, this moment, in this room, and all other rooms where I sought work, is a liability. Everyone saw the movie. Some – quite a few actually – read the book. There is no explaining what happened. Makes no sense. Melanie says she can't even explain it to her mother. The way it's supposed to be according to her mother, and according to all other moms and dads; you work hard, you prosper.

So...what experience do I have in casinos? That's one of the questions. Well, I watch my wife play the slots once in a while.

What experience do I have in the world of GAMING? Well, I play the horses every chance I get.

They want references. Do I refer them to all the newspapers that have published me, including *The New York Times*?

Do I refer them to the publisher that sold a million copies of *The Ice King*?

Would I want those calls to be made? I can only imagine the laughter.

Except for the usual name, rank and serial number, I hand in a nearly blank application form to the harried clerk behind the counter. I figure that I am the only human who has ever flunked an application form. The clerk, a kid with a Spanish accent, says, "What's this?" I explain that I'll need to talk to someone. He says that's against procedure, first the application, filled out in full, then the interview. I figure this to be the end, back home I go – famous author returns, tail between his legs. Best I could tell Melanie is, I tried.

That won't pay the bills. Trying is not an option. I must try harder.

"Can't I just talk to someone?"

"That's what you're doing," he says, and that's a fact.

"I mean..."

"I know what you mean," he says, almost sympathetically, as it is obvious that I am, well, different.

He calls over a supervisor.

"Sorry," she says, "you have to fill the whole thing out. No exceptions."

When she leaves, the kid says, nicely, "What's the problem?"

"No problem except that I need to talk about this."

"I don't make the rules," he says with a shrug. "I just work here like everybody else."

Just then a door opens from one of the offices and out steps a guy who has the appearance of show biz, Hollywood. He's handsome and slick and walks with the authority and impatience of a man with bigger things on his mind. He's got flair. My kind of guy, under the circumstances. There is nothing clerkish or routine about him. In fact, he seems out of place, as if he does belong in Hollywood. He's got a Robert Evans way about him.

I wave, to get his attention, and he responds. This is exactly the man. He's doing the interviews for slot attendant. He's a shift manager, a high position in this world.

"I just need five minutes," I tell him.

"You got it," he says.

We're in his office and we click. We get along beautifully. Because...because I tell him the truth. No choice anyway. He can look me up. The computer is right there, on the desk. So I tell him everything and his eyes do pop when I mention *The Ice King*, a movie that he saw (of course) and enjoyed. He is kind enough not to ask, specifically, what has brought me to this level. He's cool.

But I make him promise not to reveal those details about myself.

"No problem."

But, he says laughing, "You've got to promise to give me a part in your next movie."

"Deal."

He asks if I understand about the pay...$8.25 an hour.

I understand.

But the Benefits, he says, are a big plus.

That's what brought me here, I say.

He says he's been in tight spots himself, so he knows how it is. He never thought he'd end up in the casino.

"You just need something to tide you over till your next movie comes along, right?"

"Right."

"This is only temporary, right?"

"Right."

He further explains that the Benefits don't kick in until after three months, those three months when you're on probation.

So temporary means at least three months – and who knew there'd be three months upon three months upon...

Who knew this would turn out to be a job? Maybe a career.

Suliman Veejay became my trainer. I was part of a group of five, the rest of them kids, and I resented every minute of the indoctrination. Suliman was kind and patient with me. He showed us all the machines, how they were the same and how they differed and explained the varied duties and responsibilities of a slot attendant. I kept asking questions, thinking I was still in journalism, still a reporter. I kept forgetting that I was in training for a job, as an $8.25 an hour slot attendant.

No, I was not forgetting, and that was the problem. I was not forgetting at all.

But hell, I had a job.

"That's something we should appreciate," I'm telling Melanie after she visited the doctor and after she picked me up at the bus station in Mount Laurel.

There is nothing to whoopee about as the result of my New York meeting with Sylvio, still nothing to celebrate. That publisher was asking too much. But Roe Morgan – still alive with Roe Morgan. So I am trying to turn that into something, as we're leaving the Dunkin Donuts; like people who do alchemy. The trick is to make something out of nothing. The trick is to keep Melanie upbeat.

"Of course I appreciate it," she says somewhat unconvincingly. "I know how hard you're working. You think I don't know?"

"I also mean about Roe Morgan."

She doesn't respond. That name has become poison to her as well, obviously.

"But Sylvio is high on Roe Morgan," I persist.

Still no response.

Finally, she says, "We both know it's some other kid Roe Morgan wants. You're second banana. We also know that you're ten times the writer of...."

She starts to weep, softly.

"The doctor?"

"No. I'm perfectly fine."

"That's something."

"Yes," she says. "That's something."

"What's more important than..."

"Oh, Jay!"

"Okay, I know."

Now she's really sobbing. She'd been driving, driving us home from Cherry Hill, and we had to pull aside for me to take over the wheel.

She's really sobbing and I wonder if this is the time, the time to tell her about that offer from Shelly King and Bob Foster. I had kept it from her and don't know why. Really don't know why. I do know. I hated it, that's why, and was afraid that she'd not understand the mockery of being paraded around the casino floor as an AUTHOR. She'd only see the bigger paycheck. Or maybe not. She'd see it as further luring me into casino life; goodbye to all our dreams. Maybe this way or that, I didn't know, and so I chose not to bring it up for a test. But this would be the time.

"What?" she says, snapping out of the doldrums.

Yes, book signings, book parties, advertising, public relations, newspaper coverage, radio, TV.

"They want to make you public as an author, in a casino? A public spectacle?"

"That was the offer."

I tell her that Bob Foster, our president, was very nice.

"I'm sure he was," she says tightly.

"I'm sure you'd like him."

"I'm sure I would."

"So there it is."

She's thinking and with that her features are turning to granite.

"You mean you'll be walking around with a sign?"

"That's the idea."

"A sign that announces you as an author and mentions the movie."

"Yes."

"You realize that mocks you."

"Oh yeah."

"You understand that contaminates our movie. Those memories are holy to us."

"Yes they are."

"I hope you didn't say yes."

"I didn't."

"Thank God. What did you say?"

"That I'd get back."

"You want my answer?"

"I think I know."

"Not for a million dollars."

"I was hoping you'd see it in that light."

"My God, Jay, the indignity."

"That's what I thought."

"You'd be a monkey in a circus. No, they can't do that to us."

"At least as a slot attendant I'm somewhat anonymous."

"Please don't remind me."

"I'm only saying..."

"I know what you're saying."

Back home, there's a slight change, there's a bounce. Yes there is this. The hours. Nine to five. Not quite. There would be evenings and late nights, but no graveyard.

"That's the only plus," she says. "But it is something to consider."

"I know."

"These hours are killing you, Jay. I hate to tell you this, but it's made your temper short, and you don't even look the same. We never have time together."

"So, not so fast, right?"

"I hate this choice. What should we do?"

"What do you think, Mel?"

"I don't know."

"So we can't say no, not so fast."

"I guess."

That's pretty much how we leave it; not so fast. Strange turn of events, once we'd thought it over. Suddenly it had merit. We never even got to the money part, or the part where I'd never have to wear that green uniform again, or the part where people would stop whistling to get my attention, just the part that I'd have decent hours and be there for her as a husband.

* * *

I'm over at the bank and Debbi Interlante, the teller, asks what's new. I hate that question but I like Miss Interlante. I hate that question because nothing is new. She's been telling me for months that a very famous writer (besides me, of course) lives right in the neighborhood and does his banking right here, with her, and wouldn't it be terrific if the two of us got together.

I have been thinking about this. I could use a writer to pave me along the road to his editor, or at least to endorse, that is blurb, my novel that can't seem to get published. A good word from someone, someone big, could help and so happens that this writer of Miss Interlante's is someone pretty big, Bryan Denman. He lives here in Voorhees? Not in Haddonfield?

Asking a favor from another writer, it is done all the time, but humbling, yes, it is humbling. But I think of Melanie and remember that there is also a livelihood to be made and let's face it, we are desperate, so maybe it is time for some groveling. I think he forgot that, King Solomon, when he wrote Ecclesiastes, in which he said there is a time for everything. He forgot groveling. A time to be proud, a time to grovel.

He usually comes here at around this time, Bryan Denman does, according to Miss Interlante, so why don't I just wait around and she'll make the introduction. Sure enough, some ten minutes later, that's him. I know he's got something like number 15 on *The New York Times* bestseller list, and that is pretty good, since Dan Brown and JK Rowling have all of the above slots sewn up.

So we are introduced and it is Caulfield's dream of meeting the writer. This is not always excellent. Best to admire your heroes from a distance. Bryan Denman is not my hero, necessarily, but he is a novelist who is not cursed and that's near heroic. We shake hands, he does his business with Miss Interlante, and we stroll out to the parking lot together. I'd rather he not see my car, so I walk him to his, very snappy Mercedes. He's a big man, tall and wide, double-chin, hair back tight in a pony tail, bad teeth, late forties, tweeds and jeans.

Right off he says he never heard of me (except from Miss Interlante), never read me. Never goes to the movies, either, and if my novel was turned into a movie, can't be much good. He knows Sharon Glazer out there in Hollywood, and no wonder she's finished; all those remakes, including *Manchurian Candidate, Stepford Wives, Sabrina, Psycho, Out of Towners* – all guaranteed to flop, which they did. Why can't they leave well enough alone? Why do they keep trying to improve on perfection? Can't be done. Classics are classics for a reason.

They keep pressing the refresh button hoping to duplicate the original. That's plain lazy. Well, we agree, it's all corporate, hence, bottom line.

Bryan Denman tells me that Sharon Glazer offered him a contract but he turned her down. (I don't believe him.)

He asks, from out of nowhere, if I believe in God. I say yes. He asks why. The distribution of skills, I explain. There is always someone to play the tuba.

I must be a conservative, he says. I say no, I am not political. But he insists. Again, no, as I go on to say that I am neither to the right or to the left. Both sides are wrong.

He gets into his car, starts it up, and says he'd be happy to help me any way he can. (Miss Interlante told him that I am among the literary cursed? Must be.) He knows I've got something new making the rounds and that an endorsement from him could make all the difference. Do I write for love or money? he asks. I say love first, money second. He says I've got it backwards.

Is this where I grovel? Do novels have a soul? Yes. That's why, love first.

"No, you've got it backwards," he says.

To prove that – that writing is a business – he offers to blurb me, praise me to the heavens, but... without reading my manuscript.

"Wish I had the time to read other people, but I don't."

"That's the deal," he says, gunning the soft engine and edging off. "Let me know."

As I am left eating the dust of his Mercedes, I'm thinking. Is larceny good? Is this classic moral dilemma? This is done all the time, right? What makes me so holy?

Anyway, I think I'll pass. No thank you.

Chapter 18

They swarm in off the buses like cattle. They practically moo.

In no time you lose your faith in the goodness of humanity. The psalmist got it wrong. We are MUCH lower than the angels. One week on any casino floor will cure your idealism. People are snippy, testy, cranky, nasty, grumpy, grubby, sly, sneaky, vulgar, fat and ugly. Most nights you wish upon a flood. Destroy this mess and start all over again. Nice try, but God's experiment didn't work. Philosophers, scientists and theologians don't have the answer. Slot attendants do.

We see the lady in all her jewels crawling after the single twenty-five cent coin that bounced off the brimming tray. We see it all and it is not good.

There is another side, to be sure, but that's not what comes sloshing in. Mark the guard says, "What makes people go stupid the minute they walk in that door?"

So maybe it's not the people, it's the casino environment (see under: greed) that causes them to plunge into depravity. Otherwise, back home in Iowa, surely they're okay.

The only people you trust, here on the frontlines, are the people you work with, and it is true that some of them speak the language of "he don't" or "I ain't gonna" and they'll not be found with Brahms in Philadelphia or with Beethoven in New York. They've never heard of the Kimmel

Center or the Lincoln Center, and it's never the Met, but rather the Mets. For them it's jazz or hip-hop. They move to a different beat, but they've become your friends. You trust them. They trust you.

This Friday – and it is more crazy than usual, a zoo – Mark the guard, who knows the ebbs and flows from his many years on the job, tells me there are bad vibes in the air. George, his alter ego, or rather the ghost from his past life as an engineer with Henry Ford, has come to him with that signal. "Something's wrong," says Mark. "Someone's going down."

I'm in Zone 10, where the Hot 7s draw the most unruly crowds (it's non-stop for me here) when Mark approaches with that hunch of his.

"I don't know what it is," he says.

He's been around long enough to trust his nose.

Same here. Maybe it's because upstairs, Toledo Vasquez wasn't there to clock in or to stand in line to get his assignment and key. He was nowhere around.

But Jeff is doing double-duty. Jeff Milgrim is a new hire. He's about 28. He'd just finished his three month probation and apprenticeship and we formed a quick bond when he found out who I was. He wants to become a poet and belongs to a poetry club in Margate. He's had two years of community college and is enrolling again for courses in writing, despite what I told him, that courses in writing ruin a writer, those academics, they take all the music out of a sentence, although, depending on the professor. Jeff keeps asking me to read his poetry and I keep reminding him that I am not good at poetry, the reading or the writing. In this I am nearly alone, for I have yet to meet anyone who is not a poet.

Jeff also wants to talk politics. He has scrolled me on Google and came upon this: "Who are these professors who are babysitting our children and feeding them pabulums of anti-Semitism?" But I refuse to talk politics and have taken a vacation from writing politics. One voice against so many and it starts to hurt when you find yourself so outnumbered. They want to do it again and my journalism is not going to be enough to stop them.

So Jeff is working the floor first time alone. He's covering two zones at a time, 8 and 9, and that is odd for a rookie, and for a Friday night, one man, two zones. He's doing all right, jumping from jackpot to jackpot, from hopper jam to hopper jam, and I've already told him that I'm available if he needs help. These are busy zones, 8 and 9, armpit hell, especially on weekends.

There is murmuring. A mutiny is about to erupt, there in Jeff's two zones, when a group of squatters takes over the entire row of the Cotton Candy machines. They're not here to play, just here to rest, but they're taking up seats that are desired by real gamblers who demand their right at those machines. So it's one group, from the suburbs, against another group, from the inner city, and it's about to get racial. There's shouting and the shoving is about to begin. The squatters won't budge, now as a matter of respect, but lucky for Jeff, and probably for the rest of us, the suburbans disperse with plenty of hard feelings all around.

When he's caught up, Jeff ambles on over and asks if it's true that I'll be teaching a class in writing, right here, after hours. I explain that, no, not writing, but English, maybe; for our foreign co-workers. Oh, he was hoping for a class in writing. He'd love to take part. I am wondering how word filtered down so fast, and I hadn't even agreed. Nothing's been agreed.

"Hey, Jeff, why two zones?"

He shrugs.

"I don't know. I think I'm filling in for someone."

188

I take it to mean Toledo. So where is Toledo? Supervisor Omar steps up with his usual scowl and snarls "enough" and Jeff disperses. I zip back to my rounds in Zone 10, where there's plenty of disgust at my neglect for three jackpots ringing away and six hoppers waiting to be filled, and after I get it all calmed down, after the children have been momentarily pacified and tucked in, here comes Carmella, radiant as ever, and smiling that Spanish smile. She should know about Toledo. But she says, "Just because I have a jealous husband does not mean you have to avoid me."

"Avoid you?"

"Yes, Jay, you are avoiding me."

"Never."

She leans in and whispers. "We can still play."

I tell her to make herself scarce. Omar is in the vicinity and on the warpath.

"I don't care," she says. "I can get a lousy job like this any place. I don't need this."

Sure enough here's Omar, miffed.

"What's going on?"

He snaps her back to her zone. As she vanishes back into the mob, she gives me a farewell swivel and wiggle. She sure does know the tricks, that Carmella.

But where is Toledo?

This, Zone 10, is where you're always behind and where they face you breath to breath, poke you in the ribs and whistle for you to come fix their machine.

New problem. The machines aren't taking the new twenty dollar bills. It's always something.

They're always losing, most of them, and that never helps. Even when they win, and you congratulate them, they tell you they're not even close to getting even. They're never satisfied and nothing makes them happy and what a strange place to visit, a casino, to get miserable. There must be better places for this.

It's Friday night, for sure, because every seat is taken, every machine's in action, there's movement like entire armies advancing and retreating, and there's more than the usual laughing, hacking, cackling, sneezing, wheezing, coughing, groaning, clanking, whooping, and somewhere the ear-splitting, bloodcurdling screech of a woman who's just hit a jackpot. The lights are dim and the air is thick and urgent. The natives are restless.

I get into it with one beer breath who keeps whistling for me. He's been waiting an hour for his hopper jam to be fixed. He's got a bus to catch. They always tell you it's been an hour and there's a bus to catch. I tell the guy to please be patient, a supervisor is coming, I've made the call, but it's Friday and it's busy, so please; I'm speaking firmly.

"You think you're tough?"

"Just doing my job, Sir."

"You're nothing, you know."

"Hey."

I walk away. Suliman taught me that at the start. Walk away.

A few minutes later Omar finds me amid the mob and says a customer took down my name and number because I'd been rude. Beer breath, no doubt.

Omar disappears because there is so much other business.

Humberto Valdez is doing the payoff and hopper fill run. He's that tall kid that I did not like at first, always so zany and full of punk and rap and hip-hop, but I've come around. He's really a nice kid, once you get to know him, once you get him to sit down and quit making a show of himself. He's got speed, which is what you want on payoff/hopper fill detail, and now he's moving all around, joking with the players, many of whom respond favorably. Humberto knows how to work a room. He nods me over.

"Did you hear?"

I move along with him and help him empty some bags.

"What?"

"Our hombre Toledo. He's in trouble."

"What trouble?"

"Big trouble."

But the clatter of coins makes it too difficult to talk and anyway, he's already five rows down.

"Later, man," is all I can make out.

I find Roger Price over by the Magic Diamond machines where he's helping someone tuck in one of those new 20s. I know he's going in for a heart operation and I feel terrible for him. It always happens to the best of us, these things. Omar is healthy and Roger Price is sick. That's the way it goes.

Roger then moves along to pay off a jackpot and when he's done and still moving to pay off the next jackpot I ask him what's going on. He doesn't even look up. Actually he can't because he's counting out five one hundred dollars bills to this customer who has her arms and hands out like it's the first money she's ever seen.

"What's up, Roger?"

"What's up" is a good one. It's replaced whatever. "What's up" is all over the place. Back in my neighborhood it used to be – Oh yeah?

He says, "The less you know, the better."

I realize that Franco DeLima isn't around, either. Toledo is gone. Franco is gone. Is there something to add up here or something to subtract?

"Can't wait to get out of here," says Roger, paying off another jackpot.

But what a way to go, straight to hospital.

Back in my zone I'm running around like a rat in a maze. These Hot 7s are planted in a circle, a carrousel. I'm saturated with sweat inside the green uniform and am having second thoughts, about everything, but particularly that offer from upstairs, which does sound good, if it weren't so bad, so bad about being on display. Can anything be worse than this, Friday night, Zone 10? At this moment, no.

Actually this is a compliment when they give you Zone 10, Friday night, the roughest zone of all. They don't assign this to just anybody. I must be making a name for myself.

"Please don't do that," I tell a lady who pokes me in the ribs.

"But I keep calling you and you're not coming over."

"These people were first, ma'am. I'll be over soon as I can."

"Are you people on holiday or something?"

"Just busy, ma'am."

"This place is awful."

A black lady asks why I rushed over to help that white lady first. I explain that's because she WAS first, had her hand up first. The black lady says I'm a bigot.

I wonder, at this moment, if we will ever get over this, from both sides.

Mark the guard comes over because someone has complained that the chair she was sitting on made her fall off. Mark will have to make out a report.

Of course the chairs by the machines are all loose, lumpy, worn and torn. Fat Ass America needs to get on a diet.

The one good part about this zone is that they're pros. They don't ask stupid questions. They play the machines like virtuosos, like Serkin at the piano. Except that they're expressionless; their faces a showcase of rowhome vacuity. We all know why they're here; to get even with life, to make amends. Life cheated them, so here they come to get what they figure is owed them. That's why they're so quick to get nasty when even the casino cheats them, or rather refuses to pay off. Some pray to one machine, one god; others move from machine to machine, serving other gods.

But where is Toledo?

Our horny supervisor, Maggi Holt, stops by to help me clear out a jammed hopper, and then informs me that she's "met a guy." He's an accountant in the Bronx and it could be love. He could be the one. She still wants to get laid, though. "Oh, Jay," she says, "I can tell you've been around, quite the lady killer." Ancient history. "I'll get you in the sack before this is all over. You're a cutie pie."

"You say that to all the guys, Maggi."

Actually she does. I remember Mark the guard telling she's hit on him as well – and who else? Not much to be flattered about.

"Maybe," she says before leaving, "you're afraid of me."

"Maybe I am, Maggi."

"Maybe you're not so good in bed."

"I'm terrible in bed."

"So let's find out."

"Bye, Maggi."

I hardly remember. Melanie and I are saving it up for when we celebrate.

So where is Toledo?

Beer breath whistles for me again and when I don't respond he makes a dash for me and I think he really wants to fight. I could take him, but then everything goes.

I explain, again, that the people who fill the hoppers and make the payoffs – they're a different crew.

"I thought you were all the same. Scum." He says that he's already reported me.

This, at a moment like this, is when you remind yourself that your book sold a million and a half copies domestically. You attended your own premiere.

Never mind overseas. They even translated it into Chinese and Japanese. That must be something, being a translator.

I've got those books in my den, from all over the world.

Yes, this is the time to remind yourself that you've got back class and back class is always dangerous.

Guys like this beer breath, of course he's ticked off. He takes it 9 to 5 from his boss, then his wife, then his kids, then his in-laws, so here you are, so available.

At the start of my break I stop off at the Million Dollar Club, Zone 1, the high roller territory where Marty Glick is on duty in his tux. Marty is all right. He also married from a catalogue, mail order, just like Flint. Actually, Marty was first, and that's what prompted Flint. Whenever we get together, the three of us, we compare American women to foreign women and American women always lose.

Marty usually takes home a thousand dollars a night, in tips. No riff raff for Marty. He's rich, just bought a new home, and his Filipino wife drives her own Mercedes. Marty's zone is right across from the craps tables where sometimes there's a half million dollars riding on the next toss of the dice. It's much more pleasant, much more Monaco, much more Bond, James Bond around here, and no wonder we all want a turn. But this is not Marty's job, it's his career. He's not looking for anything else. This is just fine.

The Egyptian guy who plays the same $10 game every night motions me over and says he just heard from Bob Foster, our president, that I'm a celebrity, that I wrote a movie or something. I say all of that was a long time ago. I figure he'll want more information, and he does. "So what

are you doing here?" he says. Just then he hits a jackpot and
Marty rushes over to congratulate and write it up.

Good timing. I hate that question. What are you doing
here? I'm doing here what I'm doing here. What are you
doing here? Where should I be?

The clerk in that bookstore up the street got that
question kicked off, six years ago. She was really quite
attractive, this sales girl at Borders in Marlton. When *The Ice
King* sold out and Hollywood signed on, and I walked in for
another book, Thomas Pynchon's latest, she said, "What are
you doing here?" She thought I'd moved to Hollywood. Real
authors don't hang around New Jersey.

Marty asks me to join him at the cage where he's going
to collect the cash to pay off the Egyptian. Marty wants to
know if I'm destined for supervisor or shift manager or
maybe something even bigger. Word has gotten around that
I'd had a confab upstairs. "No such luck," I say. He refuses to
believe, as many times as I deny. "Just remember that I'm
your pal," he says. That's either a signal, or he's afraid I'm
taking over his zone.

But where's Toledo Vasquez? I am getting butterflies.

Upstairs in the cafeteria Bob Michaelson offers to sell me
a genuine Rolex for fifty dollars. He's got so many businesses
on the side.

"This will stop once you become a state trooper, won't it,
Bob?"

He's laughing. "It's a genuine Rolex."

"I've also got a genuine bridge to sell. Wanna buy?"

I find a quiet table to do some writing. The TV is on,
some final game of a playoff. I used to be so big on sports.

"Can't make it on this salary," says Bob Michaelson.

So I'm at this quiet table trying to write, but nothing's
coming. There's the usual nutty crowd acting up, but that's
not what's stopping me. I'm used to thinking and writing

around noise. Anyway, they honor my privacy. They accord me reverence and I return that reverence. It didn't start off that way, but that's how it's ending up.

But I can't write. I am all written out. I don't know what they want out there, Roe Morgan and his crowd. They want yarns? Yarns they want? They want golf? Well, Sylvio is giving it his best. Maybe, just maybe Sylvio can succeed where I failed. Of course Melanie is right. This can't go on. This isn't my life. I'm fooling myself if I believe this is what I've been cut for. My contentment with this is a sham.

She is also right that it is cruel of me to keep insisting that I am a slot attendant, end of story. End of story, end of dreams. It was cruel of me to keep rubbing it in at that party in Haddonfield, for which I am not sure she has completely forgiven me, and I can't say that I blame her.

As I'm finishing up my 40-minute break, Carmella arrives. Her break has just begun. I marvel at how stunning she is, Carmella. Now here's someone who could have done better. What a creep, that husband of hers. She whispers, "I love you," and whizzes past. I don't know what this is all about and where this is going. Then she says something in Spanish. I don't know what it means. Toledo would know. He'd be the man to ask, when I see him.

Which I do. I'm back downstairs on the casino floor, or, that is, just reaching the landing off the escalator, when it's all stopped, like freeze frame. There is a parade marching by, people in uniform on drill, of some sort, faces professionally tight, and in the middle of it all is a sunken figure, Toledo, in handcuffs.

The players hardly stop to notice this procession, but for the rest of us, this is a moment. We're paralyzed. We're stricken. This could be one of us, and in fact it is, it is one of us, and one of our favorites. What a sight – Toledo like this, proud kid, too, put to shame. His arms are shackled behind his back. He seems so small. They've taken the starch out of him.

I'm trying to find his eyes, to offer some sign, that I am with him, but they've got him good and surrounded, and besides, his head is down, down to the floor.

Someone's got his head clamped down as he's being displayed through the aisles. This is their lesson to the rest of us. See! This is what happens. You're next.

This could have been done differently, with dignity, but this is not about dignity, it is about disgrace, and seldom have I seen a man so disgraced.

This is today's version of a public hanging, or an auto-da-fe.

Then it's over. They're gone. He's gone.

There's no time to reflect. Back to work. But this hurts.

Howard Glass, there he is, as usual, drooling down his shirt, at his Wild Cherry machine, and I spot him before he spots me. I walk over, taking giant steps, and when he sees me he leans back and gives me that grin and is ready to insert the needle. He thinks he's got me again. Before he can open his mouth, I point my finger in his face and tell him that I know where he lives. He turns pale.

* * *

A week after all that, after they took Toledo Vasquez away in handcuffs, Franco DeLima crashes through the eighth floor of our parking garage. The eighth floor is a new addition and six months earlier two elderly women had the same deadly tumble. The concrete barriers had since been rebuilt and declared safe by State Inspectors. Still, nobody wanted to park up there, it made the papers. So that floor, the eighth, was reserved for employees only. We all parked up there, Toledo included.

Franco DeLima's death is ruled an accident. But there are suspicions that it may have been suicide, or foul play.

Chapter 19

I'm on the bus to New York and Sylvio and though I expect the best, I've developed a new strategy, or a new attitude, which is that whatever will be will be. I know this is the oldest strategy there is, but it's new for me. I figure, look, I have done my best, what more do you want, what more can I do?

As Melanie is driving me over to the Mount Laurel bus station, I start getting fidgety. Here we go again, another trip to New York and another bottom of the ninth. How much of this can you take? But then, as always, we pass Cole's Cemetery, and for the first time I give it a thoughtful glance, and am comforted, because what more can life do to you than that, and isn't this the sum of it all anyway? Does anything really matter?

Is this a thunderclap, I wonder, an epiphany, that nothing matters, that we're all in the same boat? Big is the same as small, rich is the same as poor, smart is the same as stupid, success is the same as failure, strength is the same as weakness, faith is the same as disbelief, because, as the man said, all is futile.

Granted, as we have it from another wisdom; you may not succeed, but that does not absolve you from persisting.

So I'm persisting.

Melanie had wanted me to wear something else. For luck. They're always wanting you to wear something else. Maybe even a suit, a suit and tie. Are you kidding? I asked her what it is with you women anyway, you women and clothes? What is this fixation on shoes? Don't you know that's the last thing we notice? No, it's the only thing we NEVER notice about women.

So for this power meeting with Sylvio I'm dressed casual, as usual, and still have two hours to kill, so I stop off at the Big Library, to do some browsing, and find that there is no such thing, it's all so overly systemized that you can't find a single thing and you sure can't take some book off some shelf and sit down and have a read. No, you have to know exactly what you want and then go through a whole rigmarole. It's all too confusing. The librarians were nice, though, if unhelpful.

But the library is a frightening place. A billion books! Why would anyone want to read one of yours? Why would anybody care? Nobody cares.

When I got on that network Morning Show right after the movie came out Matt asked me if I got into any bar fights, given the fight scene in the movie and the book.

"You've never been challenged?"

I said I never go to bars. Most of the time you'll find me in libraries and it's been quite some time since I've had a fist fight with a librarian.

Actually he didn't refer to the book, only the movie. They only want the movie. Amazing.

But it is different when one of them writes a book, TV personalities, where it's all self-promotion and cross promotion. I'll scratch your book, you scratch mine; meanwhile there are thousands, maybe millions of real writers out there who go unseen, unheard. No thank you. I guess this is sour grapes. Yes, it is sour grapes. But still, there ought to be a law.

After the library I visit the Grand Hyatt to check myself out in the bathroom. You don't want to arrive sweaty over at Sylvio's. I like the Grand Hyatt because it's got a busy lobby and the help in there can't tell you apart from a guest to a loiterer, which is what I am, technically, a loiterer. I don't have a room. If someone should ask, I'd be in trouble, but no one does. That's why I like this place.

Because I am a loiterer I pretend that I'm waiting for someone and I have a name picked out just in case, Mr. Collingsworth. I don't know such a person but it sounds right. Sounds like a businessman and an important businessman. This lobby is itself a place of business, people in groups poring over papers and individually tapping on computers and talking into their cell phone. I've also got a cell phone.

In the bathroom, this is where I worry about getting trapped and someone yelling, "There's a loiterer in there!" In fact, as I'm worrying about this, a cleaning man does step in and as I'm washing up he does seem to be giving me the once-over, but it's probably my imagination. After he leaves a guy walks in and he's not kidding me, he's right off the streets, and I wonder how he got in here...he's not one of us.

I think maybe I'll have a drink at that bar upstairs, and that's what I do, I have a drink, vodka straight up. The bartender asks what kind, what brand, and I tell him any brand will do, as I really cannot tell one from another. Can anyone? Can anyone really? "Oh," I say, "Smirnoff." I figure that sounds professional. So I have one Smirnoff and then another and then a third. I figure we're all supposed to be drunks anyway, writers. All writers are drunks or something.

There are peanuts and snacks, quite exotic snacks, on all the tables and I help myself and keep helping myself until I am quite full. This is supposed to be lunch with Sylvio, but I know about such plans. Lunch will come if we've got a deal. Before that, no lunch. So I fill up. Back in my hungry days in New York I knew every hotel, the good bathrooms from the bad, and where you could fill up, just from going from hotel to hotel, from snack to snack. You never had to pay.

Sometimes, when I needed a full course, I'd become a guest at a wedding, or Bar Mitzvah, or any of a hundred business receptions.

Sometimes you're stopped but usually nobody asks, or you get so good at this that you wait until a crowd arrives for distraction.

There is no excuse for starving in New York. The man who said "there's no such thing as a free lunch" just never knew his way around hotels.

So now, a bit tipsy, but in control, I'm in the lobby of Sylvio's building and decide to take the plunge, take the elevator, as a test of my new philosophy, which is, who cares? Really, who cares, and so what if the elevator gets stuck and the doors never open. I don't care. I don't give a damn. It's out of my hands. Fate will decide. Fate always decides. You're just a flunky in all this. You're nothing.

That was my old philosophy, merely merging into the new. I'm nothing. You are nothing. We are nothing. We are all nothing.

Is it possible that I really want the elevator to crash? Yes, it is possible. Is it possible that there is a death wish ticking somewhere inside me? Yes, it is possible. Is it possible that I do not value life as I once used to? Yes, it is possible. Is it possible that I am fed up? Oh yes, that is very possible. Is it possible that they have smashed you against the rocks so many times that you don't even care if you win or lose? Indeed, very possible. Is it possible that bitterness is all you can taste and that nothing, absolutely nothing, will ever make you happy ever again?

You're gone. You're as gone as Maurice Richard is gone, the Maurice Richard you eulogized in your novel *The Ice King*. You wept for him and all that passed with him. They never saw him. Those grainy film clips don't do him justice. He really was the ice God! The majesty of this man and his kingdom at the old Forum in Montreal! Those blazing eyes, the black hair sweeping back as he swooped down the ice. Does anyone remember? Is there anyone left?

So tell us, Mr. Richard, how do you manage to score all those goals?

"I shoot da puck."

He never took to English. He was too proud. He was French, French-Canadian, and so he would remain until his dying day.

I shoot da puck.

That lesson surpasses hockey.

I shoot da puck.

Beat that for hard-boiled.

He died a gentle old man, Richard did. They gave him a State Funeral. Thank goodness somebody cared.

So I make it through the elevator trip all right, but Sylvio has a new assistant, a guy, a guy named Krew. He tells me it's spelled with a K. I guess it counts. For him it surely counts. What's worse than having your name misspelled? Mine was nearly misspelled in the early copies of the book. I caught it just in time.

"I hope you don't mind waiting," says Krew.

The problem is, Sylvio had to run out on an errand. Should be back shortly.

"He won't be long."

Like it matters? I've got all day. But it's always something with these people. I wonder where he goes when he's out like this. I only know he keeps making deals, so wherever he goes, it must mean a deal or some such thing. Maybe he's visiting Roe Morgan to finalize that deal with me. Maybe it's about me. Wouldn't that be nice? Seems that it's always about somebody else.

I love those rejections I used to get, even before my Big Book, the editor writing back to the agent, "We'll have to pass on Jay Leonard, but I wish to speak with you on that other book you submitted. I think we can make an offer on Gerald Gould." I told my agent (of that time) to never show me a rejection ever again. Just tell me yes or no, forget the details. I don't want the details.

"That was Sylvio on the phone. He'll be here shortly. Look around."

So I do, and most of the books on the shelves are fitness and motivational; not much fiction. So Sylvio is big on self-help. One of his writers made it big, I think.

I think it was Weiss.

I did not know that Sylvio is weak on fiction. I did not want to know. He called. He made the pitch. He called himself the hottest agent in New York.

I checked. He was.

Only I did not know he was weak on fiction. Well, so what? He's an agent. He always sells. What's the difference what he sells.

Always six figures, too.

Melanie would love six figures. I know she's waiting back home, waiting for my phone call, waiting to celebrate. I can only imagine how she feels right now. I can almost cry. She's waited so long, so long to celebrate. She still has that dress from the premiere in Hollywood. She refuses to wear it, even to soirees in Haddonfield. No, she's saving it for the next book, when we celebrate.

I know she's got two, actually three reviews to get out. She's on deadline. But I'll bet she's not able to pull herself together.

She was so nervous about this.

No, she said, she wouldn't be disappointed if lunch didn't pan out; all she wanted was an offer.

Then we'll celebrate.

I'll bet, I said, you'll probably buy new shoes.

She laughed. I love it when she laughs. Her cheeks get all red and rosy, and how her eyes light up.

"Are you a writer?" I ask Krew. He's busy doing things.

"No, I'm just filling in."

"Then you're an actor."

"Yes."

Tough to converse with Krew.

"Actors Studio?"

"I haven't been accepted yet."

"I once met James Lipton."

"I never have."

"I wonder if he's related to those Lipton tea people."

"I wouldn't know."

I ask him who he acts like. I figure it to be a legitimate question. It's always asked of writers. Who does he write like?

"Pacino," he says.

"Oh, one of my favorites."

"I've got a ways to go."

"Well, he also had to start someplace."

"But I'm twenty-eight."

"That's not old, for an actor."

"They say it is."

"That's crazy. That's old for an athlete, but you won't be scoring any touchdowns when you do Hamlet."

That's as far as I get with Krew.

Not quite.

"Actors are a dime a dozen in this town," he says after some business on the computer.

"I know what you mean."

"You keep on auditioning but you're just another number."

"I'm a writer, so I know."

"I know you're a writer."

Of course, why else would anybody be here – and we're also just another number.

"Writers and actors," I say, "have much in common."

"You mean so far as being meat."

"Hey, that's good. That's right."

"I understand you've had a big movie."

"Long time ago, Krew."

"I've read your new book."

I'm hoping this isn't a complete sentence.

"I like it a lot."

"Thanks, Krew."

"Think it'll make a movie?"

"Has to make a book first."

"I see a movie."

I hope this isn't the case. Not again.

"Book first, Krew. I don't really care about a movie. Not yet."

"I see a part for me."

"You mean the craps shooter himself?"

"Maybe not, but maybe one of those goons. You do goons well. Very convincing."

"Tell you what. You got a card?"

Yes he does and hands it over.

"Well, who knows?"

"Thanks."

"You're welcome."

"Please do me a favor."

"Sure."

"Don't mention this to Sylvio."

"Of course not."

"I don't want him to think I'm soliciting business on his time."

"For sure."

"Though I don't think he'd really mind."

"Probably wouldn't."

"He's really a nice man. He's been good to me."

"This, or waiting tables, right?"

"I do that, too."

I am getting worried that Sylvio may not show up at all. This has happened. Not with Sylvio, but with others. They just don't show up.

Sylvio does show up. This must be said. But I'm thinking about Melanie. I hope she's not sticking by the phone. I hope she's not expecting too much.

She is actually expecting six figures. I know she is. She thinks our luck has changed. She thinks it's time. She says luck has to change.

I know better. I know the racetrack and I know there is no such rule, that luck has to change.

Heeeer's Sylvio.

"Just give me a minute."

He dashes into his office. More waiting, but he's here.

"You can go in," says Krew.

So I'm in and Sylvio is just finishing up on the phone.

"We got a deal!"

Whoa.

I am ready to fly. Forget everything. I love life. Life is precious. So, how much? I'll take five figures, okay? Anything. No more slot attendant. Hear that, Mel? No more green uniform. No more graveyard. No more...okay, I'm sorry about Haddonfield. We'll go back and I will let you brag about me, me the AUTHOR, all you want. Yes, tell Gladdy to throw another party, just for me, just for us. You know

Gladdy. She'll be thrilled. Imagine, a book party. How perfect. Just don't call me an artist, okay? That's all I ask. I am not an arteest. The rest is yours.

"Really?"

"Just got off the phone with him..."

"Roe Morgan?"

"Took some doing, but I got him."

All that remains, says Sylvio, are the terms. But Sylvio is famous for six figures, so not to worry. I'm remembering how it was with Mario Puzo after he hit with *The Godfather*. He'd been plunged in debt and suddenly he's rich. His wife is trying on dresses at Saks or someplace like that and she can't make up her mind between the blue dress and the yellow dress. She's in a quandary. Silly thing, he says. Don't you know? You can buy BOTH! Soon I'll be home with my version of that with Melanie.

"Only thing is," says Sylvio, "we're not getting the kind of offer we should."

Okay, I'll take $50,000.

"The back end looks terrific, though."

He means secondary rights, paperback, foreign, Hollywood. Also, naturally, royalties from the hardcover itself, and sometimes, publishers toss in a signing bonus, just to make you happy. That in itself can add up to $10,000. Slight glitch, but only something that bothers me momentarily – back end. There is no back end. Take all you can up front. Back end never happens. That's when literature meets accounting. Accounting wins. But anyway...

"He's offering five thousand dollars."

I am not hearing this.

"As a signing bonus?"

"Wish that were so. No, that's the advance."

"That's lunch."

"Lunch money, I know, Jay. I fought like hell."

I am sure he did.

"It's a take it or leave it deal. I say take. What have we got to lose?"

I like the "we" part but it also means he gets 15 percent off that five thousand dollars, which is fair, he fought, but still amounts to peanuts.

Now we're not talking lunch money; tip money.

There's more. Roe Morgan will want me to do book tours across the country. That's lined up with the contract. That means I'll have to quit my job, for five thousand dollars, minus 15 percent. No more paycheck. No more Benefits. There is still that one good part. I am getting my book published. "It's something," says Sylvio. "I know you're disappointed, but hey, we got a deal."

"Aha."

"Look, you can't imagine how disappointed I was. I was insulted. I've never gone that low. It's a real insult."

"I imagine..."

"Yeah, I'm hurt. But who knows? Once the book gets out there, you know, book signings, TV..."

Will Roe Morgan be paying for my travels?

"That's the other thing. No."

So that's what it is. The same No Thanks – but with honey. But I cannot refuse, not so fast. There is an offer on the table, and it has been six years, 84 days without taking a fish. Obviously, I am the side deal. Roe Morgan wants that other writer, and I am the toss in. Never mind. There is an offer on the table and that is something. Is that something to celebrate? I'm not sure.

"There's another thing. He wants a couple of changes."

"He wants a yarn, right?"

"We don't want to lose this, do we?"

I'm thinking. I'm thinking.

"So what do you say?"

"I don't know."

"I can start drawing up the contract."

I'm still thinking.

"So?"

"I'll have to give this some thought, Sylvio."

"Really?"

I tell him that this offer – is this an offer? – is not exactly a life-changing bonanza.

"I tried," Sylvio says. "He wouldn't even go for six thousand."

Wouldn't even go for six thousand, the bastard. Hah!

"Let me think it over."

He walks me to the door, a move he's never made before.

"You've got a terrific novel there," he says. "They just haven't caught up to you yet. Don't despair."

Chapter 20

Melanie already knows. She's waiting for me at the Mount Laurel bus station. There was no phone call from New York to get reservations started at the Steak House. So she knows. There will be no celebrating. It's back to one dress at a time, and hold that party in Haddonfield. Nothing's changed. It's back to everything.

Slowly, back in the house, I give her the whole story.

"It isn't fair," she says.

Then we drive over to McDonald's. I've said it all and there is nothing more to talk about.

"It isn't fair," she says now at McDonald's.

That evening I'm back in my green uniform. She drives to the Lindenwold train station. I'm off to work, as a slot attendant. She had called in sick for me, just in case there'd be celebrating. But I am not sick. So I called back that I'd be late, but I'll be in. That was Omar who took my call. Roger Price is gone, taken in for surgery. Who knows if he'll ever be back.

Melanie and I are sitting here waiting for the Atlantic City train. It's late. No, we agree, that's no deal. That's a slap in the face. That's Roe Morgan. After all this time, it's still Roe Morgan. We won't give up, though. No we won't. We will not give up. There are other agents, other publishers. Anyway, Sylvio isn't strong on fiction. I'll use him if I ever write a book on golf.

"There's more out there," says Melanie. "We'll just keep knocking."

A review she wrote a month ago so pleased the writer that he sent her a thank you, as did the publisher. Yes, the publisher. So maybe here's a contact.

"So we're agreed."

"Of course," says Melanie. "That's no offer. It's a joke."

So, some satisfaction. I will call Sylvio next day to pass this message to Roe Morgan: No Thanks.

That's something.

But what about that other deal, that offer from the casino, Shelly King and Bob Foster?

Yes, Jay Leonard, Celebrity Greeter, Celebrity Author. Next, visit our cage of midgets and giants.

"We have to think about that," says Melanie, now getting very practical.

I assure her I will, I will think about that, and she assures me that something big will come along from New York or Hollywood, as these things always happen when you're not watching, when you least expect it, so for the time being, yes, this is something to consider, something to keep us going until our luck changes.

"For the better," I caution.

Don't tempt fate.

"For the better," she says.

She reminds me of my motto: Back class is always dangerous.

I've done it before, big time. I will do it again.

We're actually quite elated. Who knows? Anything can still happen. It's impossible to believe that nothing will happen. Yes, there is that publisher that thanked her. This could be a contact. So we're elated, glad to have gotten this over with; start fresh. Starting tomorrow, start fresh. We've taken the blow and absorbing and recovering and we're even planning. We're even dreaming again.

For my part, I am near euphoric. I am back to rock bottom, and that's a powerful spot to be in. Nothing to lose. Yes, when you're weak, you're strong. So I am near euphoric.

But there is something else. There was some phone call while I was gone, from one of those investigators at the casino. Yes, Franco's death was ruled a suicide, but they're thinking of reopening the case. There are questions. Apparently, further probing showed that Franco's Mazda had no brakes. Could be neglect on his part, or tampering. No wonder he crashed through the eighth floor wall.

Do I have anything to do with this? Toledo? Toledo and me together?

"Is this going to be something?" she says, nervously. "Is this something I should worry about?"

But then the train pulls up. I kiss her and tell her I love her. I do. I love her more than anything. We hug as if it's final. But it isn't. We have dreams. Something has got to give. Emerson again. "To be great is to be misunderstood." Maybe I'm not so great, but I am misunderstood. But that is bound to change. Yes, I will go on. I step out of the car, walk up to the platform and into the train. I wave to her from the window. She waves back and blows me a kiss. I miss her already. I always do.

I am off to work. I am a slot attendant.

Slot Attendant

More Bonus Essays by Jack Engelhard

Slot Attendant

Salinger Is Back and PBS Has Got Him

NEW YORK, August 27, 2013 — The theme of despair runs throughout literary and even biblical history. So J.D. Salinger, who excelled in writing about the melancholy of human existence, mainly so in *The Catcher in the Rye*, was not the first to approach the topic of futility.

Raised as a rich kid in Manhattan, something changed when he returned from serving heroically in World War II. Was it all of it or was it mostly *Dachau*? We can argue that after that singular experience *he came back a Holocaust survivor*, and as such we will never know what he knew and we will never know what he saw – except what he told his daughter, that the smell of burnt flesh never leaves your nostrils.

Salinger left us in self-imposed silence some three years ago at age 91, but he still manages to make headlines. A new Weinstein Company production of Salinger will be distributed to 200 theaters Sept 6 in advance of a PBS documentary set for January. The accompanying biography, written by dubious experts David Shields and Shane Salerno ("slapdash," according to *The New York Times*) is to emerge in print September 3.

The buzz has it that Salinger wasn't done. More Salinger books are coming one of these days, but never too soon for Salinger buffs. Apparently, if the reports are accurate, Holden Caulfield and members of the Glass family will be with us again, updated and refreshed. If the reports are inaccurate, this won't be the first time high hopes were dashed.

As for this Salinger devotee, no biography on Salinger says it better than Kenneth Slawenski, who, it appears, holds to the opinion "not so fast" about a Salinger Second Coming. Slawenski's biography is still the authoritative word on Salinger and his chapters on Salinger's wartime exploits can perhaps be duplicated, never surpassed.

But what is it about Salinger that so fascinates us? We never stopped bothering him when he was alive and when dead we will not let him rest in peace.

He wrote those novellas and those short stories – all of it first-rate American literature – and then only one full-length novel, *The Catcher in the Rye*.

Repeatedly we are told that *Catcher* is about "adolescent angst." Really? Is that why, published in 1951, the book still sells around a million copies a year?

There must be something else, something deeper that keeps us coming back and wanting more. I suggest that Salinger hit on the very thing that we would rather not touch by that touches us all – despair. Remember, happiness is only a pursuit. Despair comes without an invitation and we all know the feeling. This is the truth Salinger had the guts to reveal. He may have couched it in teenage lingo, but *The Catcher in the Rye* can be read and appreciated at any age.

Stylistically, Salinger was mostly on his own, but owes much gratitude to Mark Twain and Walt Whitman and others who articulated American vernacular.

Onto the depth of despair, here Salinger had tradition on which to rely.

In *Ecclesiastes*, King Solomon was the first to awaken us to human frailty and futility. What profit is there in all this toil when we all come to the same end? Rich or poor, the same end awaits us all, and from wisdom to foolishness, it is all the same at the time of reckoning.

Centuries later Erasmus picked up the theme of futility, arguing in praise of folly, and in favor of foolishness above wisdom. It is the fool that gets it right.

Tolstoy admired the "holy fool."

Later on we come to F. Scott Fitzgerald, mostly in *The Crack-Up* and Samuel Beckett, mostly in *Waiting for Godot*, who extend the thought that everything is useless.

"I can't go on, I'll go on," from Beckett's *Unnamable*.

No wonder Salinger turned to Eastern Religion to find some purpose, namely the Vedantic branch of Hinduism.

Did he not know that Judaism is the original Eastern Religion?

Maybe he found the purpose, after all, and that is what is hidden in that great big box that we all want opened. Did he find the secret?

Hemingway never found the secret and by his own hand refused to go beyond 61 years.

In his last years, Salinger's search was a search for God, or simply godliness, a life of constant prayer. Did he not know that in Psalms King David is the father of prayer?

The sages who codified the 24 Books of Hebrew Scriptures tried to suppress King Solomon's *Ecclesiastes*, on the obvious notion that it was too pessimistic. They changed their minds and even declared that it was among the holiest books of all, because, despite harsh truth, it ends on a foundation of faith.

In his quest, did Salinger find that moment of divine clarity? Is this our pursuit and what keeps us waiting and wanting more?

In Praise of Jeff Bezos

NEW YORK, August 9, 2013 — By now most people know that Jeff Bezos took a giant step into the world of journalism by purchasing the *Washington Post*, and nobody covers all the ramifications of such a bold move better than my colleague Rick Townley here. Townley offers an overview and an appraisal that, in my view, is right on.

As a writer who was there nearly at the start, I may have something to add, and it is all good, good for Bezos, good for readers and very good for writers. That part, the part about writers, is seldom mentioned when talk gets around to Amazon, the online company that Bezos started back in 1995. A personal observation may be worthwhile, and it amounts to this:

Jeff Bezos saved books as much as Johannes Gutenberg saved printing.

Through Amazon, Bezos started off by selling just that, books. Today he sells everything under the sun, and nobody does it bigger or better.

But on publishing and bookselling, there has been talk that Amazon trampled the competition. That is nonsense. Publishers began losing traction back in the 1980s through faults all their own when the big fish began swallowing the small fish. Today, on Publishers Row in Manhattan, where once there were thousands of different and varied imprints – today there are five.

There are rumors that soon the Big Five will be whittled down further, to the Big Four. If you are a writer, good luck.

As for bookstores, same thing. The shops-on-the-corner began disappearing before Amazon came along, all through mergers, acquisitions and consolidations.

Amazon came in just in time. Millions of books that were destined to die, got sold. Thousands of writers out in the cold, got published.

I got the call (actually an email) around 1996/97 asking if I would mind having my books (starting with *Indecent Proposal*) listed and for sale on Amazon. Are you kidding? Of course! But there was nothing so special about me. By the multitudes, writers from all over were invited to participate; their books listed and for sale.

Where has this been all our lives?

In those early years, Amazon introduced its Amazon Shorts program, where writers were urged to submit their short stories. In other words, if you wrote well enough, you were getting published – and what a new world was this for writers who had been teased and trifled by the big-time houses, and whose works were doomed from start to finish.

Now writers had a home. This is a big thing! Writing is tough enough. Getting published can be brutal in a world so uncaring. Hundreds, soon to be thousands, participated. Digitally, this is where I met some first-rate writers, John W. Cassell and Linda Shelnutt to name just two. We exchanged our stories, shared opinions, and a big bad world got friendlier.

A new universe of literature had opened up, and soon readers, actual readers, began buying our short stories and our books, digitally and in print.

All that was unthinkable until Amazon came on the scene.

Following the Shorts program, another new beginning – the Kindle. We know that readers love it, but writers love it even more, for Kindle offers another means to get published.

No longer are writers at the mercy of the Big Five, whose doors always seem shut. Now writers can bypass the snobs and go directly to Kindle.

Even big name writers, fed up with the slow and grinding process of mainstream publishing, have turned to Kindle. This includes Pulitzer Prize winning author David Mamet. He went straight to Kindle with his latest, as have many others. This is, after all, the digital age.

Theologian Abraham Heschel provides a near perfect definition of a prophet. A prophet is a person "who knows what time it is."

Jeff Bezos is no prophet, okay. So what is his secret? He knew what time it was. The 21st Century.

Hemingway and A Lost Generation

NEW YORK, July 2, 2013 — In the end, the will to die was stronger than the will to live. On the morning of July 2, 1961, Ernest Hemingway aimed a double-barreled, 12-guage shotgun at his head, pulled the trigger and thus ended the short happy life of America's most famous writer. He was 61 and we do not know what would-be books he took to his grave.

Fittingly, he often spoke of the power of silence, or as biographer Kenneth Slawenski reminds us about J.D. Salinger, the secret to great writing resides in the "fire between the words." On the temptation to write long, Hemingway remarked that there are times to resist and to "say no to a typewriter."

Was Hemingway a great writer? The greatest? That is an argument, so let us leave it at that, but without a doubt he was a prose stylist par excellence, even though his most beloved work, *The Old Man and the Sea*, was more poetry than prose, and it earned him the 1954 Nobel Prize.

He was the Babe Ruth of American literature. Often enough he did swat it out of the park. He was a boozer and a brawler but turned devotional when he sat down – or stood up – to write. Famed for that granite-like style, he claimed to have no style, only the blood, sweat and perseverance to cobble together the cleanest sentence possible. In virtually all his paragraphs there is a sense of urgency. This is also how he lived.

Writers who came along during his heyday and those that followed owe him a debt. Only with trembling fingers did we dare type even page one in the shadow of Henry

James and Herman Melville. Hemingway taught us to be unafraid. By example, he proved that saying it simple, straight and true is far more authoritative than razzle-dazzle.

Thanks to his matter-of-fact articulation, we stopped being intimidated by the flowery prose of the past. If he could say it so plainly, so could we.

Depart from embellishments, was his message, just tell it *as it is* – and this was the lesson he learned early on from the *Kansas City Star*. Later, he complained that journalism "blunts the instrument" for fiction, and yet all his novels and short stories show the hand of newspaper reporting, like this, from the opening of *The Short Happy Life of Francis Macomber:*

"It was now lunch time and they were all sitting under the double green fly of the dining tent *pretending that nothing had happened.*" (Italics added by author)

Something did happen. So now we are drawn in, and in journalism that is a lede, or lead.

On war, Hemingway's novels do not match up against Tolstoy or James Jones. Sentence-by-sentence, however, Hemingway pioneered a unique American voice.

Hemingway illustrated that simplicity, directness and repetitiveness, if done wisely and properly, can be powerful literary tools. Surely he learned some of that from Gertrude Stein, "rose is a rose is a rose," but much of his rhythmic prose was biblically inspired, like this from King Solomon's *Ecclesiastes*:

"All is futility and vanity... A generation goes and a generation comes, but the earth endures forever."

One paradox follows another in the life of Ernest Hemingway. He is still America's most famous writer and yet, most of his years were spent overseas.

He was at war against nearly all his contemporaries, but gave time and even money to literary fledglings.

He was synonymous with virility but in his first novel, *The Sun Also Rises*, hero Jake Barnes can not satisfy Lady Brett Ashley. Moreover, in real life Hemingway was stricken by bouts of impotence. A visit to a Catholic church cured him and he remained a somewhat devout Catholic until the end.

How did it all fall apart? He became depressed and paranoid. At the peak of his fame, wealth and glory, why the onset of despair? He must have known this from the wisdom of the Hebraic *Midrash*: "Man has no profit for all his toil under the sun, for life and fortune on this earth are transitory."

He complained that the FBI was tailing him. People said he was wrong. Turned out he was right. Depression and physical ailments made him increasingly incoherent and enfeebled. His doctors tried everything, including electro-convulsive therapy. Even at his worst, he was able to persuade them that he was well enough to go home, back to Ketchum, Idaho. A few days later he shot himself.

In accepting his Nobel Prize, by letter, he wrote: "Writing, at its best, is a lonely life."

Ernest Hemingway was not afraid of writing. He was only afraid of living.

Casino "Eye in the Sky"
Knew You Before NSA

WASHINGTON, June 12, 2013 — If you get that creepy feeling that you are being watched, bet on it; you are.

The Shadow Knows. Nationwide, casinos have known you like a brother, or Big Brother, even before the FBI or the NSA or the DOJ or the IRS snuggled up to you without even a kiss. If they did not do it earlier, casinos certainly did it better in what is chillingly known by dealers and gamblers as "The Eye in the Sky."

Banks of surveillance monitors are up there atop every casino in the United States watching every move you make.

They will catch you misbehaving. They surely will catch you cheating and they won't call you Shirley. They will pick you out of a crowd and make you cry uncle. Gambling has always been a metaphor for life – sometimes you win, mostly you lose – and casinos have always served as a microcosm for life in the real world.

Apparently, we, that is, gamblers and non-gamblers alike, can not be trusted to behave properly unless we are being shadowed. Acts of lawlessness are rare in the casino, any casino. People know. So they are careful. Does this argue in favor for the massive snooping going on in America today?

Heck no. Some privacy, please. We did not bargain for Sweet Land of Tyranny.

But already we are being far more cautious in the messages we send by text, email, and by telephone. That is good and that is bad. Bad because this is America and we ought to be able to say whatever we want. We should not be like so many other countries where people have to whisper.

We should not have language police.

So what's the good? Maybe it is time to bring it down a notch, all that unfiltered garbage talk that floats throughout the Internet, and maybe every idiot that has a grudge to announce against his neighbor ought to think twice, and maybe every imbecile who has nothing to say but says it anyway ought to just shut up.

Has there ever been so much road rage in America, on and off the road? Has there ever been so much stupidity in 140 characters or less?

Consider it a gain if the "eye in the sky" stops the next fool from seeking his or her 15 Minutes of Infamy.

Headlines come and headlines go, but there is still nothing new under the sun. We have it from Eugene Ionesco and H. G. Wells and George Orwell and Arthur Conan Doyle who, through their fiction, saw what was coming – arbitrary and unrestrained use of power, as happened before and will happen again. Is this where we are headed?

Franz Kafka gave us a world where first we prosecute and then hear testimony. Are we there yet?

France's Robespierre was sure that everybody was *guilty* of *something* (and he had a point there) hence, White Terror, in which everybody spies on somebody else. We get an especially chilling quote from him, which goes something like this, "Show me 20 words written by any man and I will find reason to hang him."

That is something to think about if we allow our government to get out of hand – and also, this, from Hebrew Scriptures (Mishna):

"Know what is above you...an eye sees, an ear hears, and everything is recorded in a Book."

Scary.

Me and Esther Williams

WASHINGTON, June 7, 2013 — Right now she is probably teaching the angels how to swim. Esther Williams is dead. She left us last Thursday at the great age of 91.

I met her many years ago and am still star struck. Bill Holland, my editor at the *Burlington County Times* (NJ), scanned the newsroom and found no one else around. I was the new kid. "You'll do," he said even before handing me the assignment. A star had come to our neighborhood to promote her swimming pool business.

"How would you like to interview Esther Williams?" Bill asked.

Could this be a joke?

"There is no such person," I protested instinctively. "She is a movie star."

Where I came from, movie stars were not people. They were gods. Gods cannot be approached, and some of them were so magnified that their names alone signified a mystique that was strictly and awesomely American... names like Clark Gable, Gregory Peck, John Wayne, Elizabeth Taylor, and right there with them was Esther Williams!

Esther Williams – goddess of the waters!

Such divinities truly walked among us?

"Yes, there is such a person," said Bill, laughing, and off I went to the interview, dizzy with anticipation.

Apparently, then, celestial beings did come down once in a while to visit the world of mortals.

But I still thought it had to be a joke. Me? Esther Williams?

But there she was. No longer was she the young darling that swam in all those MGM extravaganzas. But she still radiated.

Oh brother did she radiate!

But I still had a job to do. I was here as a reporter, for gosh sakes.

I had a list of questions, but forget them all. My mind was zapped. I just stared at her.

The manager of the swimming pool operation, a terribly annoying man, hovered over me, afraid of what? Was he worried that I would make a play for her? That would be logical. Was there a chance our eyes would meet, *me and Esther Williams*, and that the attraction would be so irresistible that, despite everything, we would link up and run off together?

That may have entered my mind, yes. Fernando Lamas – big deal! When you are 21 you want to have every woman.

But there would be no future for *me and Esther Williams*. I can't swim.

Finally, I came around and asked some questions – but only pertaining to the swimming pool business. Those had been my orders anyway, plus this tip-off: she was wearing a business suit. No bathing suit. Driving over, I had thought, catching Esther Williams – *Esther Williams!* – in a bathing suit would be as close as I'd ever get (at that time) to the entertainment divinity that is Hollywood.

There was so much I wanted to know. But I was an absolute tenderfoot. If I asked the wrong question, might she storm off?

Might word get back to Bill Holland, to have him say, "How dare you talk this way to a movie star?"

Anyway, that creepy manager kept breathing down my neck. I did ask her if she was planning to do any more movies. The guy tried to intercept. "I can answer for myself, thank you," she told him to brush him off.   Offering a generous smile, she replied that yes, there will be other movies, and that I would be the first to know.

I have been waiting.

So now she is in heaven. But wasn't she there all along?

On Writing A Novel in Six Weeks

NEW YORK, March 28, 2013 - Jack Kerouac told people that he wrote *On the Road* in three weeks. Never mind Truman Capote's dig: "That's not writing; it's typing."

Is it possible to write a truly good or great novel in that period of time, in one non-stop flourish of heat and inspiration?

There is a catch to Kerouac's claim: He spent *seven years* on the road before he wrote *On the Road*, so all the material he included in the book was already distilled and waiting to pop.

I could argue both sides. On the one hand, a novel needs to be revised and polished a thousand times before it can be declared done. The other argument is that the first bloom, the first rush of excitement, tells the real story. Writing a novel is like being in love. Enjoy the romance and don't ask too many questions.

Love happens and novels happen by the same inexplicable combustion.

As a horseplayer will tell you, your first choice, follow your first instinct (there is no *second* instinct) is the most reliable, and when you start second-guessing yourself, you ruin the honest moment that came in a flash, a moment that will never come round again.

Kerouac chose his speedwriting method to attain spontaneous prose. He wanted to match the improvisational rhythm of jazz and bebop.

Conventional critics dismissed Kerouac and his fellow Beats, but today *On the Road* is deemed a classic.

Back in the mid-1800s in Russia, Fyodor Dostoyevsky had no choice but to write fast. Broke and desperate, he had 26 days to produce a completed novel. If he failed, the earnings from all his works over the next decade would revert to an exploitative publisher, Stellovsky, who insisted that the work be done by November 1, 1866, and not a moment past midnight.

Dostoyevsky met the deadline by dictating his prose to a stenographer, whom he later married, but when he presented the work at the publisher's office, the publisher was conveniently not in. Dostoyevsky then rushed to a police station to have his manuscript certified in the nick of time. He called it Roulettenburg. We know it today as *The Gambler.*

This is now a minor classic. I This writer, Dostoyevsky, had no qualms about degrading himself, and when he wrote about the harrowing days and nights at the roulette wheel in the flesh pots of Europe, he knew what he was talking about. This greatest of Russian writers, along with Tolstoy, was a gambling addict, prone to bad luck. That is partly why he'd been in debt in the first place.

The novel is largely autobiographical. Dostoyevsky had this novel in mind years before he found himself in desperate straits. Though the writing, the sprouting, took three weeks, there were years of seeding and planting. So we cannot say the writing was fast, only the typing.

The Gambler illustrates that really great novels proceed liberated and unafraid. They tell it uninhibited, blemished, warts and all. Even the hero can be as flawed as any villain. There are sections in the book that make the reader cringe, both for the blunt honesty of the hero and for the choppy, uneven prose. We can tell that it was rushed. But we are hooked *because* it is so honest and unvarnished.

Or as Hemingway said of Dostoyevsky in general, "How can a man write so poorly and still make you feel so deeply?"

Readers who follow these pages will recall that I confessed to having ditched a novel that wasn't working. But what I didn't say, for fear of the kibosh, was that the very next day I picked myself up and started all over again. I started a new novel. I finished it in six weeks. I sent it off to the publisher (typos and all) before I could change my mind.

I knew that if I let it sit I would re-work it to *perfection*. No, I would rather it be imperfect – imperfect but true.

But did I really write it in six weeks? Let's say I *typed* it in six weeks and started on it at the moment of a relentless brainstorm. But to get there, it took years of gathering material, consciously and subconsciously – material that was already percolating and seething in my mind for years, even decades. Then the right moment came for it to explode onto the page. I will only say it too is about a hero obsessed by an addiction.

On average I spend two years on a novel. *Indecent Proposal* took three years. By far my shortest work, the memoir *Escape from Mount Moriah*, took 20 years.

This new one just burst. Is it good, bad, great? Usually it takes generations to find out.

My enemies will surely be waiting for the result. But we also have friends.

Don Imus to Frank Rich:
Regrets for Butchering Broadway?

NEW YORK, March 6, 2013 - Still after all these years my early mornings begin with coffee and Don Imus on Radio or TV. He's still tops, especially in getting his guests to open up as if there's no microphone picking up deep dark secrets – as he did again this morning with Frank Rich, who used to be known as the Butcher of Broadway, and for good reason.

Rich so affably offered his confessions and condolences a second time, and that made it no tidier or prettier than the first time. Rich now sings a different Broadway melody as a writer for *New York Magazine*, but back then, between 1980 and 1993, he served as senior drama critic for *The New York Times*, and here the word "critic" is not used in vain.

For more than a decade Broadway shuddered at what that man Rich might say next.

A play that opened on Friday could be shut down on Saturday after Frank Rich had his final say, and in those days *The New York Times* was most firmly the final say. Not so anymore, as *New York Post* theater reviewer Michael Riedel told Imus just the other day, noting that *The New York Times* does not enjoy the same singular power anymore, at least on drama.

Riedel, who has a knack for telling it good, straight and honest for the *Post,* is no fan of Frank Rich. He still thinks the man was too brutal.

Here's the kicker: Frank Rich thinks so himself.

This morning he told Imus and that on second thought, all those plays he savaged – well, maybe they weren't all that bad, after all.

Now we hear this? A bit late, no?

Actually we heard this before, and it's still not funny, even though Rich laughs when he says something like, "Yes, I could have been wrong."

That is not an exact quote, but it is the gist.

Years ago I heard Frank Rich make the same confession, accompanied by giggles and laughter. As a member of the fraternity of writers who knows how ruinous a bad review can be, I was not amused by the carefree and whimsical condolences Rich offered to the many Broadway artists who'd been destroyed by the might of his heartless pen.

The topic came up again this morning, on Imus, because Rich has written a book, and in it, apparently, he discusses his "second thoughts."

Yes, on second thought, maybe those plays did not deserve to be killed, along with the people whose years of artistic work were cursed into the netherworld.

I covered that in a book I wrote in 2007, here, where editor in chief Jay Garfield confronts his drama critic for getting to be too much like Frank Rich. I never thought those words would come back to life, or maybe I did for life has a habit of repeating itself for the good, the bad, and the vicious, like this, from page 211:

"Yes, Frank Rich. This man had been the theater critic for *The New York Times* but was better known as The Butcher of Broadway. In his day he had scorched nearly every play under his withering eyes, sending thousands of writers, actors, directors, producers, stagehands and angels into the pit of eternal damnation. Most were never heard from again, so all-powerful was this executioner for *The New York Times*.

"Finally (and for whatever reason) he got switched to another beat and now he could speak his mind, and so on a morning radio show – Imus, I believe it was – relaxed and entirely happy with himself, he confessed that most of these plays, on second thought, weren't all that bad. Some were even good and maybe excellent. But he destroyed them and why? Well, because he felt like it and because he could.

"Then, after saying all that, he laughed, never mind all the people he had ruined, and all the dreams he had dashed."

So once again Frank Rich gives his regards to Broadway – and still not funny.

Dear Writers:
Suppose Your Novel Sucks?

NEW YORK, February 26, 2013 - All things considered, it could have been much worse. Some writers put 10 years into a book, and only after giving it all that blood, discover that it was all in vain. I only put in a month of sweat, or thereabouts, and woke up one morning with something of an epiphany, like this: hey, this novel sucks!

This would have been my 11th published book and my ninth novel and I had it figured from beginning to end, which is mistake number one. If you've got it all figured out so perfectly then surely you can never surprise yourself, and if you can't surprise yourself, how can you expect to amaze the reader?

A novel has to breathe and if you've got every scene charted out, you're suffocating the baby.

Besides, a novel should never be perfect. It is usually the imperfect ones that are the great ones, like James Jones' *From Here to Eternity*, which is full of bad writing, but incredibly alive. Like Hemingway said of Dostoyevsky, "How can someone write so poorly and make you feel so deeply?"

Beethoven's Ninth Symphony was full of mistakes, he thought so himself, and yet it turned out to be his preeminent triumph.

Hemingway thought his *Across the River and into the Trees* would be his finest work. He was thrilled about the progress he was making. He kept reminding A.E. Hotchner that passage for passage, chapter for chapter, he had never written so well — and what happened? The book turned out to be about some grumpy old colonel, which nobody liked. (Well, some did and some do.)

I stopped the bleeding before it was too late. Each morning when I'd start back to work on it, I found that no matter how many pages I'd written the day before, I was still on page 66. This was inexplicable and entirely weird. How can I still be on page 66 after hours of writing?

But it proved that I wasn't skipping along as I usually do for the works that succeed, and I have had successes and failures, and haven't we all?

I even went back to those novels of mine that did succeed (I number them at nine) and in them tried to figure out what worked before against what wasn't working out now. In all my novels from before, something got turned on, something clicked. The secret was simple (especially for *Indecent Proposal*): in one place my heart was in it, I was aflame, full of passion, and in this place, this new place, I was simply writing to conform to plot.

The characters never talked back to me, never argued with me, never stood up for themselves, and when none of that happens, you're writing cardboard.

I found this attempt at a new novel to be drudgery, and no matter how many times I told myself to keep going, that I will find the people, I will find the passion, I will find the excitement, I will find the voice, the novel refused to give itself up and refused to move. Still page 66. Nothing was *happening.*

(By the way, the working title for the novel that will never happen was "Welcome to Sogora." If you ever see a novel by that name, it wasn't mine, or my fault.)

Lesson number two on writing: If you can change the names of your characters midway, you've got nothing going.

You are inventing, not creating. You are faking it, and with this discovery I went to bed that night. In the morning I glanced over a few pages and declared them to be officially dreck. I announced myself done with this project. I actually felt good.

I actually felt creative for making such a decision. Yes, knowing when a thing isn't working, and being done with it, that too is part of the creative process.

I talked to the primo novelist John W. Cassell about this.

"Didn't we agree?" he said, "that it's on page one hundred that we can tell if a novel is working or not?"

Eureka! That's how it was when Joan insisted, against my wishes, that she was going to take up the sultan on his million dollar offer, even as I kept saying no, and she kept saying yes. She kept saying yes and I could not stop her. She won, as did the novel. All that happened on page 100, when I stopped typing and began channeling, or rather when I gave in, stopped being in control and judgmental, and instead, let people behave as people behave.

Inspiration can't be the moment of clarity that happens only at the start. Inspiration, if it's real, has to keep moving you page to page.

I've already got a new novel started. I will let you know when I get past page 66.

JFK, Marilyn, Elvis:
Trashing the Dead with Books

NEW YORK, February 20, 2013 - I slept with Marilyn Monroe.

Can you prove otherwise? That's right. You can't, and that's my point.

Or, as they'd say around my home, "Too much information, Dad."

I say the same about books that keep coming out about dead celebrities, told by people who were intimate with them, or so they say.

I do not need all that information.

Let me depart from books for a second to talk about a film that was made for HBO about Hemingway and Gellhorn, starring Clive Owen and Nicole Kidman. This was okay as these specials go, but I did not need those sex scenes, and I turned my head when I knew what was coming, a momentary glimpse of Owen's back end, meant to convey Hemingway in heat, in addition to his posterior.

Thank you, but I don't need that about an American legend. Nor do I need all those tell-alls that defame the reputations of people we revere and idolize.

Is this an American thing, this need to destroy our heroes? I call it Sleaze Lit.

Again on HBO, here we have Alfred Hitchcock as "mad about that Girl" – and nothing else. He comes off hateful and humorless and now dead, of course.

In other words, we get one side about people no longer among the quick.

Out comes a book by Rita Moreno (one of my favorites) and today I learn that Brando was a sex machine and that Elvis was a dud.

I may never visualize Brando the same way again, and certainly not Elvis who, over the years, I've come to appreciate.

There is a good and legit bio of Elvis by Peter Guralnick, but that is literally a different story. In fact, real biographies by real biographers belong in a different category than gossip mongers, and frankly, I don't know what to make of Kitty Kelley and Andrew Morton. I will more or less trust that the research was done.

Norman Mailer did his book on Marilyn (guessing all the way), and Peter Manso did his book on Mailer, but these are biographers who make no other claim.

We're talking about those authors who claim to have shared their lives, and bedrooms, with our gods. Can we believe what they say?

Remember, they can say whatever they want....anything about anybody...as long as that person is gone.

The actor Frank Langella wrote a book in which he makes minced-meat out of nearly everybody, particularly those who are no longer around to defend themselves, like a particular sweetheart of mine and of the silver screen, Anne Bancroft. Do we really need to know that she was so vain that only the mirror was her friend?

More important, is this really true?

Or is this just one man's opinion? Or is it one man getting even?

Mel Brooks can't be happy and I'm not happy, for this is not biography and it is not memoir, it is bitchery.

Yes, I know, that's what sells. I also know that when a prospective peeping tom approaches a publisher the question goes like this:

"Can you spill the beans? Can you dish the dirt?"

Langella also scandalizes John F. Kennedy, and who hasn't? Seems to me that nearly anyone who was in or around the 1960s has since "revealed the truth" about our handsome 35th president. For a time I believed all those stories about his supposed lechery. But as these books and movies started piling up and piling on, I began to wonder.

If true, when did Kennedy have time to inaugurate the Peace Corps and get us to the moon?

I am starting to think that Kennedy was absolutely loyal to Jackie, like a monk, and that he planted the gossip himself to distract us from knowing that he was in constant pain. Either way, some respect maybe for a president who was assassinated?

Not quite. A lady named Mimi Alford caused the latest stir. She wrote a book (who hasn't?) and appeared with Meredith Viera on TV to talk about her steamy affair with Kennedy, some of which got into perversion. As we get it, she started off as an intern, then named Mimi Beardsley, and next thing you know she was canoodling with the president in bed and in swimming pools. (Oh those interns!)

That happened in 1962. She broke the news 2012.

Is all that true? Maybe it doesn't matter as long as we enjoy watching the dead squirm. How reliable are memoirs anyway? See as revealed here.

Now it's back to my book, "How I Scored with Ava Gardner."

Adultery, Anyone?

WASHINGTON, DC, February 8, 2013 - In a book just published, and getting deservedly good reviews, *I do and I don't: A History of Marriage in the Movies*, author Jeanine Basinger asserts that we can't seem to get it right at home or at the movies. Infidelity lurks from bedroom to silver screen, and, as I define it, the love of sex and money is the root of all great fiction.

In real life, surveys mislead as to who is misbehaving, but online there are hundreds of website choices for "hooking up," single or married. On surveys and statistics we only know what people are saying, not what people are thinking, especially when it comes to sex.

Writers of fiction do it best, and on this topic I do have a say. I've been told that I started a new baby boom from what gets started on page 228 of *Indecent Proposal*. Too often I've been asked to define the novel and my standard response is that if I could define it in a single paragraph I would have written the paragraph instead of the book.

However, *temptation* comes close to the mark, and as I've already written, sex is nothing. Temptation is every-thing...and anyway, sex is not for girls.

I'm okay with Basinger naming David Lean's *Brief Encounter* as perhaps the best take on infidelity at the movies, even as the film was minus any scenes of lovemaking, drawing chuckles from reviewers in France who found it so "very British" for a film to feature sex but without the sex.

Ditto for *Madame Bovary* and *Anna Karenina* as contenders. There, too, most of it was flirtation and temptation.

Likewise, in books or in film, presenting married couples in the act of sex, does nothing. Who cares? That's what people are supposed to do, to be fruitful and multiply. *When it gets illicit*, that's when the fun and the drama begin. "All happy families are alike" – Tolstoy's opening line for *Anna Karenina.*

So thrilled as I was to be mentioned in the same pages as Leo Tolstoy, and Gustav Flaubert, and astonished that she missed James M. Cain's *The Postman Always Rings Twice*, Basinger was mistaken to surmise, on page 142, that *Indecent Proposal* (the movie) "floats on an unlikely story."

Not quite. After my novel came out, followed by the Paramount movie, I counted a hundred letters spilling the beans on oil rich sheiks who offered a million dollars (more or less) for a night of love — and the many Hollywood actresses willingly sharing their bedroom charms for the cash.

I had no idea that this was going on (and still going on) when I wrote the book. We may think we are creating when in fact we are merely taking down dictation.

All that got me to wondering where we are, ethically, in this Real Housewives/Page Six world where nearly everything goes. Is there anything left that's taboo? The movie *Indecent Proposal* premiered April 7, 1993, so we're approaching a 25th anniversary. The novel was published four years earlier. In each instance, there was shock.

Someone out there said it better than I could.

Writing for NPR (National Public Radio), Jimi Izrael ranked *Indecent Proposal* number one on a list of "Five Great Films about the Perils of Infidelity." Izrael complained (as did I) about Amy Holden Jones' "jerky script" but cited the novel as "a gut-wrenching study on love, money, and trust that sparked dinner party conversations for years afterward here."

Back then, women's groups blasted me for sexism, even when they'd only seen the movie and not read the book. To my defense comes a recent Amazon UK review from Thomas Hardy for the Kindle edition of the novel: "Indecent Proposal is probably the ideal example of why a screenwriter should never be allowed near a great writer's work." (His words, not mine.)

Still, back then, even as the novel kept selling and getting fine book reviews, and even as the movie broke box office records, I took it on the chin from movie reviewers coast to coast. The New York Times and Roger Ebert were overly generous about the movie, but the rest of them were overly hysterical.

My guess was that people simply did not want to be challenged like this – like what would you do if you were impoverished and were offered a million dollars to perform a sinful act that could change your entire life? Movie reviewers expected a popcorn outing and were vexed and offended when asked to go back home to *think* and face up to a too-near-to-home moral dilemma.

Robert Redford, though I had nothing like him in mind, rather an oil rich sultan, even liked the script and especially the novel despite or maybe because of its "hard-edged writing" and "flagrantly sexual theme." He said, "Yeah. It will work." Sure did. The movie took in $260 million at the box office worldwide and made everybody rich in Hollywood, and sales of my book zoomed here and around the globe.

So nobody got hurt except for the critics.

The novel, and even the movie, got personal, and touched America deep into its Puritanical soul. On live TV, Matt Lauer chuckled and asked me if my novel was based on personal experience...hell no!...and on live radio, Larry King asked, "Why only a million dollars?" True, I had not thought of inflation.

I also did not think that we'd turn as blasé as the Europeans, who take sex casually and often.

When I asked columnist Liz Smith to please get women's lib off my back, she wrote, "What are you complaining about? Your book is a runaway bestseller."

Nowadays every sitcom comes with overt sexual titters and nearly every movie opens with two or more people in bed and nudity is ho-hum.

I refuse to rate my book or my movie on the scale of infidelity and I refuse to judge the behavior of my characters.

Sex is about love and nothing else and let someone else, not me, be the judge.

I write and I publish because there may be one person out there with whom I've made contact in a world so brutal and lonely.

Salinger, Roth, Hemingway and the Wilderness of Writing

WASHINGTON, DC, January 16, 2013 - Philip Roth has quit writing and nobody knows exactly why though I can guess. Salinger wrote only for himself, for his own pleasure, and considered getting published a nuisance, a bother and an intrusion. F. Scott Fitzgerald's last royalty check amounted to something like six dollars and change. He said, "Why am I doing all this writing. No one's reading me."

Hemingway was so unimpressed with his Pulitzer, his Nobel, his wine, his women, his fame, his books waiting to get written, that he committed suicide.

John Kennedy Toole ("A Confederacy of Dunces") won his Pulitzer too late. He kept getting rejected and answered right back with his own suicide.

Dear world...How's that for rejection!

Both a doctor and an auto mechanic (people I admire) marveled at the fact that some of us can turn emotions into prose.

I explained that we are all geniuses at something. The trick is to find out what it is.

Writing novels, as I do, is fun, and more than that, once the inspiration kicks in there is nothing compared to the exhilaration when the words begin to flow, and there is no stopping us once we get started. There is no choice but to write and as I have said plenty of times, you don't choose writing, writing chooses you.

But that's the writing itself that I'm talking about, and in that period when the going is good and the words (from above?) keep coming so fast that even the keyboard can't keep up – in that period we are charmed and blessed. At these moments, as we write and lose track of time, we create a universe and discover continents. We become gods and kings.

In the publishing we turn ourselves over to our readers and trust that we will get a fair hearing. We don't ask our readers to love us, only to understand that a novel is tender and precious and easily broken when trashed. We worked long and hard to get it done and deserve leniency for the effort alone – and for having the guts to stick our necks out where there may be multitudes waiting to do us harm.

This is an especially tricky time for writers. We find ourselves squarely into the teeth of a technology that permits anyone to comment on our work without telling us who they are, so that by remaining anonymous they enjoy a tyranny. Bygone writers faced their accusers.

All around I have been lucky with reviews though we don't know what a new day will bring, but on getting published it has been a drag from day one, and yet there have been some astonishing successes, which only recently I have come to appreciate. I keep saying that every work of art is a failure because we never get it exactly right, but even so, sometimes we click and our books get praised, become bestsellers and get made into movies...and for that much I can vouch.

But generally all true writers – all true artists – are failures. We are dependant on the mercy of strangers.

I even wrote a novel about a novelist, his triumphs yes, but oh brother the rejections, the hardships, the bills. I knew what I was talking about.

I am reading the biography of David Lean the great director of "Lawrence of Arabia" and am astonished at his feelings of inadequacy even after scoring success after success. Even at the height of his fame Hemingway had trouble getting a press pass to cover World War II. Even after "The Catcher in the Rye" Salinger had to keep proving himself at The New Yorker. (Read Kenneth Slawenski's fabulous bio on this.)

Today I have begun writing a new novel and I wonder if it's worth the trouble. I keep hesitating as I consider my predecessors and about their weariness and despair and the uselessness of it all. Fitzgerald in "The Crack-Up" extended King Solomon's despair in Ecclesiastes. All is futile and futility.

Readers will misunderstand, as is to be expected, but some will misunderstand the work purposely and viciously.

Once the work has been done and is out of your hands you have no say. Onward your readers become gods and kings. They, not you, interpret your work, and this is their duty in this, the final act of intimacy, more intimate than sex, this give-and-take between writer and reader.

But who will be around to read this book of mine? Will we all be tweeting by the time it's done – tweeting instead of reading, and tweeting instead of writing? Already the language has changed and already we have a generation trained and conditioned to express themselves in 140 characters or less.

I notice this even at the movies where a typical scene in today's films runs no more than about 10 seconds. Our attention spans are devoted to the next commercial.

I also notice that the finest writing these days comes not from our novelists but from our screenwriters. (Is this why Roth quit?) True that so many films are junk but also true that good films keep getting done, and the writing is good and sometimes very good. I cannot write a screenplay because to me words are notes, sentences are music, and I need rhythm to keep moving from paragraph to paragraph.

Rhythm is something you have or you don't. Read the first paragraph of Hemingway's "A Farewell to Arms."

Read the opening lines to James M. Cain's "The Postman Always Rings Twice."

Read Kafka to find that a writer does not and should not care if his works get read. Kafka died before seeing his novels in print.

The work – it's only the work that counts. Forget the rest.

Tips for Becoming A Better Writer from A Writer

NEW YORK, November 6, 2012 – Writers and editors periodically ask me if I have any advice about writing and I usually, actually always, say hell no. Writers, speaking mostly of fiction writers, don't like to be told.

We don't like rules and we don't like tips. We are all different and respect must be paid for the uniqueness in all of us.

That said, as a public service and free of charge, here are some tips and rules gathered from my years in the trade.

Jack Engelhard's Tips and Rules to Become A Published Writer

GET TO THE POINT: Get that hook going right at the top. This is how it works in journalism. We want to grab the reader's attention immediately If not sooner.

TAKE YOUR TIME: When writing a work of fiction (or fact) remember, you've got all the time in the world to win the reader's attention. There is no need to get it all said right at the start. You've got plenty of pages to go. Don't get fooled by people who tell you that the hook is how it works in journalism. You are writing a book.

WRITE SHORT: Short, tough sentences always succeed. Think Bukowsky, Fante, James M. Cain, but most of all, Hemingway. He learned how to condense from Scriptures and from Gertrude Stein. Fitzgerald's dreamy type of writing is old hat and it is Hemingway who is now regarded as our greatest writer.

WRITE LONG: Every writer has his or her particular style, so it makes no sense to heed advice from anyone who tells you that writing short, clipped sentences is the way to go. Ridiculous. Today, it's Fitzgerald who is regarded as our greatest writer. Hemingway is old hat.

KEEP YOUR READERS IN MIND: You want to reach a wide public. People are waiting for your first or next book. So unless you are writing a diary or a laundry list, you want your work out there, to be appreciated by all. You want to cover all the bases so that you can please as many people as possible.

WRITE FOR YOURSELF ONLY: If you write with your readers in mind you are cheating both yourself and the reader. You will never make everyone happy, and you shouldn't even try. Remember, people are not waiting for your first or next book. Nobody cares. It's a jungle out there, believe me.

GO TO SCHOOL: Learn from the experts, first high school, then college. Let the professors tell you how it's done.

FORGET SCHOOL: Professors will scuttle every original thought that runs from your mind to the page. They are killers. It's all about grammar and punctuation with those people. Our best writers never went beyond high school and this includes Hemingway, Faulkner and Salinger. Fitzgerald stayed at Princeton for maybe a cup of coffee. If they had gone to college you never would have heard from them again.

DO NOT WORRY ABOUT POLITICAL CORRECTNESS: Say it all. Don't be afraid!

BE AFRAID: Editors will accept only so much boldness and controversy. If you really write what you think you have no shot. If it's politics, think Mahmoud Ahmadinejad as your editor. (Say it all anyway. This is still America...until the United Nations lords it over your Internet.)

GET AN AGENT: Traditional publishers will accept your work only if it is submitted to them through an agent. Agents are easy to find online.

NEVER MIND AN AGENT: Literary agents are impossible. They can not be found and when they are found, they never respond. If they do respond they do so after you have aged by some three to four months. After this, they will tell you that your work is quite wonderful – but not quite right for them. Then they will wish you "good luck" but they don't really mean it.

GO DIRECTLY TO A MAINSTREAM PUBLISHER: Fat chance. There are only seven publishers left in the United States of America and each time I check the list, I find that the number has been reduced – so that by the time you read this there may be only three or two left, or maybe one. Meanwhile, there are a thousand opportunities by going Independent – and this, small press and e-book publishing, like Kindle, this is the future. Truly great writers like Mark Twain and Walt Whitman self-published.

SO FORGET MAINSTREAM PUBLISHERS: Period.

GO MARKETING: If you get published, you are sure to land on TV and get big sales.

FORGET MARKETING: Sure you ought to try. But chances are you won't get on TV unless you are a TV personality and have your own show.

LET YOUR SPOUSE OR MOTHER REVIEW YOUR BOOK: Good idea.

LET YOUR EX-SPOUSE OR MOTHER-IN-LAW REVIEW YOUR BOOK: Not a good idea.

TAKE ALL THE ADVICE YOU CAN GET: Learn from other writers, especially those who have succeeded.

NONSENSE: Go it alone...and besides, all writers have mostly failed...but never give up!

The Obit Uris Never Got

NEW JERSEY, July 1, 2003 – Leon Uris deserved better. The obits were a disgrace. They read more like a spiteful book review, rather than an appreciation for the man who gave us the romance of Israel. But let's not be fooled -- for these obits were an attack upon the Jewish State, not Uris, who merely served as a prop, a decoy.

The cheap shots came from intellectual stormtroopers who decide for us what is good, what is bad, what is high-minded, what is low brow... Like this, which appeared all over the news media: "Uris is not well regarded by critics, many of whom consider his writing crude and simple. People who think Saul Bellow, Bernard Malamud and Cynthia Ozick are major Jewish writers would say he's just a popular writer... He tells a good story, but he's not of lasting literary value."

Huh? This belongs in an obituary?

For my money, Uris towers over Bellow and others on the strength of Exodus alone. And if Exodus is not of lasting literary value, I don't know what is.

Oh, I know what they're talking about. He was no stylist. First of all, there is no such thing as style. Of course there is, but that's for us, the readers, to decide. There is no Supreme Court to rule on style, and anyway, style is no factor in deciding a book's greatness. Dickens (in my view) was a terrible stylist, as was Dostoevsky, and James Jones was a terrible writer, but a great novelist by weight of From Here To Eternity. These were all great novelists.

No, the snotty obits were reprisals upon Israel, and had nothing to do with literature and everything to do with politics.

How many writers "created" a nation within the pages of a book? Non-Jews by the millions (never mind Jews) know and love Israel only through Exodus.

Uris died at the wrong time; anti-Semitism is up, Israel is down. Today it is not proper to glorify Israel, as Uris did. Today it is proper, it is fashionable, to slap Israel around.

Here's a secret: Newsrooms carry obits well in advance for people of achievement. As I write this, there's news that Katharine Hepburn just died, but you can be sure that the obits for her were written years ago. Back a generation, someone was in such a hurry to present his beautifully-written obit on Hemingway that he got it published all over the wires while Hemingway was merely recovering from a plane crash.

Hemingway, very much alive, said he loved what was said about him. Uris would not be so pleased.

Surely, over the years Uris' obit kept being rewritten in reflection of how the world viewed Israel and the Jewish people at the moment. Back then, a guilt-ridden world embraced the romance of the Jewish people returning to the land of their Fathers and Mothers. The mood has changed. The mood is ugly and the obits on Uris symbolize that change and that ugliness. Our tenured intellectual elite (think Oxford, Columbia, the BBC, NPR....) have fallen in love with homicide, terrorism, anti-Semitism.

Uris showed us David winning against Goliath, but this world covets Goliath... Hence the scorn upon the man who wrote Exodus.

In a class that I visited as a lecturer, a student mocked Proverbs. "Anyone can do that," he said. "Go ahead," I said, "write one." Of course, he was stumped.

I say the same to Uris' scholarly critics. "Go ahead, write me an Exodus."

We have lost a great man, a great writer, and he deserves to be hailed.